DEADLY DECISION

C G Penne

'Deadly Decision'

Other books by C G Penne:

Novels:

Raw Heritage

Climatic Crisis

Short Stories:

Never Assume and Other Stories

It Started with the Milk

Hidden Intent

For Adrian

Chapter One

Professor Bingwen Zhang sat back in his swivel chair absent-mindedly twiddling his pen. Frowning, a worried expression in his eyes, he was totally absorbed in thought. From the papers scattered on his large, old-fashioned solid oak desk, it would be fair to assume he was working on the lecture that he would be giving to his students tomorrow at Cambridge University where he held the post of Head of the Virology Department. That would be the wrong conclusion however, because his thoughts were centred on his son, Qiáng.

“Darling, it’s so dark in here!” Olivia exclaimed as she appeared in the doorway of her husband’s study, a tall, elegant figure of indeterminate age.

Bingwen looked up but didn’t answer.

Olivia glided effortlessly as though she was walking on air towards the huge sash window behind the desk and pulled on the drawstring cord. The heavy brocade curtains made a swishing sound as they shut. Then she moved across the thickly carpeted floor to turn on the light. She opened the door and turned back to look at Bingwen.

"I'll leave you to work, darling, but do put on your desk light, you will damage your eyesight".

Bingwen got up from his chair.

"Don't disappear, my love, I want to talk to you about Qiáng".

"Oh! I see – what about him?"

"Come, let's sit down by the fire. What will you have?" he asked.

Establishing herself in one of the comfortable armchairs, Olivia looked up at her husband, "Campari and soda for me, please" she answered smiling.

Returning the smile, he went over to the rather ornate cabinet in the corner of the room, selected two bottles, mixed his wife's drink and after handing it to her, he poured himself a whisky and soda.

They sat opposite each other for a couple of minutes sipping their drinks and then Olivia put her glass carefully on the occasional table. She sat back in her chair, smoothing her skirt, and folding her hands one on top of the other in her lap, looking expectantly at Bingwen.

The study was on the ground floor of their eight-bedroomed house which was surrounded by five acres of land. Unbeknown to the couple, a shadow had appeared on the stairs situated in the wide hallway. The shadow was that of a young man in his early twenties, tall, just touching six feet with a shock of black hair. He had slightly slanting brown eyes like his father but his nose was aquiline and his upper lip noticeably curved like his mother. At this moment he was wondering if his parents were talking about him. He wasn't suffering from paranoia but rather his curiosity stemmed from the suspicion that they were discussing recent events that might end in serious repercussions for him.

He tiptoed down the stairs, crossed the hall, stood outside his father's study hardly daring to breath and listened intently.

"So, you can see why I'm concerned, can't you, my love?" Bingwen was saying.

Olivia had her arms folded now, looking down at her knees.

“Well maybe the rumours you have heard from the university are wrong. He is about to graduate and maybe someone is jealous of that. Perhaps someone is not doing very well and when they asked him to help them cheat, he refused. After all the Dean was very complimentary on his performance and was sure he was in for a double first” she said at last but the expression in her eyes told Bingwen that she was also very worried.

They fell silent for a while.

“If that terrible incident hadn’t happened when he was a boy and, remember darling, there were other times too where there was more than a hint of concern then I would think twice but in view of past events and now these rumours, I can’t see any other option; we have to seek advice”, he said.

“But if we do that and ………………” she faltered not able to go on.

“But if we don’t………………”

The door creaked slightly.

A shadow could be seen on the wall of the staircase as noiselessly it disappeared, but Bingwen and Olivia were sitting at the wrong angle to see the shadow.

“I have a couple of hours more work to do for my lecture tomorrow, my love, so I think we have to leave it tonight and discuss it again tomorrow evening” said Bingwen taking Olivia’s glass.

“I’m going to bed then. I know your ‘couple of hours’! Just don’t work on too late, darling” she said smiling, her mood lightening for a moment. Then just as suddenly, her expression became more serious, “Yes, we must talk more about Qiáng tomorrow. It’ll be alright, won’t it, Bingwen?”

“I hope so, my love, I do hope so” and he kissed her gently on the lips.

In the event, Bingwen managed to finish his lecture preparations within two hours and at one o’clock in the morning he turned out his desk lamp and went upstairs to bed.

It was 4.00 a.m. when Bingwen’s hand reached out to the bedside table to turn off the alarm clock radio. He pressed the stop button on top of the alarm several times but to no avail. The tune was persistent seemingly becoming more and more shrill. His brain kicked in at last. It wasn’t the alarm clock radio.

“Wake up, wake up, Olivia. Fire, there’s a fire!”

Olivia was already waking up as Bingwen shouted.

"Oh my god!" she uttered as she swung her legs over the side of the bed.

"Qiáng – we have to get Qiáng!"

Bingwen picked up the phone on his bedside table. The line was dead.

Frantically, he looked for his mobile, but he must have left it in his study.

"Have you got your mobile, my love" he asked.

Olivia looked for it.

"No, it's not there! I must have left it downstairs somewhere!" and briefly she thought that odd as she always put it on her bedside table at night.

Bingwen was at the door. He tried to open it.

"I can't open it, my love. It seems to be stuck!" His stomach was churning at the possibility the door had been locked. Wreaths of smoke were coming from under the doorway now and Bingwen turned, a look of horror on his face.

"Qiáng! Qiáng!" Olivia shouted unable to keep the emotion from her voice, "we have to get to Qiáng!"

“I know, I know, but first we have to get out of this room so that we can”.

Bingwen covered his face with his dressing gown, signalled to Olivia to do the same and ran to the window. Having undone the lock, he tugged at the lower window.

“I can’t open it!”

“Have you unlocked it?”

“Yes, of course!”

“Try the other window!”

Bingwen went to the other window in the room.

“I can’t open this one either! The way the windows are constructed with small squares of glass I don’t think I can smash them, but I’ll give it a try!”

Bingwen picked up a chair and battered one of the windows with all his strength. He succeeded in breaking a pane or two but little else.

Suddenly there was a loud bang behind them.

They both turned. Terrified they threw their arms around each other.

“We’re going to die and Qiáng is all alone. I love you Bingwen” she sobbed.

“And I love you very much too, Olivia” and he kissed her lips tenderly.

The fire ripped relentlessly through the room consuming all in its path.

The crimson and orange flames together with the huge columns of thick black smoke could be seen for miles around as one side of the beautiful Cotswold stone house turned to ashes in the winter night.

The nearest house was located about four miles away where an old man lived on his own. He suffered from insomnia, and it was he who alerted the fire brigade at around 4.20 a.m. when he spotted the fire.

Chapter Two

DS Jack Allan had never needed more than five hours sleep in any twenty-four-hour period. Perfect for his line of work and today found him as usual at 3.30 a.m. in the gym area of his open plan flat situated above a warehouse on a small industrial estate just outside Cambridge.

Allan enjoyed a good workout at the start of his day but unfortunately all too often he had to sacrifice his me-time for the demands of his job. Despite this, Allan wouldn't have traded his work for any other. He was currently through thirty minutes of his one hour run on the treadmill and working up a healthy sweat.

Part of a team that had recently successfully brought a serial killer to justice after months of painstaking and methodical investigation, he was feeling good pounding away, his arms and legs in perfect rhythm. He slowed to walking and then stepping off, he strolled over to his rowing machine which was set on the highest tension where he moved backwards and forwards with ease.

His mobile vibrated and rang out the jazz tune he had selected. Having replaced the handlebar of the machine carefully he ran over to the kitchen where his mobile lay on one of the surfaces.

"Allan" he said answering the call.

"Sorry to disturb you, Jack, but you're needed over at Rosedene Grange, Perrydene, just outside Ely. There's been a serious incident and suspected arson. DI Hopkins is on his way to the scene now. I'll send you the directions".

"Thanks" he said as the directions from DC Szymanski arrived.

Putting down his mobile, Allan quickly showered, pulled on his clothes, picked up his phone, jacket, two bananas, two apples and left. Munching on an apple, he jumped down two stairs at a time bursting through the exit door while zapping his car.

On the way, he picked up DC Julia Szymanski from her home. Julia was a broad shouldered, rather spare woman, with a bird like face. A long, thin pointy nose and small, glittery eyes that bore into you as though she knew exactly what you were thinking. Her mouth was thin and determinedly straight. She had short cropped highlighted blonde hair and together with the red lipstick that never seemed to come off her lips, she exuded a formidable façade masking her natural empathetic nature. DS Allan was one of the few people that had an unnerving effect on her. She hadn't worked with him very long, six months in fact, but she respected him enormously for his already renowned abilities. His boss, DI Jim Hopkins was confident that his subordinate would not be long in making Detective Inspector. Admittedly, it was a begrudging acknowledgement of Allan's abilities, as normally Hopkins had little respect for anyone who had come in at officer level just because he was a graduate. He himself had worked up from the bottom rank, but he had made an exception in Allan's case although he often took delight in making sarcastic comments to him just to ensure that Allan knew who was boss. Nevertheless, Allan had progressed smoothly from Detective Constable to Detective Sergeant and Hopkins knew his subordinate was destined to speedily climb the ranks.

Jack arrived at the scene fifteen minutes after his boss.

"One hell of a fire, sir" Allan remarked as he came alongside his boss.

“Yep, observant as ever, even at this time of the morning, Jack” Hopkins quipped with humour in his voice.

Allan had an enormous respect for Hopkins and tended to ignore his sarcastic comments just as he did this one knowing that, despite his boss’ habitual sarcasm, respect was mutual. The Chief Fire Officer came over.

“The blaze is coming under control for the most part now” he said addressing Hopkins, “two bodies have been found in what was the main bedroom. Pretty gruesome – they were obviously hugging each other at the end. This job never gets any easier” he said.

“We’ve checked occupancy, and it looks like it was just the couple living there permanently, Professor Zhang and his wife. Their son, Qiáng who doesn’t live at the Hall was also staying at the house by all accounts. He’s a student at Cambridge, home for the holidays.”

“No sign of the son’s body, you say?” asked Allan.

“Nope. There are personal effects in his room though indicating that he was staying at the Hall at least recently, but he may have gone back to university or perhaps he is visiting friends?”

The detective nodded, “We’ll check. In the meantime, we need a fire investigator”.

“Consider it arranged”.

DS Allan began munching on his second apple. He hated fires. Especially when people had perished, in fact, ever since his childhood when his neighbours’ house had burnt down killing all four children and their parents. He had been best mates with one of the four and had known then that it would haunt him to his dying day.

Allan’s feeling was that they should be as quick as possible in locating the Professor’s son before he found out from some other source his parents’ horrifying fate. He said as much to Hopkins who agreed.

Three days later, there was still no sign of Qiáng. The fire investigators had completed their work and filed a report for the urgent attention of the police.

Jim Hopkins emerged from his office after a long phone call with the Super. He strode through the main office and knocked on the top of Allan’s desk.

Jack looked up at his boss.

“Yes, sir?” he said.

Hopkins sat down on a chair in front of Jack’s desk.

“Have we received the report on Professor Zhang’s house fire from the investigators yet?”

“Yes, sir. I was just about to bring you the report” he said handing him the file. Hopkins took it and quickly scanned the contents.

“It seems the fire was deliberate. The source of the first fire was paraffin along the carpet directly outside the owners’ bedroom. The second fire was set off by the front door, also using paraffin. Someone wasn’t taking any chances. Someone wanted the Professor and/or his wife dead. This is now a murder enquiry”, he commented throwing the file down on Jack’s desk.

“OK so have we managed to locate the son......Qiáng?” asked the DI.

“No, not yet. The university haven’t seen him, but we are still talking to his friends and their parents and obviously grandparents and relations. Apparently, he is exceptionally bright, brilliant by all accounts and destined for a double first”.

"Do the usual digging into the professor's relationships with his colleagues and students at Cambridge University. Likewise, his financial affairs, debts and so on. Follow up on the wife and the son and chase the rest of the forensic report too," said Hopkins.

"On it, boss" he replied, immediately getting up and walking over to DC Szymanski's desk.

"Julia, I want you to conduct interviews with all the Professor's colleagues and his students at the university. See what turns up".

Next, returning to his desk, he sat down and picked up the phone.

"Good morning. Allan here, I need the rest of the forensic report for the Zhang case. No, it can't wait. This is a murder investigation, and I want that report now. No, now" and he put the receiver down abruptly.

Chapter Three

DC Szymanski was on her last interview with the late Professor's colleagues. So far, she had ascertained that the Professor had been highly respected for his research and was well liked as a colleague. He seemingly had no enemies.

Professor Beale was a tall man with an over-ebullient face. He strode into the room, hand outstretched to shake hands with her.

Greetings exchanged; Szymanski began her questioning.

"So, as far as you know, then, nothing was concerning your colleague, sir? Everyone liked him and he had no work issues?"

"Well.................."

Julia waited while the professor looked around sheepishly and then at his hands. Finally, he drew breath and spoke.

"Well....er.... yes.....there was something. The day before he er....er....er.... passed away, he mentioned that he was worried about his son, Qiáng".

“In what way was he concerned?”

“Well.....er....” and Professor Beale paused “well....er...I don’t really know, he never told me. I think we were interrupted or something before he could tell me”, he finished lamely.

“Are you sure that he didn’t tell you why he was worried?”

“Er...yes.... yes, quite sure but er......”.

“Yes?”

“Well, there were rumours flying around that Qiáng was involved in some ...well...unsavoury business”.

“Unsavoury business. Would you like to clarify, Professor?” Szymanski asked having difficulty keeping the irritation out of her voice. She felt as though she was extracting the Professor’s teeth.

“It was...well....er...it was something to do with a financial scam that young Zhang was running. It was rumoured that he was making a huge amount of money”.

“Why wasn’t it reported to the police?”

"Partly because there was no evidence. Zhang's computer was looked at by our technical department, but nothing was found".

"How did these rumours start?"

"Miles Peterson brought it to the Dean's attention but then the most unfortunate thing occurred".

"Yes?" again Szymanski visualised a dentist's chair.

"Miles Peterson fell from the window of his digs and was killed" he said.

"Was it possible that Peterson committed suicide?"

"No. He was a happy, confident individual who was doing very well with his studies and heading for a First. To our knowledge he had no particular problems and there was no suicide note. The coroner's verdict was accidental death".

"Did Professor Zhang know about these rumours; he worked at Cambridge University?"

"Yes, indeed Professor Zhang will be very much missed. His virology research has done much to advance his field. These events happened a few months back and I am not sure that Professor Zhang had heard the rumours. He is always very focussed on his work and usually totally unaware of such matters".

"Well, thank you, Professor Beale, you have been most helpful". They shook hands and she departed.

Szymanski punched Allan's number into her mobile as she sat in her car following the interview with the professor.

"The interview with Professor Beale was very interesting, sir" she said not offering a greeting. "It would seem that our Professor Zhang was worried about his son. There were rumours about, to quote "an unsavoury financial scam" that the young man was running although Professor Beale did his best to suggest that Professor Zhang didn't know about the scam and therefore his worry was unrelated. At a guess he wants to avoid any scandal for the University. What is even more interesting, sir, is that the student who was blowing the whistle on Zhang conveniently fell from his second-floor digs and was killed."

"Yes, that is very interesting. I think I would very much like to interview Qiáng. I've been to see Qiáng's closest friend at the university, Mike Browne who said that Qiáng thought most of the students were immature and boring. He kept himself aloof. From Browne's description this Qiáng sounded a rather unlikeable, condescending and arrogant person. Mike said he had no idea where he was. Qiáng hadn't seemed any different or concerned about anything last time Mike had seen him at a lecture on the day of the fire. Certainly, he seems to have disappeared off the face of the earth. No-one seems to have heard from him at all since the day of the fire. Zilch about the wife either – no previous form or underworld connections. Came from a nice upper middle-class family, private school, finishing school etcetera, etcetera".

Allan rubbed the side of his nose, a habit which always helped him to think.

"It's essential we find Qiáng. So, start by interviewing the rest of his peers. Perhaps we can glean where he might be hiding out or, alternatively though unlikely, if there is any hint that he might have come to harm. In the meantime, I will pay a visit to his grandparents. I would like to know more about this guy's background. So far, he doesn't sound an endearing character according to his close friend and the fact we can't find him seems suspicious. We know it was arson, and he wouldn't be the first offspring to kill its parents. Let me know if anything turns up in the interviews".

"Yes, sir".

Olivia Zhang's parents' house was large and imposing set in several acres of Surrey countryside. As Allan approached, he thought something didn't add up. If Qiáng Zhang came from such a wealthy family, why did he feel the need to amass more money through fraudulent activity. Albeit he could be jumping the gun, and the rumours were in fact unfounded apart from the untimely death of the student Peterson. It could be coincidence, of course, but then when had he believed in coincidences?

"Good afternoon" he said standing a respectable distance from the front door holding his identification in front of him for a sufficiently long time to allow the rather aristocratic tall thin gentleman to examine it.

"I do apologise Detective Sargeant, but we are not ourselves at the moment as you must understand. You have come about the fire?" he asked in a shaky voice.

"Yes, I am so sorry for the loss of your daughter and son-in-law, Colonel Fortescue. I would appreciate a few moments of your time; I have a few questions to ask".

"Yes, yes, of course. Come in, come in".

The Colonel led the way to a lovely room which boasted a real fire encased in an imposing marble mantlepiece. He gestured to an elegant, if somewhat uncomfortable, Queen Anne chair.

"I'll just go and fetch my wife, if you'll excuse me" he said forlornly.

Fiona Fortescue was every bit the English country gal dressed in a tweed skirt and brogues. Allan wondered if he had accidentally sat in a time machine and been whisked back into a bygone era.

Allan got up to shake her hand, but Fiona waved him away and sat down on the chintz sofa opposite. She had clearly been crying as her eyes were red-rimmed, but she was not one for displaying her emotion for all to see. She sat demurely sporting a Hermes pure silk scarf which brightened her somewhat dull twin set.

"I'm sorry for your loss" began Allan, directing his gaze to Mrs Fortescue to which the latter graciously inclined her head.

"I'm here today because of your grandson, Qiáng, who is still missing. Have you heard from him at all?"

The married couple looked at one another and both shook their heads.

"Are your people sure he wasn't in the fire?" asked the Colonel.

"Yes, we're absolutely sure, sir. I'm sorry but I do have to ask this question but did your daughter, as far as you are aware, have any connection with anyone who might wish to kill her and her husband?"

"No, certainly not! That is an affront to our daughter, Detective" said the Colonel getting up from his chair again.

"Sit down, dear, the policeman is only asking these questions because he has to" said his wife getting up from her chair and placing a placatory hand on his arm.

The Colonel shook his head vehemently and allowed his wife to persuade him to sit down.

"You see, Colonel and Mrs Fortescue, what we find extremely puzzling is why your grandson has disappeared. We cannot locate him at all at the moment. Do you have any idea where he might have gone?"

"Detective Sargeant, what are you suggesting? I shall take it as extreme impertinence if you are now inferring that somehow my grandson is what do you call it, on the run and that he may have been instrumental in starting the fire. The poor young man has just lost his parents. I demand an apology".

Allan didn't apologise but let fall a couple of minutes before he broke the silence. He was looking quizzically at the Colonel.

"I haven't suggested or inferred anything detrimental about your grandson. Indeed, he may, and I sincerely hope not, be a victim himself but at present, I'm merely mentioning that it is strange that your grandson cannot be located. However, we are now sure from the forensic evidence that the fire was deliberately started and that is arson. Two people are dead as a result, so this is a murder enquiry, Colonel".

Allan allowed another couple of minutes silence to allow this to sink in.

"Did you know that your son-in-law, Professor Zhang, was worried about Qiáng?"

"No, no" they exchanged glances "No he never mentioned any concerns. What would he be worried about?"

"I was hoping you might tell me. Qiáng isn't, for instance, ill?"

"Not as far as we are aware" Fiona replied.

"One final question if I may" he said without pausing for their permission to speak "what sort of boy is Qiáng? I'm trying to get a sense of what was worrying the Professor. Whether he might be struggling with his studies, with the pressure from his peers or his teachers perhaps?" Allan refrained from mentioning the rumours and he knew full well that Qiáng had no problems with his studies or pressure from anyone, but he didn't want to lead the Fortescues - he wanted to ascertain their understanding of their grandson.

"Qiáng is a brilliant scholar, has a great wit and is an excellent sportsman. Destined for a double first I understand just like his father!" announced Colonel Fortescue.

"I'm sure he is and thank you very much for your time, Colonel and Mrs Fortescue" and he got up to go.

As Allan was getting in his car he glanced up at the house and noticed Fiona Fortescue looking at him intently. He had a peculiar feeling that Fiona wanted to tell him something. He looked down at his gear lever and when he looked up at the window again, the woman had gone. Allan shrugged; he was probably reading too much into it.

The following morning, DC Dev Patel rushed up to Allan as he walked towards his desk.

"The DI wants a word … now!" he said breathlessly.

Allan did an about turn and headed up the stairs to Hopkins' office. He knocked on the door and summoned, he walked in.

Hopkins did not greet him with the usual nod and smile. Instead, he had a thunderous look on his face.

"I've had a complaint, Allan" he began, calling him by his surname and without asking him to sit down which was always an ominous sign.

"May I ask from whom, sir?" Allan asked in a deferential voice.

"Colonel Fortescue. Apparently, you were insinuating that his daughter may have had sinister connections and that there was suspicion of his grandson being a criminal!"

"Sir, firstly, I apologise if I have upset the Colonel, but I was merely pursuing lines of enquiry in order to find the arsonist and to find their grandson. I asked whether they knew of any reason to believe that their daughter knew anyone who could have wanted to kill them, and I suggested that it was curious that their grandson couldn't be found and that he could himself potentially be a victim. If you would like me to apologise to the Colonel, I will be happy to do so" he ended and resolutely held up his chin.

"No need, Allan but try not to blot your copybook again, will you. I will sort this one out. That's all, thank you" he said dismissively.

Allan closed the door quietly behind him, took a deep breath, ran down the stairs, then stopped by the coffee machine and purchased one cappuccino and one expresso. Walking up to Szymanski's desk, he proffered the expresso to his colleague and sat down on the spare chair nursing the cappuccino.

"So we've been through Professor Zhang's financial affairs with a fine toothcomb and it's so squeaky clean I am wondering if it can be true. Seriously, there is absolutely nothing to indicate any underworld connection, fraudulent dealings, nothing to hint at a reprisal of some sort," he said, frustration obvious in his voice and on his face, "What have we got so far. Two people who have burnt to death in a deliberate fire. A son who has gone missing. There is no ostensible reason for anyone to kill these two people and why has Zhang junior disappeared? His photo has just been distributed to the authorities as someone we are actively seeking to help us with our line of enquiry. Hopefully, he will soon be found. He is our best bet but if he is the perpetrator of this crime, what would be his motive? If he was planning on doing something like this and obviously thought, he would get away with it why would he bother with the fraud stuff? Something's definitely off about his fraudulent activity because also, if he is innocent of the murder of his parents and for some hitherto unknown understandable reason he hasn't been found, why bother to risk being found guilty of fraud when you know that you come from an extremely wealthy family and you are going to have an excellent very well-paid career ahead of you with a double first from

Cambridge that would be a certainty. It doesn't make sense! So, it is possible that he is a victim too and the rumours of running a scam are untrue. The only real two points of interest so far is that firstly, Professor Zhang was obviously worried about something concerning his son which could be the damning rumours at the university. Secondly, today when I interviewed the grandparents, I had the feeling that the grandmother wanted to tell me something. That's not much to go on!" mused Allan.

"Maybe make a media announcement to the general public to try to locate Qiáng?" suggested Szymansky.

"Yes, I'll speak to Hopkins and also say I think there should be a full-scale search of the area to make sure he hasn't been killed and his body dumped in the immediate area because that is a possibility. He may indeed also be a victim" said Allan getting up at the same time as draining his coffee cup. He picked up Szymanski's cup and idly mused how she never seemed to lose that lipstick, it seemed to be a permanent fixture. Maybe she had been born complete with vermilion lips! Dismissing these frivolous thoughts, he walked in the direction of his office, throwing the used cups in the waste bin as he passed by.

Later that day he was summoned again to Hopkins' office.

"Good afternoon, sir" said Allan to DI Hopkins as he went into his boss's office having heard the summons to enter.

This time it was the usual greeting.

"What have you got for me, Jack?"

"Financial affairs are in order, no connections with the underworld, Professor Zhang and his wife are beyond reproach. Szymanski has interviewed a colleague of Zhang's and apparently the Professor was concerned about something concerning his son. Rumours were flying about that Zhang junior was involved in serious fraud. I've interviewed the grandparents, and I think there is something they are hiding about their grandson. So, if I could suggest a full-scale search of the area around the house for the body of Zhang junior who could be the intended victim but somehow the plan went wrong. If we don't find his body, I think a press conference with a media appeal should be launched to the general public stating that any sighting should be relayed to the police but that he should not be approached. He may be a victim, or he could be the perpetrator".

"Yes, I agree. I'll organise one for later today and let you know the time. I will want a complete brief from you and your involvement in the questions and answers".

"Sir" said Allan as he got up and swiftly left the office.

The search having drawn a blank the following day a press conference was held and a media appeal launched.

Hundreds of calls from the public were received by the incident team alleging sightings of Qiáng some of which were dismissed immediately after further questioning and some were put on a list of possible follow-ups.

Allan sat at his desk staring out of the window next to him. Nothing made sense. Something didn't sit right with this case and he had always been at odds with that feeling.

A colleague tapped on his desk to draw his attention.

“Sorry, sir” she said “there is a woman at Reception says she needs to tell you something relating to the Zhang case. Says her name is Mrs Fortescue”.

Allan got up knocking some papers on the floor as he did so.

“Pick those up and put them on the desk, will you?” he said in an authoritative voice that indicated that was an order not a request, belying his current status and indicating that he was soon to rise to a higher rank.

Fiona Fortescue was sitting clutching her handbag tightly which was the only insight into the turbulence inside her as outwardly she was as elegant and composed as she had been the previous day.

Allan approached her and the two shook hands.

“Would you like to come this way?” he said and led Fiona into a nearby meeting room.

Closing the door and indicating a chair he said, “I understand you have something of interest to tell me?” He sat down in a chair opposite.

“Yes, well, I don’t really know. It may be of interest, or it may be incidental”, Fiona replied.

“Let me be the judge of that”.

“It was a long time ago. It must have been at least eight years now maybe more when Qiáng was a child. He had a cat. A lovely creature with a beautiful black and white coat”.

“Go on”.

“Qiáng was in the garden and my daughter and son-in-law had been entertaining some guests in the house. The guests gone; they went to find Qiáng. There is no way to describe the depths of disgust and repugnance they felt when they found out what their son had been doing. The cat was dead, stabbed through the heart and Qiáng was dissecting it. He had blood all over him. They questioned him of course and he said he just wanted to know how a cat’s system worked and what it looked like. At first, they thought, well Bingwen thought, that help should be sought for Qiáng, but my daughter said that he was growing up and she was sure that other children had committed far worse acts. She felt they should wait and see if there were any repeat performances. In the end Bingwen felt, and I must admit when we heard about it we agreed, that Qiáng has a brilliant mind and sometimes child prodigies have a thirst for knowledge that take them to a level that a lesser intellect would deem unacceptable. He was, you see, trying to get a better understanding of a cat's anatomy. I suppose they were right about his brilliance. As you know he is likely to attain a double first at one of Britain's top universities. So, there you are, Detective Inspector, that is what I had to tell you and I have probably wasted your time".

"No, not at all. Just one thing you said eight years ago or thereabouts, is that correct?"

"Yes".

"Thank you very much for coming in, Mrs Fortescue, and please don't hesitate to let me know if there is anything else that comes to mind".

"I would ask that you don't tell my husband that I have been to see you. He wouldn't understand".

"There is no reason, at present, for your husband to know and thank you again for coming in".

They shook hands and Mrs Fortescue left.

Allan made his way back to the main office, sat down in front of Szymanski's desk and relayed the essence of Mrs Fortescue's story.

"It begs the question whether someone had it in for Qiáng and by association his family because of something terrible Qiáng did to them, their pet or someone associated to them. Obviously, the cat incident was eight years ago, so is highly unlikely to be relevant although it can't be dismissed altogether. Grudges can be held for a very long time."

"Well forensics have found something else interesting. The paraffin can was found buried in the woodland about a mile from the Zhangs' house and a tiny piece of fabric from what might be an anorak has been extracted from the handle of the can. Forensics are on it now, which might shed some further light".

Allan's mobile rang.

"Allan…." and he sat up straight, listening intently.

"Well, well…. really…..ok….we'll step up the search" he said.

"Things are moving fast now. That was forensics. The windows were glued shut in the main bedroom. That meant that no-one had a cat in hell's chance of getting out with the fire at the doorway and the windows immoveable. Conversely no other windows tested for glue. Get a list together of every shop that sells paraffin in the area within a radius of five miles".

“On it, boss”.

In total Allan and Szymanski questioned six different retailers.

“How many people have you sold a can of paraffin to in the past seven days?” asked Allan to the white-haired Asian man behind the counter, having shown identification.

“Only one” he replied.

“Can you describe him for us?”

“Yes, of course. The young man was about six foot tall with dark hair. I would say he was mixed race, oriental and Caucasian but I don’t know that for sure”.

“Was it this young man?” Allan produced a photo of Qiáng.

The Asian man, putting on his spectacles, looked closely at the photograph.

“Yes, yes it’s him” he replied confidently.

Back at the station the two detectives sat down in Allan’s office.

“On the surface of it, then, it would appear obvious, having been identified by Mr Ahmed at the hardware store, that Qiáng killed his parents?" said Allan looking thoughtful.

"I'm not sure, sir. He may have been asked or forced to buy the paraffin by person or persons unknown. He may be in imminent danger. We don't yet have the report from forensics on the fabric found on the petrol can, do we?" replied Szymanski.

"No, we don't but I don't buy that he was coerced, Julia. I mean he is a young man in his early twenties and brilliant to boot. How could someone have got him to buy it and what reason would someone give him? What about the incident with the cat? That surely backs up the theory that he did it. After all what young child in their right mind would kill a cat for anatomical understanding!?"

Julia nodded pulling the corners of her mouth downwards.

"My money is on Qiáng being behind all of this but nevertheless it is still a matter for conjecture and the theory that he was somehow persuaded to become an accomplice is possible but not probable in my view. He has a brilliant mind and is undoubtedly a cold character if we can believe his friend Mike. This Qiáng is supercilious and in all probability very precocious but that doesn't necessarily make him a killer and there is just a small possibility that he too has been harmed or killed" and Allan leant back in his chair putting his arms behind his head.

"Ummm. As you say, we need to find him. So where do you think he might be?"

"That's a very good question, Julia. We need to step up the search for Qiáng – he is the key to answering three vital questions in this case".

"And they might be?" Szymanski leant forward in her chair.

"Who killed the Zhangs, what was their motive and what has happened to Qiáng?"

Chapter Four – 5 Years Later

DI Jack Allen was scrunching an apple as he ran down the flight of stairs from his flat taking them two at a time. Reaching his car a couple of minutes later he switched on his blues and twos and drove out of the car park at a rapid rate. He had been called to a crime scene where there had been a domestic which had resulted in horrific injuries being inflicted by the husband. Arrived at the house, even his strong stomach that had experienced many terrible sights, turned to jelly when he saw the corpse of the deceased wife. He struggled to keep his apple down. The body was decapitated, one leg and one arm had been sawn off and the hand of the sawn-off arm had been stuffed in the victim's mouth whose sightless stare he couldn't rid from his mind for a long time afterwards. The husband just stood there completely calm and said she deserved it. As far as the law was concerned it was an open and shut case.

Jack's mobile rang.

"It's Jane, Jack" said his sister as though he would have some difficulty recognizing her voice.

"Hi, listen this isn't a good time. Can I call you back?"

"No, you bloody can't. There's never a good time with you, is there? It's always work comes first. Just like dad. You'll end up like him. I can't believe you let your marriage fail in favour of work….".

"Look Jane, can we cut to the chase, please. Otherwise, I'm going to have to go" Jack cut in.

Jane audibly took a deep breath.

"Okay. Mum has had another fall. You know what she's like still insisting on doing her gardening. Anyway, she's been taken to hospital, and I can't go. Phil and I are just about to go on holiday to Crete as you know, and I think it's time you took responsibility for our remaining parent. You have to admit I always step in. It's always me that has to deal with things for mum, well, this time I can't".

"Jane, you have to understand that it's difficult for me to get leave at the drop of a hat. I'm up to my neck in it at the moment".

"Well, I leave it to you to decide which is more important, Jack, your job or mum" and she hung up.

When he got back to the station, after having immediately completed a crime scene report on the domestic, he went upstairs and knocked on

DCI Walters' door. Hearing the summons from within he opened the door and went in.

"Good afternoon, sir".

"Sit down, Jack" said the DCI in response. Bob Walters had nothing but respect for his subordinate who had first excelled under Jim Hopkins as the latter had always known he would. Then Jack successfully applied for the position of DI when he stepped into Hopkins' position after the long serving officer retired. Jack had initially missed his old boss but was soon fully engaged in his new role. That was two years ago. He was in line for further promotion and heading up the ladder with amazing speed although the one-to-ones that Walters had had with Jack indicated that although he would be capable of a higher rank than DI, Jack was very satisfied with the involvement in cases that he was afforded in his current position and which he would largely lose if he moved up.

"I attended the crime scene this morning concerning a domestic, sir. Really nasty business and I've submitted my report".

"Thank you, Jack" the DCI knew that his DI wouldn't have taken the trouble to come upstairs just to tell him that and waited for the real reason for his visit.

"I do apologise, sir, but I need to take some leave of absence. My mother has had quite a bad fall and possibly a stroke. She is in hospital and my sister who would normally take care of things is away on holiday. I know it's short notice, but I am the only other sibling and……"

"What are you doing sitting here, then, Jack. Off you go. Your leave of absence is granted. We all have personal matters to deal with from time to time and just looking at your record here" he said turning to his screen on the corner of his desk and tapping some keys "it looks as though you are due several weeks of leave. How long would you anticipate being away?"

"No more than a week, probably less".

"Very good, Jack, keep me informed and I don't need to tell you to make sure that Szymanski is up to date with everything".

"Of course, sir" and Allan stood up and left, his long legs reaching the office door in three strides.

That had been mid-morning and now he was on his way to Warminster Community Hospital. He made the M3 in good time and sped down the fast lane thankful that there was little traffic. The good luck continued, and he was soon on the A303.

Arriving in Corton, Allan decided to go to his mother's house before going to the hospital. His sister had emailed to him a list of personal items that their mother would need.

He parked up on the drive of the three-bed detached cottage which was located in a leafy lane just past the village church. It was set back from the road, a large front garden with rhododendron bushes screened the house from passers-by and traffic although both were few and far between. The garden was immaculate; largely from the work done by the house owner although nowadays there was a little help from a local gardener.

Allan found the front door key under the pot of geraniums which stood amongst a variety of other potted plants either side of the porch. He went in and closed the door. He stood there for a minute in the hallway running his fingers through his thick, black hair and breathing the familiar smell of his childhood home, a mixture of beeswax polish and scented roses. He walked into the lounge and over to the sideboard with its array of family photographs. Looking at them thoughtfully he then selected one of his father and himself. He remembered that day. It was sunny and warm by the river and his father had been teaching him how to fish. He rang a finger over his father's face including the perpetual cigarette that hung from his mouth. Fishing had been his hobby, he said he found it relaxing and peaceful, therapeutic. It had helped him cope with the stresses of the job until it didn't, and he had turned to alcohol for his relaxation. He thought about the day that his father died. It was cirrhosis of the liver that caused his death, but a tumour had also been found on his lung probably caused by the twenty a day that he had smoked from his early twenties. Allan sighed as he put the photo down. That wasn't going to happen to him. He missed his father. He had had a wicked sense of humour and was devoted to them both when he was there. Both mother and son had known that he had to do his job and understood that he would rather have been with his family. He knew his mother missed him enormously. She had been devastated by her loss. He sighed again as he put the photograph carefully back in its place.

He went upstairs to the main bedroom and began putting together the bits and pieces on the list. He was taking his mother's dressing gown off the back of the door when a piece of paper floated out of one of the side pockets. He stooped to pick it up and, although he knew he should have put it back in the pocket without reading it, out of curiosity he unfolded it. It was a doctor's report, and he took a moment to fully take in what it said. He read it through twice so there was no mistake.

He sat down on the edge of the bed, the paper loosely held in his hand, staring straight ahead at the wall in front of him.

Did his sister know? Had their mother told Jane? He didn't think she had. If she had, Jane would surely have told him. He looked at the date on the letter. Two weeks ago. Their mother was so independent she wouldn't want a fuss, so it was highly likely she had just kept this to herself. Poor mum. She'd lost her soul mate. When he had died, she had been devastated although she knew deep down that his untimely death was a tragedy waiting to happen because of his excessive smoking and drinking. He had been a good husband and father; the drink hadn't made him violent or abusive in any way as many alcoholics were. Then after a while mum had dug deep and was enjoying her later years. Now this bombshell.

He packed up the remainder of the things, went downstairs and made his way to his car having locked the front door and put the key in its secret place.

When he got to the hospital, having stopped by a florist shop on the way, he asked at reception for the whereabouts of Mrs Sarah Allan and having been directed to Aylward Ward he entered a small room with six beds in it. He walked to the end bed on the left and there looking quite frail lay his mother, her eyes closed. He sat down by the bed and held her hand. She stirred and turned her head towards him. Her pallor was pale, but the smile was still there as she opened her eyes and realised her son had come to see her.

"You shouldn't have come, Jack. I'm alright. Just had a silly fall. I tripped on one of those uneven flagstones. You know what it's like. Anyone could do it not just aged people like me. You are busy and I'm holding you up from your work" she said lightly.

"Mum, I wanted to come and see you" and he showed her the flowers which she always appreciated.

"Thank you so much, dear. They are just the thing. Very cheery and pretty. I'm sure one of the nice nurses will arrange for them to be put in a vase.

Allan nodded.

“I’ve also bought you a few personal items” and he opened the bag to show her.

“Thank you again, son, very thoughtful”.

“Oh, it’s Jane you have to thank, not me! I just followed her instructions which were very comprehensive!” he laughed.

“But seriously now, mum, you really must think about moving into a warden assisted flat. You are all on your own there at that house and sometimes Jane can’t come and I’m a long way away now. You need to be able to call on someone quickly if needed” he said solemnly but avoiding mentioning going into a home.

“Nonsense, Jack. You know I love that house and I still enjoy gardening. There is no chance of me going into some pokey little flat without a garden. You should know me better than that!” she retorted and then her expression changed to one of sadness.

“But you know, son, I miss Poppy. You and Poppy were so good together. You knew each other as kids, you grew up together and everyone always knew you would end up together. I wish you could patch things up" and she looked sorrowfully at him.

"There's no chance of that mum, you know that. It's history now".

"Many couples go through what you have been through, and they come out stronger for it. You know why she did what she did, don't you?"

"Yes, I do mum, but I was hurting as much as her. I lost a baby son too. She chose to find consolation in the arms of another man and the day I found her with him was the day I lost my family. There's no going back. The trust has gone and without it there is no relationship" he paused and looked at her considering whether to continue.

"Have you met someone else?" she said smiling, her mother's intuition kicking in.

He laughed.

"How did you guess?"

"I didn't know but I'm right, aren't I?" she was beaming now.

"Yes. She's amazing and I can't believe she's interested in me. She's a very independent person and is all for us remaining in our respective apartments. She's a doctor and understands about shifts so no arguments there".

"What's her name?"

"Vanessa".

"That's wonderful news, Jack. I would so love to see you settled and happy. That would be the best thing that could happen for me".

"Thanks mum, but let's not race ahead too far. We've only been together for a short while. Anyway, it's you we should be talking about not me!" he admonished her, smiling.

They talked of other things then. Of times gone by when his father had been alive. Of her gardening group and how she had won the local Bridge Club competition. He talked a bit about his colleagues but not about his work.

"I'll just go and have a word with your doctor while you have a little rest, mum, ok?" he said at last getting up but still bending over to continue holding her hand.

"Okay dear. I am a little tired now. That's fine".

He went in search of the doctor and found him talking to a nurse along the corridor.

"Excuse me, are you Dr Fraser?"

The doctor turned and looked at him through his black framed spectacles.

"I am and you are?" he said with a professional smile.

"Detective Inspector Jack Allan but I'm here on a personal front about my mother Mrs Sarah Allan".

"Ah, yes. Let's find a quiet room to talk in" he said excusing himself to the nurse he had been speaking to and marching at a rapid rate down the corridor. He quickly found a quiet room and he waved Allan into a seat.

"May I call you Jack?"

"Of course, doctor".

"Jack, how much do you know so far of your mother's condition may I ask?" said the doctor looking at him with a concerned expression making Allan feel even more perturbed than he had a moment ago.

"I read the contents of a letter that by chance fell out of my mother's dressing gown pocket. It seemed to indicate that she is beginning to display signs of Parkinsons".

"Right" and the doctor took his spectacles off and lowered them to his lap then pushed the arms back and forth looking down at them seemingly considering his next words.

"Jack, there is no easy way to say this. Yes, your mother is suffering from some early symptoms of Parkinsons but while she has been here, we have taken a couple of scans and given her a general check-up and I am so very sorry to have to tell you that your mother also has stage four lung cancer".

Allan sat stunned and speechless for what seemed hours, and which was in fact only seconds. This was totally not what he had been expecting and was indeed far worse.

"No that can't be doctor. She has never smoked and has taken care of herself despite everything. No, this must be a mistake" and he looked for confirmation that this could be possible but the doctor, having put his spectacles back on, was shaking his head in a sad and placatory way.

"I wish I could give you the hope you need but I can't. The first scan has shown up a massive tumour on your mother's right lung and this was corroborated by a second scan. There is no doubt".

"How.... how long has she got? A couple of years with treatment?" asked Allan wiping the tears away but even as he asked, he knew it was far less time than that.

"Maximum six months but be prepared it could be a lot sooner".

"Then are you saying it is palliative care?"

"Yes, I'm afraid so but for a time she will be able to remain at home and independent with the aid of pain killers".

"What about trying treatment first. There may be a chance that could work. As I understand it everyone gets cancer from time to time, and they never know just like my mother didn't know and the cancer just disappears of its own accord. We could at least try the treatment, after all if she hadn't had the fall, no-one would have been aware that she had cancer".

"I understand how you feel, Jack, and if there was the slightest chance that treatment might work, believe me we'd be starting it immediately but there is no chance at all that any treatment would work".

Jack looked down at his hands trying to get a hold on his emotions.

"Have you told her? Does she know?" he said in a broken voice.

"No not as yet. Would you like to break it to her, or do you want us to?" the doctor asked softly.

"I don't know. Yes, I think really, I should be the one" he said distractedly.

"Of course, and if you have any further questions or change your mind and want us to tell her, don't hesitate to find me. Once again, I am very sorry, Jack. Please feel free to stay here as long as you like".

The doctor's bleeper sounded, and he got up and walked to the door, opening and shutting it quietly, leaving Jack with his face in his hands silently sobbing.

After half an hour Jack wiped away the tears again, found a toilet and rinsed his face in cold water at the sink, patting it dry with one of the rough NHS paper towels. He stood at the sink, his hands resting on the rim and looked himself in the eye in the mirror. He had to be strong for his mother. It was going to be the worst shock of her life and he needed to be there for her. He decided not to text or ring Jane. She was on holiday. No need to ruin it. There would seem to be time when they returned for her to be with mum before the inevitable happened.

Jack returned to his mother's bedside.

"I already knew, Jack" she said raising her hands and holding her son's face in them after having heard the terrible words.

"How so, mum?"

"The pain. I've had very bad back pain lately and a cough that hasn't shifted. Then a few days ago there was blood when I coughed. You just know, don't you, when there is something wrong?"

They talked until she fell asleep, and he promised to come and see her again the next day.

He called in at the local pub for a meal on the way to his mother's house and then crashed out in front of the television. He woke up at four o'clock in the morning after having some terrible dreams about running from something or someone, but they continued to chase him. He had woken up in a sweat. Donning some sports gear that he found in his old room he went for a five-mile run. He was starving when he got back and raided his mother's fridge. Breakfast was not as healthy as normal, but he scrambled some eggs and was halfway through it when his mobile rang. He looked at the time. Walters was calling at six-thirty. Something was up.

"Sir?"

"Jack, I'm sorry to disturb you. How is your mother?" asked Walters.

"Not good news, I'm afraid, sir" Allan said not trusting his voice to remain stable if he elaborated.

Walters seemed to understand and refrained from asking Allan any further details.

"I'm sorry to hear that, Jack, but I need you back here immediately, I'm afraid. How quickly can you be here?"

"I'll leave right away. I'll be with you around lunchtime" he said.

"Good. Quick as you can, Jack" and the DCI hung up.

Chapter Five

Francesca Cunningham walked across the wide south-facing lawn towards the marquees that had been set up for the annual summer party held in the grounds of the splendid Cambridgeshire mansion. The party had only been held for the first time in May two years ago and so it was this year. Already it had become a major event in the calendars of all the residents of the small village in which Misslethwaite Hall was situated.

"I think there should be some garlands of flowers around the entrances to the marquees" she suggested in her sing-song unaccented voice.

"What a good idea, Lady Cunningham" replied one of the staff that had been hired for the event. Francesca didn't officially have a title but from the time she and her husband moved into the Hall the villagers called her Lady, and it had stuck.

She smiled and nodded. Francesca was tall and slim, twenty-four years of age but because of her poise and confidence could be mistaken for thirty years. Her blonde hair scraped back into a ponytail accentuated her fine bone structure, perfectly arched eyebrows, and wide smile, displaying perfectly even very white teeth. However, it was her eyes that everyone noticed, not because of the colour, which was an altogether uninteresting sort of hazel, but because of the expression; a mixture of interest and aloofness which made her alluring to all. She was very well liked both by the staff and the villagers.

Because Francesca was awarded the title 'Lady' by the locals, they felt they had to call Piers Cunningham 'Sir' and so it was that Sir Piers Cunningham ran down the steps onto the lawns and putting his arm round his wife's tiny waist kissed her lightly on the lips.

Piers was a full four inches taller than his wife at six feet two inches but as Francesca generally wore three-inch heels, she usually didn't appear to be a great deal shorter than her husband. He was also twenty-five years her senior, distinguished looking with silver-grey hair, but his physique was that of a much younger man.

"Everything under control, darling?" he asked in a deep, rich, well-educated voice.

"Yes, I'm very pleased with the progress so far. There is still much to do before tomorrow but I'm sure everyone will have a terrific time".

"Just like last year then! A repeat performance, darling".

"And what have you been doing this morning?" she asked archly.

"Oh, just boring business. My son is on his way over and should be here this evening so make sure there's an extra place at dinner".

Before she could answer his mobile rang.

"Damn! Sorry, darling. I must take this!" he said moving away and blowing her a kiss.

Francesca continued giving orders and making suggestions for the decorations and arrangements for the following day and then went in to speak to the housekeeper regarding dinner.

That evening the dinner table was laid for three but only Piers and Francesca were seated as the soup was served. Suddenly, the sound of a deep, throaty engine could be heard. Small stones from the wide gravel drive showering from the wheels of the black Porsche announced the unmistakeable arrival of Freddie Cunningham.

"Sorry I'm late, I got held up" he said bursting into the dining room where his father and stepmother were already seated.

“Well at least you are consistent in your habits, Freddie” was his father’s dry greeting.

Freddie sat down in the chair between his parents.

“Must take after you then, dad!” he said with a wide grin.

“Francesca has been working hard on the arrangements for tomorrow. You are, of course, coming!” said his father between mouthfuls of asparagus soup. It was rather more of a statement than a question.

“Try and stop me!” was the reply not without a sarcastic tinge.

“I know you think this is a waste of time, Freddie, but the villagers really look forward to it and it’s a way of cheering people up when there have been so many problems for them to cope with lately. We are very fortunate and it’s good to help those that are not so lucky in life” said Francesca looking directly at Freddie.

“Very commendable, oh wise and charitable stepmother” and he got up from his chair and made a mock bow.

“Yes, your father is right, you are consistent, certainly in your rudeness and thoughtlessness”.

“That will do now, I think. Apologise to Francesca, Freddie” instructed his father.

Francesca glared at Freddie, and he stood up once again.

“I have been instructed to apologise to you, Francesca, and so I do” he said unconvincingly.

After dinner, Piers and Freddie installed themselves in Piers’ study for a father and son chat.

Francesca went into a drawing room that she kept for herself, to go through last minute details for the next day.

Suddenly she found herself concentrating on the voices in the next room which had become raised.

“That is the most stupid idea I think I have ever heard!” Piers was saying in a raised voice.

“But, dad, it’s not. You know it makes sense. When I spoke to you this afternoon, I wasn’t kidding. Unless we do this, all our dreams, I mean, the project won’t come to fruition. Desperate measures. You know if this fails.......”

“Shhhhh…”

The voices lowered again and there was no more shouting.

Francesca sat there for some minutes digesting what she had heard. ‘All our dreams…project …. desperate measures’; what dreams? what project? what desperate measures? This didn’t sound like anything to do with the pharmaceutical company that her husband owned and where her stepson was a junior director. What were they talking about? In the end she gave up searching for the answers and went up to bed.

Piers and Freddie sat in Piers’ study. Piers was sitting upright with his hands steepled, his elbows on the desk.

Freddie sat opposite him lounging back, his hands crossed in his lap.

“You can’t back out now” Freddie was saying, “there’s too much at stake”.

“I am backing out Freddie and I suggest you do to. I don’t think you realise what you are doing, what you are getting into”.

“I absolutely know what this is about. The company needs this. You know it is floundering, and this will save it. Our competition is too strong for us to survive much longer. We need this life saving injection of funds".

Piers was shaking his head.

"No, Freddie. That is my final word on the matter" he said firmly and standing up he continued, "Now I need to get on with some paperwork. Freddie, good night, and don't think for one minute I will change my mind in the morning".

Freddie got up, glanced at his father with an unreadable expression and left the room without a word, closing the door quietly behind him.

Francesca, dressed in a beautiful rose-pink negligee, was brushing her hair in front of their dressing table when her husband entered their bedroom.

He walked across and gave her a kiss on the lips and the tip of her nose. Then he walked over to their dressing room and started to unbutton his shirt.

"What is going on, Piers?" said Francesca turning round on her stool to look at him.

"What do you mean, my love?".

“I heard raised voices. You were arguing with Freddie in the study” she said.

Piers hesitated before answering.

“Oh that!” he said at last. “Nothing for you to worry about, darling. Really, there is no need to be concerned. Everything is fine! It was just a little disagreement about the company, that’s all”,

He bent over and kissed the top of her head. She looked up at his reflection in the mirror and smiled but her eyes expressed the concern she still felt.

The next day was a glorious one. The weather forecast had been right. It was only May, but it seemed more like July. The sun was shining brightly, the sky a brilliant blue and the lawns were beautifully green, the sprinklers having been on and off throughout the night. There were garlands of fresh flowers; red, pink, orange, apricot and white were among the colours adorning the marquees. Tables had been laid with crisp, white, linen tablecloths. There were piles of sausage rolls, quiche, savouries and salads of all kinds. Delicious desserts and elaborate gateaux were abundantly available. There was red and white wine and plenty of beers with squashes and fruit juice for the children and those who didn’t drink alcohol. On the lawns croquet had been set up. Bat and ball poles. A fortune teller sat outside one of the marquees at a table, a set of tarot cards to the ready. A Punch and Judy show, coconut shies, and archery were amongst the excellent entertainment to be enjoyed on this perfect summer day.

To the left of the main area was a large swimming pool and changing area. A notice had been put up to advise parents that they should accompany their children if using the pool, but everyone was welcome to use it. Loungers had been placed by the pool for those who were sun worshippers. No detail had been overlooked; no expense spared.

Francesca looked radiant in a yellow sundress with red detail. Her striking blonde hair hung down her back in loose curls and some tresses had escaped over her shoulders. She was smiling as she looked around her.

“Perfect, just perfect” she thought.

At 11.00 a.m. the villagers would be arriving. Not all the villagers would attend, of course, some houses were used for summer holidays, occupants of others would be on business. Francesca was expecting about two hundred and fifty guests. She didn’t know if she was pleased or concerned that Freddie had decided to join the party. She fervently hoped her stepson would control his rudeness and not ruin the day. For the moment he seemed to be enjoying himself in the pool. Hopefully he would get dry and dressed to conduct his host duties along with herself and Piers and welcome everyone as they arrived.

Francesca went to find her husband and finally caught up with him standing under the shade of an old apple tree by the lake that was shimmering in the strong sunlight some way from where the fun and festivities would take place.

"Hi, darling. Are you okay? Only people will be arriving in droves very soon, and I think we should be ready to circulate?" her voice went up a decibel as she threw the question to him.

"Yes, everything's fine my love" he said turning to her, but his reassuring tone didn't match the worried frown.

He reached for her hand and raising it up to his lips he kissed it holding her eyes with his. Then he put his hands around her waist and gently pulled her towards him. He kissed her on the lips and then kissed her again more passionately.

After a few moments where they were locked in a tight embrace, he took her hand and led her up towards the entrance gates where the first arrivals had appeared.

The next half-hour was spent shaking hands with the guests until Piers and Francesca thought their hands would drop off from overwork. Francesca periodically looked round expecting to see Freddie walking up to undergo his hosting duties.

"If you are expecting to see Freddie, you won't, darling, so don't over exercise your neck in the futile belief he will appear".

"I know, darling, but one lives in hope" she replied, smiling weakly at her husband who she knew was right.

The stream of guests finally dried up and Piers and Francesca walked arm in arm smiling around them at their guests and watching the ever-increasing throngs of people who were to be seen queuing for archery, outside the fortune teller's tent, in fact everywhere there were queues for the entertainment. Children were laughing and shouting to each other in the swimming pool and adults were enjoying the champagne, the wine and lavish food that was spread over several tables. The whole atmosphere was one of fun and enjoyment. Francesca felt flushed with pleasure as she approached the happy scene and squeezed her husband's hand. He squeezed her waist in reply.

It was against this happy scene that the contrast of the ensuing events would always remain stark to those who witnessed it.

Suddenly without warning first one adult then another, then a child and so on fell to the ground like soldiers killed at a battle. People screamed, children started to cry, hysteria set in. Francesca just stared, shocked, at the unfolding scene before her, totally unable to move. Then she turned to her husband, but he wasn't there. She looked round wildly trying to locate him. Adrenalin kicked in and she started to run, across the grass, up the steps and into the house. Grabbing her mobile she tapped 999.

"Police, ambulance. Come quickly. Something dreadful is happening here. People - children are falling over. They are on the ground".

"Can you give me the number you are calling from please?"

Francesca gave her number.

"I will ring you back on this number if we get cut off. Try to keep calm, Francesca. We will send help. Approximately how many people have been affected?"

"I don't know. About.................."

"Francesca? Francesca?"

All the while outside, more and more men, women and children had fallen to the ground. Francesca lay on the floor; the mobile had slithered under the large, mahogany hall table as she crashed to the floor. Her eyes were staring, her mouth open and her body unmoving.

Ambulance and police sirens were heard minutes after Francesca's frantic call.

DS Julia Szymanski had been in the police canteen getting a late lunch when she received the call about the incident at the Hall. She immediately called DC Dev Patel.

"You've heard obviously" she stated without preliminary pleasantries.

"Yes, just had a call but no real detail" Dev replied.

"Good. I'll pick you up in fifteen and fill you in" she said abruptly. She put on her siren and blue lights and arrived there in ten minutes.

When she arrived at the three-bed semi-detached on the outskirts of Cambridge where Dev lived with his parents and two sisters, the front door opened before she had time to alight from the car. Mrs Patel stood looking at Szymanski with a welcoming smile, pushing her blonde bob behind one ear.

"Dev won't be a moment, Detective Sergeant" she said respectfully as Szymanski approached up the crazy-paved garden path.

"Good afternoon, Mrs Patel. How are you?" Szymanski asked politely breathing in the ever-present aroma of lemons that seemed to always emanate from Dev's house although admittedly she had only been there a few times.

"Very well, thank you".

At that moment Dev came rushing down the stairs. He was of medium height, but if he had one distinguishing feature it was his feet that seemed to be several sizes too big for his frame.

"Sorry, Julia" he said his blue eyes, the exact same colour as his mother's, looking apologetically at his senior.

"Let's go" said Szymanski nodding a goodbye at his mother.

The two detectives were the first on the scene. Patel's mouth involuntarily dropped open at the horrific sight. Szymanski outwardly remained completely calm and focussed. Inside her stomach churned and she felt sick. She stuck a mint in her mouth and offered one to her colleague which he gratefully received.

Szymanski moved towards the crowd and picked on an adult still standing but who was clearly in a state of shock.

"What happened here? Take your time" she said with a sympathetic tone and a comforting smile.

At that moment a women approached her running, waving her arms and shouting. At first what she was saying was unintelligible mixed as it was with her crying, the tears streaming down her face.

"I'm Detective Sergeant Szymanski. Madam, please calm down otherwise I can't help you" Szymanski said in a reassuring manner. The woman was clutching her arms and sobbing but eventually calmed down enough to explain her distress.

"My boy, my son, Timmy, he's not here. I can't find him. He's gone. Someone has taken him.

Where is he? Where is my son? Where.... where....?" and the hysteria rose in her voice once more.

Szymanski took out her notebook.

"Can we find somewhere to sit down Ms....?" Szymanski looked about her, glimpsed a summerhouse a short distance away and led the woman there.

"Mrs Swan, Susan Swan" she managed sniffing loudly. They were sitting on the bench in the summerhouse at the southern edge of the manicured lawns.

"Mrs Swan when did you last see Timmy?" Szymanski asked.

"He was in the swimming pool. I've been there and some of his friends they're...well they're...." and she stopped and gulped unable to speak.

"I know this is very difficult Mrs Swan and I repeat take your time, but I must understand all the facts before I can begin to help. Are you saying that his friends are dead?"

"I'm not sure but they weren't moving" she whispered.

"And your son wasn't there?"

"No, no he wasn't. I've looked everywhere, Sergeant, and he has just disappeared".

"Is your husband around Mrs Swan. I think someone should be with you".

"He's around somewhere. What I want is my Timmy" and she wiped her eyes and nose with her tissue that had numerous holes in it from overuse.

"I assure you, Mrs Swan, we will do everything in our power to find your son".

The ambulances were in the process of taking people to hospital or going straight to the morgue and some seemed to recover.

After finishing talking to Mrs Swan with reassurances that they would do all in their power to find little Timmy, Szymanski called Allan and gave him a rundown on the situation. Allan told her to give the order to seal off the area and get forensics there to check the food and water. He was thinking poisoning of some sort, he told her. The possible kidnap of two children was of tantamount importance and to prioritise establishing the facts relating to their disappearance as quickly as possible.

Walking towards the trestle tables filled with food and sporting all sorts of hot and cold beverages, she saw out of the corner of her eye a young attractive woman stumbling towards her. Very unsteady on her feet she had a look of horror on her refined face.

Szymanski ran towards her and took her by the arm, guiding her to one of the trestle benches. When she had calmed down a little, Szymanski began her questioning.

“I’m Detective Sergeant Szymanski, Cambridgeshire Constabulary. Can you tell me your name, please?”

“Francesca Cunningham” she replied.

“Your husband is Piers Cunningham who owns Cunningham & Son?”

“Yes,” she whispered, tears now streaming down her face.

“In your own words what happened here, Mrs Cunningham?” she asked.

“Please call me Francesca, detective” she said with a sob in her voice.

“Francesca, please tell me the exact events leading up to when people started falling over”.

“I don’t know” she stammered “my husband and I were walking back from welcoming our guests at the main gate, and everyone was enjoying themselves in the swimming pool, queueing for the fortune teller, eating, drinking, laughing and then suddenly people started falling to the floor as though they had been shot but there was no gunman. I ran to the house to phone for the emergency services. I thought it might be food poisoning, but I didn’t really know what it could be. It was just indescribably ghastly, like something out of a horror movie. I managed to make the call but in the middle of it I must have blacked out like I suppose some of my guests did. It was like someone, or something hit me. One minute I was standing and the next moment I was falling. I don’t remember anything else”.

“How are you feeling now?”

“I feel I’m in a nightmare. None of this seems real. I don’t feel too bad physically but ……”

“Yes, I can imagine. I need to ascertain some facts. So, you and your husband hold a gathering every year, I understand. Is that correct?”

“Yes, we do. That is correct” replied Francesca wiping the smeared mascara across her face.

“You said you thought it might be food poisoning. Which caterers do you use?”

“Minows. They are always excellent. I can’t think that any of their food was sub- standard, and they have very stringent hygiene rules which is partly why we use them. It was just that I couldn’t think of any reason why people should just fall to the ground en masse” she replied clasping and unclasping her hands.

“Did you notice anything odd before or during the event, even the slightest seemingly unimportant thing could be very important?”.

She bowed her head in thought, her hands now either side of her, grasping the edge of the bench, her knuckles white with the pressure.

Looking up after a couple of minutes she looked Szymanski straight in the eye.

“There was one thing, but it couldn’t have anything to do with this” and she nodded towards the latterly festive area.

“Let me be the judge of that” replied Szymanski sternly.

“Well, there were two things really. Last night my husband and stepson had a disagreement of some sort. I don't know what it was about, but I heard raised voices. It didn't last long, and everything was fine this morning. Freddie and Piers were talking amicably over breakfast but my husband disappeared just as guests were about to arrive, and when I finally found him by the lake, he was troubled. There was something on his mind without a doubt".

"Did he give any indication of what that might be?"

She shook her head.

"Do you know where they both are now?"

"No. I don't" she said getting up suddenly alert. Shading her hand against the sun she cast her eye all around her.

"I'm sorry but I must go and find them. What was I thinking sitting here talking to you!"

"Francesca, you have had a terrible shock. You should see a paramedic before you do anything else. In the meantime, can you describe your husband and stepson, and we will try to locate them".

A shadow fell over them as a tall dark imposing man appeared. Piers went straight to his wife and pulled her towards him.

“Thank god you are alive, my darling” he said hugging her tightly.

Francesca was too overwhelmed to speak and just looked up at him, tears once again streaming down her face.

Szymanski coughed and they both turned to her.

“Very glad you are alive and well, Mr Cunningham. I would like to ask you a couple of questions if I may?” said Szymanski standing up, putting her at eye level with Cunningham.

“Of course, Detective....?” asked Piers Cunningham with a slight incline of his distinguished head.

“Detective Sergeant Szymanski, sir. Can you tell me what the disagreement with your stepson yesterday evening was about?”

There was a moment of hesitation before Cunningham answered and Szymanski could bet that she wasn’t going to get the absolute truth. Cunningham was uncomfortable but he was good at hiding it.

“Oh that! That was nothing. My son is a director at my company, and it was a work-related matter” and he displayed a perfect set of very white teeth enhancing a charming grin.

"May I ask how you know about our conversation?" he added looking directly in Szymanski's eye.

"Following on from that though, sir, according to your wife, you seemed troubled this morning just before the guests arrived. As this is an annual event hosted by yourselves it would seem to be a time for enjoyment so I presume whatever was on your mind must have been very concerning?" asked Szymanski totally ignoring Cunningham's question.

"I have to say Detective Sergeant Szymanski, I find your questioning impertinent. If something was on my mind it was a private matter and there is no reason at all why I should answer any more of your questions. My wife and I are going to look for our son and establish the situation regarding our guests. I bid you good day!" and he gently but firmly led his wife away.

Szymanski went in search of Patel and caught up with him finishing an interview with one of the casualties who was wrapped in a blanket sitting on the steps of an ambulance. Black vans having taken away the dead there were still several paramedics treating patients.

"So, what have you gleaned?" Szymanski looked questioningly at Patel.

"Well apart from the missing child Mary Peters……."

"Just hold on a sec a missing child did you say?" interrupted Szymanski.

"Yes, that's right, her parents who were not affected it would seem, can't find her anywhere – why?"

"Ah that's interesting. Very interesting. Because a little boy called Timmy Swan is also missing" Szymanski took a mint out of her pocket and absent-mindedly stuck it in her mouth sucking on it loudly. She proffered the packet to Patel who waved a hand.

"What other information did you gain from the interviews of survivors?" asked Szymanski staring ahead, her eyes focussed inwards on her thoughts.

"Not a lot really. They all seem to have been enjoying themselves and then they blacked out.

No-one saw or heard anything out of the ordinary".

****

Having popped into the hospital and explained to his mum that he had to go, work called and promising to be back as soon as he could, Allan had run to his car, putting his sirens and blue lights on.

Racing along the A303 towards the M3 his mind switched from personal to professional thoughts. From what Walters had told him this case sounded potentially complicated. He needed to find these children quickly and establish what if anything the connection was to the collapse of some of the guests.

While he was driving, he thought about his team which he had pulled together over the last two years. Overall, they were a good fit. Julia had been promoted to Detective Sergeant now and Dev, of course. They had both stayed with him when he had been promoted to DI and then Barry, Peter and Sophie, all of them were exemplary police officers, and he was lucky to have drawn them into his team. However, there were a couple of things about two of his team that were slightly concerning. Recently, Amy had shown signs of being restless and had applied for promotion unsuccessfully. By all accounts she felt unappreciated and was pretty miffed about being passed over. He made a mental note to give her a pep talk. Mike was his other concern. He had a gambling habit which he wasn't aware that his boss knew about. That could be a problem especially as he understood his habit was getting worse not better. Again, he made a mental note to speak to Mike when he had the chance.

His thoughts were interrupted from time to time as he was in constant contact with Szymanski for the duration of the journey and consequently was up to speed when he arrived a couple of hours later.

"Right! We need to organise a search of the area for these missing children" said Allan to Szymanski and Patel.

Within two hours a police team had been drafted in to conduct the search. They spread out in a long line and scoured the surrounding area.

Allan's DCI appeared in the middle of proceedings.

"Nothing so far, sir" said Allan answering his boss' enquiry.

“I’m getting flak from upstairs, Jack. We must find these children and find them fast!” Walters said in an agitated manner.

“Yes, sir, understand sir” said Allan thinking that was a statement of the obvious.

“Do you, do you, Jack? Understand? I don’t think you realise the pressure I’m under. The Super is already breathing down my neck” Walters said turning to look at his subordinate.

Allan studiously avoided looking at him and tried not to smile. They were all under pressure and surely the most important issue was finding the kids not pleasing the Super, but he kept his thoughts to himself.

The light was failing now, and both Walters and Allan agreed that the search should begin again in the morning at first light.

“So, what do you make of it, Julia?” asked Allan when the two of them were back at the station that evening.

“Two children have gone missing. Some guests have died and some survived. Some have not been affected at all. It doesn’t make any sense!” said Szymanski.

“No, I agree. It would be too much of a coincidence that the missing children and the guests afflicted with maybe food poisoning, were not connected. We need the forensic report on the drinks and food. I would be surprised if that didn’t yield something. The question is where are the children? Why have they gone missing? Most puzzling though is what the connection is between them and the afflicted guests”.

Chapter Six

Five o'clock in the morning the following day saw Allan lost in thought. Having completed his usual workout, he was munching on a super healthy breakfast of probiotic yoghurt, a mixture of nuts and seeds, strawberries, and black grapes washed down with mango and orange juice. A Press Conference had been due for nine o'clock and he was scheduled to speak. He got up, walked over to the sink and began washing up his bowl, spoon and glass when his mobile started to ring and vibrate.

"Allan" he said in his usual abrasive style.

"Sir, sorry to disturb you at this hour but I thought you would want to hear this straightaway. The two missing children have been found or rather they turned up at their homes about twenty minutes ago," said Szymanski.

"Do we know what happened to them?"

"Well, here's the thing. Apparently, from what I can gather so far, the children don't remember anything!"

"Right. First call off the Press Conference and the search. Meet me at Timmy Swan's house in an hour. If the children arrived home a short time ago no-one is going to be asleep, and we need to find out if the children remember something but perhaps are too afraid to speak".

"Yes, boss, see you in an hour".

On his way to his car and his mobile rang again.

"What the hell is going on, Allan? I've just heard the search, and the Press Conference have been called off. I assume the children have been found, have they? Either that or you have finally taken leave of your senses?" Walters shouted so loudly that Allan held his phone several inches away from his ear, an unmistakable irritation in his boss' voice.

Allan tentatively held his mobile to his ear again and with his other hand he smoothed back his thick, dark, hair, an amused smile dancing on his lips.

"Sorry, sir, I was just about to call you with an update. You're absolutely right, of course, the children have in a sense been found.......".

DCI Walters having calmed down slightly at Allan's flattery immediately began fuming again.

"What do mean 'in a sense'"? he interrupted, shouting loudly down the phone.

“I mean, sir, that the children just turned up at their homes. Paramedics have examined them, and they seem fit and well with no signs of abuse. Apparently, they don’t remember anything. DS Szymanski and myself are going over to each home now to interview the children and again, sir, I apologise that I didn’t manage to catch you before you rang me”.

“Okay Allan, carry on but make sure you inform me immediately if there is any news” he barked and clicked off.

****

There was an uncomfortable atmosphere around the Cunningham breakfast table. Francesca hadn’t eaten a thing and could barely swallow her tea. Piers looked like thunder and Freddie was stone faced.

“Do you think the children are alright? Perhaps they are playing a prank? It was such a horrid ending to what should have been a fantastic fun day for everyone” Francesca broke the suffocating silence, the news of the children turning up not having reached them.

“Let’s hope so!” replied her husband looking directly at Freddie.

Freddie steadfastly took an interest in his breakfast and didn't look up.

Francesca got out her handkerchief, wiped her eyes and started to sniff.

"I'm sure they will be fine, darling" Piers said seeing his wife's distress and endeavouring to allay her fears. He placed his hand over hers.

"Yes, Francesca, Dad's right. Don't worry about it! They'll turn up!" Freddie added and looked defiantly at his father.

"Where were you yesterday, Freddie? We couldn't find you anywhere" asked Francesca.

"I was around and about. Never in one place for very long. I was mingling with the guests, and you probably just missed me all the time. Then I went for a drink with Miles and James at The Good Shepherd hence I wasn't back until very late but I'm a big boy now and allowed to stay up after nine o'clock!" he said laughing.

Piers got up abruptly from the table and strode out of the room.

Freddie wiped his mouth with the napkin and made to get up also.

"Don't go Freddie, I want to ask you something".

Freddie sat back down,

“Freddie, what were you and Piers arguing about the other evening?”

“Arguing, who says we were arguing?”

“I do! I heard you and you were both raising your voices!”

“Well, if our voices were that raised, and you were eavesdropping then you should have heard what it was about! Might I suggest in future that you don’t eavesdrop then you won’t be curious, and you will give everyone a rest!”

“Don’t be impertinent, Freddie!”

Freddie smiled superciliously as he got up.

Turning at the door he said, “Have you tried asking your husband?”

****

Allan and Szymanski were seated in the Swan’s small but comfortable lounge. Susan Swan was bustling about making tea and offering biscuits, her eyes still red from the crying. Stephen Swan was sitting with Timmy on the sofa opposite and Susan joined them having placed her cup and saucer carefully on the coffee table between the sofas.

"Thank you for the tea, Susan. Now Timmy I just want to ask you a few questions about your day yesterday at the fête. Is that alright?"

The small boy nodded but he noticeably cuddled up further into his father's arm.

"So, what happened when you went to the fête? Just tell us what you did when you got there".

Timmy fiddled with his fingers and stared down at them.

"There's no need to be afraid, Timmy. We are here to help, and nothing is going to happen to you. We just need to know about all the fun you had yesterday, that's all. Okay?" encouraged Szymanski.

"I like swimming, so I went to the pool with my friends. We were jumping in and out. We used the slide, then some of us played ball in the water and some of us swam up and down. Then I heard screaming, and I could see people falling over".

He stopped and continued fiddling with his fingers.

"So, then what happened, Timmy?" nudged Szymanski in a soft friendly tone.

"Then nothing. I don't remember anything else" he said.

"So, you were swimming, playing ball and generally enjoying yourselves. Then you saw people fall over. That must have been worrying. Did you try to find your mum and dad? Did you go over to some of the people and try to find out what was the matter? Try to remember, Timmy, what you did".

Timmy shook his head.

"I think, Inspector, that is enough for today. Timmy can't remember. He has had an ordeal, and he is clearly upset".

"Okay Stephen, I understand but there is just one more question I need to ask your son," said Allan.

Stephen nodded his agreement.

"Timmy, can you remember how you got home? Your mum and dad tell me that you just arrived at the front door. They heard the doorbell and there you were standing on the doorstep. Were you playing a game and thought it was fun to hide from your mum and dad for a while?"

Timmy shook his head violently.

Allan held up his hand to prevent Stephen stopping the interview.

"Just one more question, I promise. Timmy, can you remember did someone drop you in a car outside your house? Were you in a car?"

"I don't know. I can't remember!" and the little boy started to cry.

"I'm sorry but we are obliged to ask these questions to try to establish what happened and if they were abducted, by whom. I'm sure you understand?" said Allan addressing Stephen Swan.

"Yes, Inspector but *you* must understand that our son is traumatised from something. He's a good boy and I would be very surprised indeed to discover that he went missing on purpose" replied the little boy's father.

The two detectives thanked the parents once more and left.

Back in the police car they sat for a moment each deep in thought.

"What do you make of the boy's loss of memory?" Allan asked.

“I don’t know, sir. It’s certainly strange, particularly as he can’t even remember how he got to be on his doorstep”.

“Yes, it almost seems as though he has been brainwashed into forgetting a particular timespan. So, he remembers being at the swimming pool and nothing after that until he arrived home. Either he was brainwashed, which seems a little on the dramatic side and which begs the question why anyone would brainwash a small child or more likely he is too terrified to tell us. Let’s now find out little Mary Peters’ experience” and Allan fired up the ignition.

It was a ten-minute drive to the Peters’ house. By contrast to the Swan’s neat semi-detached this house was a rather shabby looking end of terrace ex-council property in need of a coat of paint and the garden, a lawn mower. They walked up the cracked concrete pathway and rang the doorbell which somewhat surprisingly worked.

The door opened a crack and a burly looking man with unkempt greying hair stared belligerently at the two police officers.

“Good morning, Mr Peters?” asked Allan with a friendly smile.

"Yeah, who's askin'?"

"Detective Inspector Allan and Detective Sergeant Szymanski, sir" replied Allan and they both proffered their identification for inspection.

Darren Peters gave the badges a cursory glance.

"Well? Wotever you've 'eard and wotever you fink I ain't done it" he said.

"We are here about your daughter Mary. We would like to talk to her briefly, if we may, about what happened at the fête".

"She don't want no more upset with it so nah, you may not talk to 'er" and he went to close the door.

Allan winced at the double negative but quickly put his hand on the door to prevent it closing.

"We really need to speak to your daughter, Mr Peters, Mary may not be aware but she could have information for us about who abducted her and Timmy Swan. I'm sure you realise how important it is to understand exactly what happened to them".

"It was probably just kids mucking about and they are frightened to tell us 'cos they know we'll give 'em a good 'iding" sneered Peters.

“Perhaps you are right, sir, but if you’re not, then other children might be in danger. Unless there is some other reason you don’t want us to speak to Mary?”

“Wot yer implying?” demanded Peters.

“I’m not implying anything, sir, but I would ask again, just a few minutes with your daughter and, of course, you will be present too”.

Peters considered for a moment and grumbling under his breath he grudgingly opened the door to allow them to enter.

Once in the lounge/diner, Allan pulled up one of the dining room chairs to sit on as one of the armchair seats was missing, displaying the springs beneath. Szymanski took the remaining armchair.

On the settee Mary sat close to her mother who was stroking the little girl’s hair back from her forehead. Peters had by now disappeared somewhere in the house.

“Thank you very much Mrs Peters for allowing us to speak to little Mary here, it is much appreciated” began Allan.

"That's alright Inspector but can you no' be too long abou' i' 'cos our Mary is still gettin' over it".

"Of course. Now Mary, your mum tells us that you are still getting over it. Can you tell us what 'it' is?"

Mary looked up with a puzzled expression at Allan and then at Szymanski who smiled at her. She turned away and buried her face in her mother's side.

Allan and Szymanski exchanged the briefest of glances.

"Mary, we want to catch the people who took you away from your mum and dad but to do that we have to ask you what you remember. Can you do that for us?"

Mary slowly came out of hiding and glanced at the detectives before looking down at her hands.

"Mum and dad asked me the same question and I told 'em I don't remember nuffink. Just that I wos in a queue to have my face painted and the people started to fall down round me. The next fing I remember is standing on me doorstep".

"So, Mary, you don't remember who brought you back home or how?" asked Szymanski.

The little girl shook her head.

Allan and Szymanski thanked Mrs Peters and left.

Back at the station, Allan called together his team.

“You’ve all read the case file. Anyone with any thoughts?”

“Yes, sir, there doesn’t seem to be a plausible explanation as to how the children were abducted. However, if the children were taken, it would appear that there were two perpetrators involved because Mary and Timmy were in completely different areas?” said Barry.

“Good point. Anyone else?”

“In my opinion, in view of the lack of evidence that the children have been in any way harmed or abused, it is probably a childish prank to have some fun and when they realised that they had caused so much worry and concern they became frightened and decided that the best course of action would be to keep silent” suggested Sophie.

“Ordinarily, I would be inclined to agree with you, Sophie, but I have a gut feeling that something bigger is at play and that the children were abducted. But what happened to them and why can’t they remember anything? Why were they abducted? No stone should be left unturned, and I would like all the villagers to be interviewed to just to cross the ‘t’s’ and dot the ‘i’s’. It could be that one of the guests unwittingly observed something out of place, something odd”.

“Do we need further help from uniform?” questioned Julia looking at Allan.

“No, I think our team will be enough to deal with this. Organise it for later this afternoon and evening. We should get most people home from work at the end of the day”.

Allan’s mobile rang, and he signalled to the team that they had finished and could go.

“Allan” he barked.

“Morning, Jack. Thought you would want the feedback from forensics on food and drink” said Stewart Strange, Head of Forensics.

Allan sat up in his chair.

“I’m all ears” he said.

“Well, I’m sorry to have to say that there’s absolutely nothing to report”.

“What, all the food and drink was perfectly harmless?”

“Yes indeed. Doesn’t really help does it?”

"No, it does not! Thanks, though for coming back so quickly, Stew. I owe you".

"How about that long-promised drink some time?"

"Yes, I'll buzz you".

Allan crossed his office, opened the door and called out.

"Dev, no need to chase forensics, we've heard".

"Sir" Patel said in acknowledgement.

Walking back into his office Allan sat down and absent-mindedly arranged his three pens and four pencils in a completely straight line and then placed his desk pad above them exactly in the middle. His dark brown eyes were looking inward at his thoughts.

That afternoon, the village hall had been commandeered and by three o'clock the village interviews were in full swing.

Desks had been arranged in three rows of five apiece and people were standing in queues waiting to be interviewed. Most were resigned to waiting. A few were grumbling they didn't know why they were there as the children had been found. Further the 'food poisoning' episode was bad but there was nothing they could do about it.

Allan strode over to the side of the hall where there were several stacked chairs and arranged them two and two at some distance from each other. He indicated to Szymanski to take a seat on one of them. He took a seat on one of the other chairs at a distance from her. Then he indicated to the next interviewee and Szymanski did likewise.

Allan was not amused when he got one of the moaners of this world.

“About bloody time!” commented the miserable looking middle-aged man with a down mouth as he sat down with a thud on the small-seated chair which struggled to accommodate the man’s fat physique.

“I do apologise for your wait, sir…….” began Allan in an assumed placatory manner.

“I don’t know why we are here. The children are safe by all accounts and how can we help with the food poisoning?” interrupted the grouch.

“I can assure you that the slightest detail could be very important to us in understanding what happened to Timmy and Mary. So can we proceed?” Allan said with firmer emphasis and without waiting to hear the man’s protestations he took out his notebook and carried on in a determined manner.

"May I take your name, sir?"

"Percy Bowman" was the sulky reply.

"When did you arrive at the fête?"

"At the start. We queued to get in".

"And what did you do at the fête?"

"Well, I didn't get my face painted that's for sure" he snorted but when he realised that his little joke hadn't had any effect on Allan he begrudgingly continued.

"I went to get the grub and a beer first. It was quite a spread. I saw, Andy, a mate of mine and we chewed the cud for a while. Then I went over to one of the marquees where the slot machines were. Thought I'd try my luck. Next thing I know there's a lot of kerfuffle outside the tent and I went to see what was happening".

"What exactly did you see then?" Allan cut in.

"There was a lot of screaming and running about. Some people were lying on the ground. I couldn't make head nor tail of what had happened".

"Did you see any children?"

“No can’t say as I did. Oh yes, I could see some in the swimming pool”.

“Good and did you see any children wandering off from there or anyone lurking around? Someone maybe you hadn’t seen before. Or maybe a villager acting strangely?”

“Everything happening was strange but no, no I don’t recall anyone in particular….oh hold on a minute, yes, I did see Freddie Cunningham near the pool but it was only a glimpse. My attention was focussed mainly on the people on the ground”.

Allan was scribbling in his notebook.

“Did you notice whether Freddie was talking to any of the children in particular?”

“No, no as I said I only saw him briefly, just an instant really”.

“Just one final question, Mr Bowman. Did you see anyone or anything unusual around the trestle tables where the food and drink was?”

“No, I can’t say I did”.

“Okay, well, thank you very much for your time. Much appreciated”,

Percy Bowman managed a smile and a nod and got up to go. Then he turned round to face Allan.

"There was just one thing that seemed odd, it's probably nothing but………."

"Go on" and Allan sat forward in his chair eager to hear.

"The people who fell seemed to be in groups. What I mean is that there were like clusters of bodies. Whole areas didn't have anyone lying on the ground. It just seemed a bit odd that's all. Almost like they were targeted. Don't suppose that's any help at all, is it?"

"On the contrary, Mr Bowman, you've been very helpful. Thank you".

Percy grunted and moved off.

The interviews went on until early evening when all officers went back for a debriefing outside Allan's office.

"So, anything interesting from anyone?" Allan was standing in front of the white board which boasted a small amount of writing and stickers with connecting lines drawn between them.

"Yes, sir, one of the villagers saw Piers and Freddie gesticulating at each other near the lake early on in the proceedings but they were too far away to hear what it was about" said one officer.

"That's my understanding, too, from one of the villagers" confirmed another.

Allan added that to the whiteboard.

"A Mrs White who I interviewed said she noticed Piers and his wife in earnest conversation by the lake, but she wasn't quite sure of the timing".

No-one else had taken down anything of importance.

"So, what have we got here.

- 2 children went missing for 15 hours or so but returned seemingly unharmed however with total amnesia for that time.
- 20 guests were struck down from an unknown cause - 2 fatally.
- Piers and Freddie were seen arguing by the lake.
- Piers and Francesca were seen having a heated conversation.
- Freddie was spotted by the swimming pool shortly before the two incidents.
- One villager was struck by the way victims had fallen; in clusters rather than

scattered. I found that out from Mr Bowman, grumpy old sod but interesting information, nevertheless".

"Question – were the heated conversations with Piers between he and his wife and then with his son about the same thing? That would be interesting to know because if so, it begs the question was Piers up to something that the other two disagreed with? "

"There again Freddie was spotted by the swimming pool just before the children disappeared. Was he the abductor but if so, he probably wouldn't have had time to lure both Timmy who was in the pool and Mary who was in the face painting queue located at the far end of the paddock, without anyone seeing him. That again begs a question – were there two abductors?"

"Last but not least and in my view perhaps the most intriguing point is that people affected seemed to be in clusters and not scattered".

"We haven't yet interviewed the survivors, sir. Most are out of hospital now, perhaps they saw or heard something before they were struck down?" Dev said.

"Also, we can't be sure that the children are not too frightened to speak. It seems a bit odd that neither can remember anything at all about those missing hours?" put in Szymanski.

"Right, so Dev, Barry, Mike, Amy and Sophie interview the survivors and see if they spotted anything of interest. Also, what they were doing immediately prior to when they fell. Meanwhile Julia, come with me, we're going to the Hall to interview Mr Freddie Cunningham".

Forty-five minutes later saw the Allan and Szymanski arrived at the gates of Misslethwaite Hall. He pressed the entry button.

"Detective Inspector Allan, Police" Allan responded to the enquiry.

There was a brief acknowledgement, and the gates slowly opened.

Having parked his black and white Range Rover on the golden coloured sweeping gravel drive outside the grand front entrance of the imposing manor, Allan strode up to the front door with Szymanski following close behind. Before he could ring the bell the door opened, and a woman answered the door dressed in black with a white apron. She was tall, nearly six foot in height, strikingly good looking with intelligent green eyes, an unusual person to be a housekeeper, Allan thought. Smiling at them, she briefly examined their credentials and ushered them in.

They followed her through the long corridor to a door at the end which when opened revealed a huge reception room with windows at either end framed with thick, richly coloured brocade curtains.

“One moment, sir. I will let Lady Cunningham know you are here,” she said.

“Actually, if it is possible, we would like to speak with Mr Freddie Cunningham” Allan said to the back of an already retreating housekeeper.

“Of course, sir. I will let him know”.

Allan was becoming impatient and paced up and down the room. Szymanski sat unmoving although she did glance at her watch a couple of times more from boredom than wanting to know the time. They had been waiting for a full thirty minutes with no sound apart from an ornate ticking clock on the rather elaborate mantelpiece.

At last, the door swung open with a flourish and in walked Freddie.

“Good evening, Mr Cunningham. I’m Detective Inspector Allan and this is my colleague Detective Sergeant Szymanski. We are sorry to disturb you at this late hour, but we would like to ask you a few questions in relation to the day of the fete”.

Freddie was blonde with slightly effeminate facial features. He was tall, thin with an air of privilege about him. Sporting a velvet smoking jacket in an opulent red he was smoking a cigarette which had a peculiar, pungent smell, Allan thought. He walked towards the detective offering his free hand.

“Pleasure to meet you Inspector. What can I do for you? Not more bad news I hope? Dreadful happenings at our fête!”

They sat down opposite each other in two large chintz armchairs.

“I understand that on the day of the fête you were arguing with your father by the lake. Can you tell me what that was about?” asked Allan his eyes fixed on the interviewee.

A puzzled expression crossed Freddie’s face.

“Arguing? With my father? Who told you that, Inspector?”

“I’m not at liberty to say but you and your father were seen gesticulating in a manner which suggested that you were arguing. So, I would just like to know what that was about” Allan persisted.

There was a long pause.

“Now I come to think about it, yes, we did have a slight disagreement but hardly an argument. I don’t see, with the greatest of respect Inspector, what concern that is of yours”.

“It would be greatly appreciated if you could just tell us broadly what the *disagreement* was about to help us with our enquiries”.

“It was a work-related matter. Does that help you, Inspector?”

“Could you expand a little more, sir” Allan used the most placatory manner he could muster.

“Really, Inspector! Okay, it was about the fact that I felt, no, correction, I feel that more money should be put into research and my father obviously disagreed and still does disagree. Are you quite satisfied now Inspector?”

Allan didn’t answer.

“Just one other thing while we are here, sir. Could you tell us what you were doing immediately after you were seen at the swimming pool?" asked Szymanski.

"What? I don't remember. Why?"

"Perhaps you could think back and try to remember. It is very important. You may, for instance have noticed something out of the ordinary. Maybe something that didn't really make sense at the time?"

Freddie visibly relaxed.

"I was wandering around being a good host, showing interest in the festivities and from the swimming pool I think I went up to the face painting and from there I really don't remember. As far as anything odd is concerned, no, I can't say I noticed anything of note".

"Okay, well, thank you for your time, Mr Cunningham. It is much appreciated and if you think of anything you feel is important then contact me directly" and Allan passed him a card with his contact details.

"Freddie please, and for the future may I call you Jack, Inspector?" and Freddie extended his hand with a warm but slightly condescending smile.

“If you don’t mind, sir, I would rather keep things on a formal basis but thank you again for your help” he said sternly while shaking hands with a firm grip.

Next morning, back at the station Allan was getting out of his car when a large middle-aged lady with unruly curly hair waddled up to him.

“You’re the detective in charge of the happenings at Misslethwaite aren’t you?” she asked.

“Yes, that’s right madam and you are?”

“Mrs Dean. My husband was one of those who died at the fête” and she gulped as she said it.

“I’m very sorry for your loss, Mrs Dean but what can I do for you?”

“You can find out why he died. No-one knows at the hospital you see. I’ve tried to find out, but they either don’t know or won’t tell me. Do you know what happened? It wasn’t food-poisoning, and he was in good health” the pitch of her voice was rapidly rising.

“The hospital doesn’t know at present and neither do I, but we will find out. I’m sorry Mrs Dean for your distress. We will certainly do our best to establish your husband’s cause of death and others who died that day in similar circumstances".

"I want closure you see and so do our children. Thank you Inspector and I'm sorry to trouble you. I know you must be a very busy man".

As he walked to his office, he determined to find answers.

Later that morning Allan, Szymanski and the team met up with their findings.

"Okay, what have we got?" asked Allan.

The team were seated outside Allan's office with their coffees and Patel had succumbed to a chocolate bar which he was consuming at a rapid rate of knots having skipped breakfast.

"Couple of things, sir, that we ascertained" said Patel, quickly swallowing the last mouthful of chocolate.

Allan nodded for him to go ahead, leaning against a table his arms folded.

"One of the patients said that one minute he was in the queue for archery and the next he was on the ground. After that it's a blank until he woke up in hospital. The interesting thing was that just before he blacked out, he noticed someone holding a small item. The person's arm was down by their side, and they were holding the object close to their leg, it was as though they were trying to hide it from view. The guy, at least he was pretty certain it was a guy, or he said it could have possibly been a woman as they were wearing a hoodie, was looking straight ahead apparently not interested in what was going on around them. He said, it may not have been anything, but the person seemed out of place, and the best thing is the patient discovered what the object was, and this is where it gets really strange," Patel paused for effect.

"Yes, well, Dev. We are waiting" said Allan impatiently.

"The patient saw the person suddenly and swiftly raise the object and spray something around and just as quickly he lowered his hand back by his side. That's really interesting isn't it, sir" Patel said excitedly.

"Yes, that is indeed very interesting," said Allan.

"Anyone else?" and Allan looked around at the team.

"Yes, sir one of the patients said he saw one of the children holding hands with someone and walking towards the entrance. He couldn't make out who it was, there were too many people in the way, but he thought it was Timmy and from the way the person was walking it was probably a man. He was wearing some sort of dark hoodie. He couldn't make out anything else and by that time there was chaos everywhere," said Barry.

"That explains why no-one noticed the children disappearing. Could the chaos have been created as a smoke screen to abduct the children? We need to search the area for that object which we now know was an atomiser and which might have been discarded. It could be a substance was sprayed that was debilitating but not lethal and it was only sprayed in certain areas accounting for only groups of people being affected. It is a possibility person or persons unknown threw it in a hedge, undergrowth or a rubbish bin nearby. For my part, Julia and I interviewed Freddie, and in my view, he is definitely hiding something. When we questioned him about what he saw immediately after being at the swimming pool he visibly tensed but as I indicated that he might have witnessed something without realising, he completely relaxed. I'm sure he was lying when he said that he and his father were arguing about whether more money should be put into research; it was about something else possibly relevant to the events at the fête. In addition, by his own admission, he wandered over to the face painting area which was where Mary Peters was taken. I'd be surprised if Freddie didn't know something about the events or is part of it himself".

"It certainly seems to point to one or both family members being involved somehow" commented Szymanski.

"Dev organise some uniform to do a thorough search of the area for that atomizer and anything else of interest. Julia and I will speak with Timmy and Mary again. I want to establish whether they were in an affected area".

Chapter Seven

It was five o'clock in the morning and Allan was preparing one of his healthy breakfasts consisting of avocado, cucumber, spinach, kale, pineapple and coconut water. He had just poured this wonderfully invigorating drink into a large glass when his mobile rang.

"Hi oh sleepless one!" said a familiar voice.

"Vanessa! I thought you were on duty" his tone was one of surprise.

"I was but Bella wanted to swap with me, so I did. You okay to come over".

"Now?"

"Yep!"

"OK I'm there!"

He thought of Vanessa while he gulped down his smoothie and quickly dressed. She was unlike any girl he had ever known. She was totally independent but for some reason found him irresistible. That was mutual. From the first moment they had met outside a health food shop when she had dropped a whole bag of shopping over the pavement, and he had stopped to pick it up, they both knew they would end up in bed together that night. That day had been four months ago. Jack was still hurting from his failed marriage but something about Vanessa had breathed new life into him. He wanted her, yes, she was extremely attractive but more than that. There was something very special about her. She was funny and interesting too. Both had agreed to keep their own places partly because they had jobs that entailed shifts. Vanessa was a doctor at the local hospital. She was just a smidgen smaller in height than Jack at six foot and like him athletically built. She had long tawny brown hair and large brown eyes. Jack was musing over her body in his mind when his mobile rang.

"No, no, no, not now!" he exclaimed.

He pressed the button to receive the call.

"Sir, there's been a fire at Misslethwaite Hall. We're needed there urgently".

"Okay I'm heading there now" he said grimacing.

Grabbing his coat, car keys and mobile, he set the alarm and bolted down the steps two at a time.

Once in his car, he activated his siren and blue lights, taking off at speed. Then he pressed the button for Vanessa's number.

"Sorry babe.........." be began.

"No worries, my hunger will just have to wait a little longer to be satisfied. Love you".

"Love you too" he hung up smiling, and then switched his thoughts to the fire.

Twenty minutes later he had déjà vu. One wing of the building in front of him was ablaze. In the distance he could hear the wail of the fire engine sirens. He ran up to where a group of civilians were standing watching, hypnotised by the unfolding catastrophe.

"Stand back, stand back" he called as he ran.

The huddled little group turned round, expressions of horror on their faces.

Reaching them, Allan waved his arm indicating that they should move back to a safer position.

"Do we know who is in there?" he asked looking round at several pairs of eyes fixed on him.

They didn't have time to respond as the first fire engine arrived, along with Szymanski and two other police cars.

Allan shouted to the officers to get a tape round the area while the firemen leapt into action with hoses and within a very short time gallons of water were being directed on the fire.

Three hours later the fire was under control and Allan and Szymanski donned their barrier clothing and walked into Misslethwaite Hall, the east wing of which was completely gutted although the rest of the Hall had remained intact.

As they entered the Chief Fire Officer appeared and explained to them that the fire would seem to have started in the east wing outside the main bedroom, although that had to be confirmed by the forensic fire investigators. Two bodies had been discovered in the main bedroom.

Having updated Allan and Szymanski, the CFO walked off to carry on his duties.

“Obviously forensics will have to identify who the bodies were through dental records, but I would be surprised if they were not the burnt remains of Piers and Francesca Cunningham. Any bells ringing for you, Julia?” Allan asked.

“Yes, sir, bells are ringing but I can’t put my finger on it”, she answered screwing up her face desperately trying to remember.

“I couldn’t either until now. The Zhangs. Rosedene Grange. Not a million miles from here although five years ago. Same format. I shouldn't be surprised if we find the accelerant can somewhere outside discarded in the bushes".

"If I recall, sir, Qiáng, the son, was never located. He just simply disappeared, and the case went cold".

"Yes, indeed. In my view, he was guilty of arson causing the death of his parents but whether he did it entirely for his own reasons or whether he was forced to do it and was then killed is up for discussion".

"How could this fire be connected to the previous one though? It's five years ago. There is nothing to suggest that Qiáng is involved".

"The similarities are too strong for it just to be a coincidence. We need corroboration as to whether the windows were sealed in the main bedroom and whether Freddie has gone missing. If he has, then the devil if I know at the moment what the hell is going on, but one thing is certain, we will get to the bottom of it. In the meantime, call the team and let's all look around for a can of accelerant. I'll get Dev to try and locate Freddie. There are altogether too many coincidences for my liking".

The team arrived about thirty minutes later and set about scouring the bushes, shrubberies and woodland around the mansion. After about an hour one of the officers called out.

"Over here, sir, I've found something".

Allan hung up after talking to his DCI who was demanding to know what progress was being made on the current situation. He had explained, much to the DCI's displeasure, that they were now looking at a potential murder enquiry.

Allan took the petrol canister from the officer's outstretched hand and put it in the large plastic evidence bag produced by Szymanski.

"Ah just the man!" exclaimed Allan, as Stewart Strange appeared from the house.

"Been here before?" Strange remarked taking the bag from Allan's outstretched hand.

"Meaning?" asked Allan raising a brow.

"I'm sure you have noticed the resemblance to the case a few years back. Must be five years or so. Rosedene Grange, I believe".

"Indeed. Five years to be exact. The thought also occurred to me. Interesting. What's the link though, that is the burning question. Forgive the pun!".

"I'll have the tests run and you'll have your report first thing tomorrow" said Strange not acknowledging Allan's quip.

"Thanks, Stew" and Allan slapped Strange's shoulder, pulling his singing mobile out of his pocket with his other hand.

Listening intently, Jack nodded now and then. "Thanks Dev" he said and clicked off.

Allan turned to Szymanski, "Right, Dev has managed to speak with Freddie on his mobile. He was at a mate's house apparently. According to Dev he sounded devastated at the news but interestingly wasn't in any denial. Dev felt his distress sounded a bit phoney".

"Maybe because the bodies were found in his parents' bedroom, he just assumed it was them though?".

"Maybe" Allan replied not sounding convinced.

Once the team were back at the station, they all assembled in the main office.

"Firstly, thanks to all of you for your speed and thoroughness in searching and locating the accelerant can. We now know that we have an arson case on our hands at best and a murder investigation at worst. So, in addition to that we have the case of people falling ill in clusters at the fête and we don't know why the children can't remember anything about the time they went missing. Therefore, have we got three different cases here or are they connected? Let's look first at the fires. We have two extensive fires in two mansions a few miles apart but also five years apart. The two fires have significant similarities. 1. Where it took place – in the main bedroom. 2. An accelerant was used; thus, it was arson. 3. In each case both parents died".

"In the first case the son disappeared, and evidence pointed to him possibly being the arsonist and murderer. In the second case, the son stands to inherit substantial wealth and heads up the family business but is very much alive and well. However, is the case of the missing children and the case of the guest sickness linked to the fires or are they separate investigations? As far as the children are concerned it could be that they are lying because they don't want to get into trouble for playing a prank. As far as the sickness is concerned that would potentially seem to have been deliberately started through an atomizer or atomizers. We are awaiting the forensics report on the contents of them and it may be they were used as a diversion for the kidnapping of the children. It would, I venture to suggest, be too coincidental that all of this happened in the grounds of the mansion that subsequently burnt down within twenty-four hours of the fête with significant similarities to the fire at Rosedene Grange situated five miles away. Bearing all this in mind I think we have us a profound riddle to solve" concluded Allan.

"I agree it is too much of a coincidence that they are not all linked," said Patel.

"The question is though, how on earth are they linked?" Szymanski was frowning.

"Let's work on the premise that there is a connection," said Allan.

"Was anything else discovered from the search for the atomizer?" asked Allan to the team generally.

"Yes sir, but not from the search. It might not be related but a woman was admitted to hospital yesterday afternoon; a Mrs Bowman" Sophie replied consulting her notebook.

“That name sounds familiar. Yes, is she related to the grumpy sod I interviewed?” Allan grimaced.

“Yes, sir, she is his ex-wife”.

“Ex-wife! Well, she sounds like a woman of sound mind. Carry on,” said Allan keeping a straight face.

Sophie struggled not to smile as did the others.

“Anyway, sir, Mrs Bowman had found an atomizer in a bin and as there was still some in it, she sprayed some on her wrist and sniffed the scent. She thought it was odd as it seemed to be odourless. She then passed out and ended up in hospital. She’s fully recovered now, and the medics can’t find anything wrong with her”.

“Where is the bottle now?” demanded Allan.

“Well, here’s the thing sir. She can’t remember what she did with it”.

“Okay, we need to arrange another interview with her and see if we can jog her memory. We need to get that bottle. I doubt whether there will be any fingerprints, but we might strike lucky. Julia and I interviewed Timmy and Mary again. Both confirmed that people had been falling all around them but that lots of people were still acting normally in other parts of the paddock. So, I think we can safely assume from the sighting of a man walking around with an atomizer and the fact that only certain groups of people were affected, that some sort of substance was sprayed in certain areas only", said Allan.

The others nodded their agreement.

"I also want to interview Freddie Cunningham again. He is hiding something, and I want to see the face-to-face reaction to the loss of his parents, and we need to bring in his alibi. I'm not satisfied that our Freddie Cunningham didn't have anything to do with the fire. Julia, you come with me to Misslethwaite and Dev you interview Mrs Bowman again."

In the car, Allan delayed switching on the ignition and turned to Julia, her thin mouth set in a noticeably more determined line than usual.

"Julia there's something up. Care to tell me?"

Julia turned to look out of the window and seemed to concentrate on something in the distance.

"Julia we've worked together for over five years now. I know when there is something up with you and if there is, that will most likely impinge on your concentration at work. So, you know I don't pry but please tell me, as your colleague and friend, what's wrong."

She turned and looked at Jack, tears in her usually hard, piercing eyes, her chin wobbly.

"I won't let it interfere with my work, Jack. I never have and I never will."

Allan remained silent.

Julia wiped her tears away with the back of her hand. She took a deep breath. She knew Jack well enough. He wanted to support and help her.

"It's Sally. We had a big, no, a colossal row last night. She's fed up with my hours. She's worried all the time that I might be injured or killed. Our son, Leo, is keeping her up at night and she says she just can't cope with him, the house, me and oh ... everything" she tailed off and resting her elbow against the edge of the car window she covered her forehead with her hand.

"I'm sorry you and Sally are having problems, and I don't suppose it will help to say what you already know, that most of us have relationship problems, it goes with the job. Have you thought about getting someone in to help Sally with the housework. Remind me, does she work?"

"Yes, she is a part-time teacher's assistant".

"So, she is getting some time away from the house?"

Julia nodded.

"It's okay Jack. Thanks for asking. I'll sort it. Really, I will".

Allan looked doubtful.

"I will sort it. Promise sir" she said assuming her professional manner.

Allan smiled.

"Good. Glad to hear it but if you need an ear, I'm here. Okay?"

"Yes. Thank you, sir, but before we go back into work gear, I know you compartmentalise your private life and your work very successfully but the offer of an ear to listen cuts both ways. I've heard through the grapevine that your mother isn't at all well and you're a close-knit family. I, just like you, wouldn't want to pry but if you want to talk about it, I'm here too, Jack" she said slipping back into informal mode again.

"I might take you up on that offer, Julia, but not now. Now we have to focus on this case. Thank you, Julia, and I mean that" he said giving her an appreciative look. Then he switched on the engine, and they sped off in the direction of the Hall.

Arrived back at Misslethwaite, they were ushered into the large reception room and a few minutes later Freddie entered attired in a crisp, white shirt, black suit, tie and shoes.

He strode across the room, hand outstretched, a suitably morose expression on his face.

"Good afternoon, Detective Inspector Allan isn't it and Detective Sergeant .... Umm?"

"Szymanski" she filled in the missing blank.

"Forgive me, Detective Sergeant Szymanski. I'm still in a state of shock as I'm sure you understand" he said with a sad smile that somehow didn't come across as sincere.

"Yes, of course, and I'm very sorry for your loss and to have to trouble you at such a time, Mr Cunningham, but there are just a couple of things we would like to ask you" said Allan with a friendly smile.

"Thank you, Jack. I'm just thankful that most of the Hall is still standing!" replied Freddie.

"Firstly, can you tell me again who the friend was that you were staying with last night?"

"Oh, I've already given that information to one of your uniforms. Did they not tell you?" said Freddie a look of frustration crossing his face.

"Yes, they did but just for the record I would appreciate it if you could tell me again" replied Allan with another friendly smile.

"Of course, Jack," he began with an insolent sneer. "I was staying with a very good friend of mine. His name is Roland Manning".

"And how did you come to meet Mr Manning?"

"How did we meet?"

"Yes, how did you first meet?"

"At university. Cambridge University, but I can't think that is relevant to the death of my parents or any of your current investigation!"

"So can I ask why you were staying with him last night".

"We were playing Bridge at the local club and then we had a few drinks. I didn't want to drive as I am sure you will agree, Detective Inspector, that would not be the thing, so I stayed at Roland's".

Allan nodded.

"Just one other question. Do you know the contents of your parents' Will?" asked Szymanski looking down at her notebook.

"I'm seeing the family solicitor today but I'm confident that I know. There are probably a few small bequests to one or two members of staff and charities, but the bulk of the inheritance will go to me. Why do you ask? What are you suggesting, Detective Sergeant?" he asked reproachfully.

"We're not suggesting anything, sir" interceded Allan.

"Your inheritance will include the family business?" he continued.

"Yes, I believe so" Freddie answered.

"Good, well, thank you for your time, Mr Cunningham. Once again, we are very sorry for your loss".

"Thank you, Jack" and Freddie inclined his head to each of them in turn.

Back in the car, Julia spoke first.

"You were a bit smarmy in there, sir".

"Indeed, Julia, just putting him at his ease. Get far more out of him that way than going in heavy. We learnt that he is going to be very wealthy. That's motive enough for arson with intent to kill. We need to look over Manning's statement and then possibly interview him and relevant members of the Bridge Club. See what we can glean and if the alibi sticks".

"I still don't see the connection with all these happenings though, sir. I don't see the connection with the cold case either!"

"If there is a connection. I've a hunch but it's just that at the moment based on scepticism for coincidences".

Allan's mobile rang.

"Just spoken to Mrs Bowman and you were right, sir, by taking her back to the moment she found the bottle, after a bit of nudging, she did remember where she found it!" exclaimed Dev excitedly.

"Yes, well where?" demanded Allan.

“There’s a village green just outside Misslethwaite, a mile from the Hall in fact. There’s a bus stop there and a waste bin”.

“Good work, Dev. We’ll retrieve it on the way back”.

“There’s one problem, it’s refuse-collection day today so I hope we aren’t too late”.

Allan didn’t reply, he put his siren on and made for the location.

At Misslethwaite Hall, Freddie poured himself a whisky soda. Standing with one arm propped on the impressive mantlepiece, he sipped his drink, a sinister smile forming on his lips.

Chapter Eight

Allan woke up to the early morning shafts of sunlight streaming in the window, highlighting hundreds of tiny dust motes. For a second, he couldn't place where he was. Then he remembered. He was at Vanessa's. She had rung late yesterday evening, and they had ended up eating a delicious but very bad for you curry and downing several glasses of wine totally against his usual healthy regime. For dessert they had themselves. It was always wonderful, satisfying sex with Vanessa. He had to admit he was a little bit in love with her, no, honestly, a whole lot in love with her, but he knew he wouldn't ever tell her. That would sound the death knell to their relationship. Although the next second he thought 'never say never'.

He lay there basking in the sunshine, listening to the clink of bowls and glasses as Vanessa gathered together a breakfast for them both. He felt lazy not getting up in the early hours and embarking on his strict gym routine. Although it was only seven-thirty, somehow, he didn't feel too guilty, in fact, he felt good, better than he usually felt with no sign of a hangover.

He was rudely awoken from his musings by his mobile ringing and vibrating.

He got up and stumbled across the bedroom floor and into the dining room where he found his mobile on the table buried under a pile of discarded curry containers and clothes which were all beginning to smell rank.

Wrinkling his nose at the unsavoury odour he picked up his mobile.

“Allan” he barked as he beat a hasty retreat into the bedroom.

“Good morning, Jack” said a cheerful Strange “I gather you aren’t at the station. Having a lie in?” Stewart Strange was well aware of Allan’s regime along with most of the force and couldn’t resist a tease.

“What have you got for me, Strange” was the severe retort from Allan who totally ignored the quip.

“Well, this may be helpful to you, or it may muddy the waters. The main bedroom windows were stuck shut. There was no way the occupants of that room could escape especially as we have determined that the fire started outside that same room”.

There was a pause while Allan digested this information.

“So, it’s almost certainly murder then. Curious” he said eventually almost to himself.

“Before you leap off to conduct your further investigations, something else that might interest you. The analysis of the contents of the atomizer which, by the way, unsurprisingly, had no fingerprints and quite clearly had been wiped clean, threw up a somewhat alarming result. The virus contained in the atomizer is unknown but is potentially lethal, in fact, could be instantly lethal if at a high enough strength. The strength of the virus contained within the atomizer was low and presumably was not intended to result in deaths, at least not at that time”.

“So, it could be that it was used as a diversion in the kidnapping of the children”.

“That was my train of thought, Jack, but you’re the detective so I’ll leave you to figure that out. Another point of interest is that we are of the opinion that the virus was manmade rather than natural. The structure of it indicates that the strength can be controlled by man. I won’t go into the technical details. Trust me on this one, Jack”.

"Yes, sure. Thanks for the info, Stew" and Allan clicked off standing for some moments staring at nothing in particular, deep in thought.

"Breakfast is served, sire, oh great one!" said Vanessa giving him a cheeky, flirtatious look.

"It was a great night and………………" he began.

"But you have to go" she cut in, realising in an instant that he wouldn't be sharing the breakfast she had carefully prepared which included all sorts of nutritious, healthy ingredients.

"I heard the mobile ring and wondered obviously. No worries, more breakfast pour moi!"

His mobile rang again and after a brief conversation he hurriedly got dressed, grabbed his things, kissed Vanessa goodbye, and left.

On his way to the station, he drove over the picturesque bridge in the village of Tillingford where an abundance of swans flapped their wings while their signets gracefully ducked their heads in and out of the water, their feathers still a grey colour. The arresting beauty of this idyllic scene was wasted on Allan as the frown on his face became ever deeper.

Having parked his car, he strode up the steps towards his office.

Szymanksi caught up with him before he had a chance to enter. “Sorry to have disturbed you, sir, the DCI wants to see you. Not sure why he didn’t ring you himself but anyway before that I thought you might like to see Freddie Cunningham speak about taking over the family business. He will be on TV very shortly speaking to employees in front of the family firm” and she pointed towards the main office where the TV screen could be seen with several of Allan’s team gathered around it.

A couple of minutes later Cunningham appeared. “It is with great sadness that I am standing here today. My parents were wonderful people, and the sorrow is almost too much to bear” Cunningham was saying wiping his eyes with a pristine white silk handkerchief.

“Methinks he doth protest slightly too much” muttered Allan sarcastically.

“Only slightly though don’t you think, sir” added Szymanski with equal sarcasm.

“However, my father would want me to continue the good work that he has conducted over the years as head of Cunningham & Son, and I have to tell you that I will work night and day to ensure that his work is continued. To set your minds at rest there will be no redundancies….." at that reassurance, the crowd of employees to whom he was making his address, applauded and cheered loudly.

Cunningham raised his hand, on his face a self-satisfied smirk.

"So, it's business as usual and thank you all for your understanding and loyalty at this difficult time".

The people began to disperse, Cunningham drove off in his state-of-the-art Porsche and the officers watching the TV went back to their desks.

"Sir, the DCI wants to see you. He said it's urgent" said Dev rushing up to Allan.

"I know, I know, thank you, Dev. Julia has already told me. Everything's urgent with him" Allan muttered this last under his breath but nevertheless he hastened his step towards his senior's office.

DCI Walters was standing upright looking out of the window, his hands behind his back as Allan entered.

“Sir you wanted to see me”.

“Yes, Jack, have we got any further with the murder, the child abduction and the rest of it”

“It was without doubt a murder sir as Strange has confirmed that the windows were stuck with glue and the fire started with an accelerant right outside the main bedroom. Strange also updated me with the results of the atomizer and that it contains an unknown potentially lethal virus. Regarding the child abduction, I’m afraid we are no further forward, and it is just possible it was a prank played by Timmy and Mary although the virus might have been spread as a diversion to the kidnapping of the children. A point of concern sir regarding the fire at Misslethwaite Hall, is that five years ago there was a similar incident not far from here at Rosedene Grange where two people were murdered in their main bedroom by the same means”.

“Indicating what precisely? That we have a serial killer that leaves a five-year gap and targets wealthy people, husband and wife in both cases for no apparent reason?” Walters was going red in the face.

“No, I’m merely saying that it is a big coincidence that this has happened twice in such close proximity, both in location and time, and there is a similarity. However, although in each case there is a son involved, that's where the similarity ends because one son disappeared, and the other is about to take over his father's firm".

"Could that not indicate a copy-cat murder?" suggested Walters.

"It could yes, sir, and I intend to interview Roland Manning, Cunningham's alibi for the night of the fire. Perhaps there was a window of opportunity when Manning was not absolutely certain that Cunningham was in his flat".

"Right, well, Jack, I think regarding the children we need to leave that be. Upstairs is on my back about manpower and a prank would seem to be the logical conclusion there. The murder enquiry must take precedence for your team. However, in view of the importance of this lethal virus, I'll delegate that line of enquiry to another team".

"Sir, in my view all of these incidents are connected, and I would appreciate it if I could have a little more time to investigate without delegation of any part for the moment".

"Very well, but I need some evidence of the connection by early next week at the latest. Carry on then Jack and keep me updated" and Walters sat down at his desk dismissing Allan by concentrating on a pile of papers on his desk.

Back in his office, he called in Szymanski and Patel.

"OK so the DCI wanted the missing children case to be dropped but I have said there could be a connection between all three incidents under investigation. He also wanted to split the murder case to be investigated separately from the virus case, but I have managed to gain some time, until early next week. I have a hunch on the murder case, and we need to start interviewing Roland Manning.

Looking at the virus what have got to go on?"

"Nothing much, sir", said the DC.

"Interview Mrs Bowman again, Dev. See if she can remember anyone around as she approached the village green. She might remember someone getting in a vehicle or a person walking away, anything would be helpful. In the meantime, Julia, we'll tackle Manning".

Later that day, Allan and Szymanski walked down one flight of stairs to Interview Room 3.

“Good afternoon, Mr Manning. Thank you for coming in” said Allan on entering the austere, sparsely furnished room with the standard one-way window, behind which sat an expert in reading mannerisms and body language.

“Good afternoon, Jack. I suspect it would seem rather odd not to come in at the request of the Police Constabulary” he replied archly.

“It’s Detective Inspector Allan for the sake of correctness and this is Detective Sergeant Szymanski” said Allan indicating his colleague who was sitting to his right.

“Do you mind if we record this interview, Mr Manning?”

“As per my previous comment, a pointless exercise asking me the question. Obviously, if I said no that would seem that I had something to hide which I have not. So, in answer to your question *Detective Inspector*, no I don’t mind” was the rather pompous reply. Manning stroked his thick blonde moustache looking at Allan astutely with his cold blue eyes through his gold rimmed glasses.

Allan turned on the recorder and voiced date, time and each confirmed those present.

"Do you understand why we have asked to speak with you, Mr Manning".

"Yes, it's about the night of the fire at Misslethwaite Hall and establishing Freddie's whereabouts at the time. Presumably to eliminate him from your enquiries. I understand that it was arson?" Manning appeared perfectly relaxed as he answered Allan's question.

"Not only arson, Mr Manning. This is now a murder enquiry".

"Forgive me, Detective Inspector, my mistake" was the supercilious answer.

"So can you go through the events of that evening".

"I've already given a full account to the police" Manning answered, moving a stray strand of his blonde hair out of his eyes. His was a foppish cut, short at the back and cut to mid-ear length at the sides.

"I would appreciate it if you could recount your recollections again".

"Oh yes, of course, just in case I should contradict myself. Well, I can assure you I won't because the account I have already given is the truth" he smirked.

There was a brief silence.

"Here we go then. Freddie came round to my place at 7.00 p.m. we had a couple of drinks and then headed off to the club where we played Bridge, that's a card game by the way, until 11.30 p.m. We then stayed and had a few more drinks, one for the road you know, and got a cab back to my place at 1.00 a.m. We both hit the sack and as I was up first the next morning at about 9.00 a.m., I got some breakfast together. Freddie emerged a little while later at about 9.15 a.m. That's it" he looked at his watch and sat forward in his chair one hand clutching the armrest as though to get up.

Allan was concentrating intently on writing in his notebook with no indication that the interview was at an end.

"So can I go now, Detective Inspector, I've got an appointment at 3.00 p.m., this afternoon and I will be struggling to make it. I think you will see that nothing has changed" and this time he got up from his chair and moved towards the door.

"Sit down, Mr Manning" Allan said calmly and authoritatively.

"So, there was a time then that you couldn't be absolutely certain that Freddie was in the flat?" asked Szymanski.

"That's absurd. I would have heard the front door to the *apartment* open and close if Freddie had gone out during the night because my bedroom is next to the front door, which makes a loud clunking noise when it shuts. So, if that's all?"

"We will tell you when the interview is concluded, Mr Manning".

"No, you will not, Detective Inspector. I have come here voluntarily, and I am perfectly at liberty to leave at any time. I have cooperated with you fully and answered all your questions. I have another appointment and it's imperative I leave now. Good afternoon detectives" he said getting up purposefully.

"Please sit down, Mr Manning. This is a murder enquiry, and we require your cooperation. We will be as fast as possible but I'm sure you would want to be seen to be helping the police in such a serious matter" said Allan in a firm, stern voice.

Manning sat down once more.

“So, I understand that you knew one another at Cambridge. What did you both study there?”

“We both graduated with a first in biochemistry” he said sullenly pushing his hair to one side again.

“And what has been your employment since then?”

“As you are probably aware already, Inspector, I head up one of the research teams at Cunninghams where Freddie has been a director at his father’s firm since he left university. His degree, and of course my own, are particularly suited to the pharmaceutical industry and now, in the most unfortunate of circumstances, Freddie will be heading up the firm”.

Before Allan could proceed with further questions, Manning got up.

“This time I am leaving, detective. I really do have an appointment, and I think I have been more than helpful to the police” and he strode to the door, opened it and closed it firmly behind him.

Allan turned off the recorder having relayed for the tape what had occurred and concluding the interview.

“Well, that’s one hunch gone” he said desultorily.

“What was your hunch, sir?”

“Trying to find a link, it occurred to me that Manning might be the missing Qiáng but there was no way. He didn’t look remotely like him. His eyes are blue, his hair blonde and his bone structure completely different”.

“Okay, that’s disappointing, but on the bright side, there was possibly a window of opportunity for Cunningham to leave the flat. Certainly, interviews with the Bridge Club members confirmed that Manning and Cunningham were both there that evening. So, maybe we should attempt to get access to Manning’s flat, or apartment as he stressed, perish the thought that he lives in a mere flat, with a view to seeing if you are in Manning’s bedroom how loud the noise is from shutting the front door?”

“Yes, that’s not a bad idea but it may be difficult to gain access if he doesn’t want to play ball. Although if we impress on him that it is a murder investigation and he needs to cooperate, that should do it,” said Allan.

“Another thing, sir, is that we weren’t aware that they both work for Cunninghams”.

“Yes, that is interesting” mused Allan.

Szymanski's phone rang.

"OK, Dev, slow down, you're not making much sense. Just a second, I'll put you on loudspeaker".

"I went round to Mrs Bowman like you asked, sir" said Dev realising why he was on loudspeaker.

"She did remember someone walking away from the village green just as she was arriving, and she remembered thinking that you wouldn't know who he was because he was completely covered in black leather bike gear and gloves except that the helmet he was wearing was particularly distinctive, having on it a skull and crossbones design together with four red circles with different colour spikes coming out of each circle. It stuck in her memory because it was out of the ordinary and contrasted with the rest of his black gear. Apparently, he crossed the road, got on what looked like a state-of-the-art motorbike and sped off".

"In which direction did he go?"

"Towards the village centre and Cambridge City. Away from Misslethwaite Hall" said Dev his excitement now spent.

"Thanks, Dev. Come back to the station now".

He had no sooner finished the call with Dev when he phone rang again.

"Allan"

"You're needed at Misslethwaite Junior School. There are several children and staff who have passed out. It's looking like the same thing is happening as happened at the Hall!" said Sophie.

"It's the school half-term holidays, isn't it?"

"Yes, sir, but this is the holiday club. Lots of activities are laid on for the kids during school holidays. It's really popular," she replied.

"Right! We're heading there now! I take it ambulances are on their way? Get Forensics there and head there yourself, Sophie. Call Dev, update him and tell him to join us there".

Allan's siren was wailing as he put his foot down.

Arriving at Misslethwaite village school, a string of ambulances and cordons met his eyes.

Allan and Szymanski made their way through people lying on the ground apparently lifeless, the sound of crying all around, and arrived at the headmistress' office. Sophie, who had also just arrived on the scene, was doing her best to calm down the distressed lady.

"Mrs Wigan, Detective Inspector Allan and this is Detective Sergeant Szymanski. Can you outline the events here as far as you know?"

"The first I knew that anything was amiss was when my deputy informed me that a number of children and two members of staff had passed out. I immediately dialled 999 for ambulances and police" the headmistress was wiping her eyes and giving resolute loud sniffs to try to control her emotions.

"We need to take a roll call immediately" commanded Allan.

"Yes, of course, detective" and she got out her school register.

They all filed out of her office and rounded up the children with the help of other members of staff. In the school hall the register was taken for the children and staff who were present, and then those children that had collapsed were also marked as present.

Back in the headmistress' office, she totted up who was unaccounted for.

"Four members of my staff and fifteen children are missing" she said in a broken, shocked voice.

“You are absolutely sure, Mrs Wigan”.

She nodded.

“Absolutely. No shadow of a doubt”.

He turned to Dev who had just joined them.

“I want as many uniform as you can muster immediately to search the surrounding area for the missing children and staff. They need also to be looking for a discarded atomizer” he barked.

“On it” said Dev already moving outside the headmistress’s office to make the necessary calls.

Allan and Szymanski left the office and headed outside.

“How many casualties?” asked Allan to one of the ambulance crew.

“About fifty altogether three of whom are unfortunately deceased”.

Allan’s phone rang.

“This is out of control, Allan. Another incident! What the hell is going on?”

“Yes, sir, but we are dealing with it”.

“Are you? I certainly hope so! I’ve got the Super on my back, and we need to have a Press Conference. I want results otherwise what am I going to tell the public?” the DCI sounded apoplectic.

“Can we hold off the Press Conference for a day or two?”

“I can stay it maybe twenty-four hours. Get some results, Allan!”.

“We need a profiler” Allan muttered.

He clicked off his mobile and immediately rang a number. A voice answered.

“Allan here Cambridgeshire Constabulary. I need you now over at the station as soon as” he said in a way that would only accept an affirmative response.

He and Szymanski walked back through the chaos in the school grounds to Allan’s car.

“What sort of person or persons would do this? What’s the point? What’s the motive?” Allan was saying more to himself than his colleague.

“We are peering through a fog at the moment, sir, and the biggest mystery, apart from finding the person or persons responsible, is the motive", Szymansky commented.

Allan fired up the ignition and they set off.

"By the way, Julia, how are things at home?"

"We're working things out, sir. Your suggestion of taking on a cleaner helped".

"Glad to be of service," he said with a wide grin.

"No really, sir, that was a brainwave. I don't know why I didn't think of that myself. We've a long way to go though, because it doesn't solve her worrying about me and the fact that I have to go at a moment's notice at any time, but we do love each other, and I feel positive now that it will work out for us".

"Really pleased to hear that Julia" he said with sincerity.

Having arrived back at the station they quickly made their way to one of the meeting rooms where the profiler was waiting for them.

Allan gave him the low down on the latest events.

"So, from the information I've just given you, what are your thoughts?" asked Allan.

"If it is one person, they will almost certainly have psychopathic tendencies. They have no compassion particularly as they are targeting children in addition to adults. They are also highly intelligent, very cold, calculating and a narcissist. The motive, and there will be one, is, as you say, currently unclear, but I would guess that will become obvious either after this attack or they may want to reinforce their power by launching another. I would doubt whether there will be more than one more attack at the most, before a demand is made. On the other hand, it could be the work of an activist group but if it is then I would be surprised that they haven't already made a demand, and I doubt they would target children to promote their cause".

"So, it would appear then that we are likely looking for one highly dangerous individual with no empathy who is extremely clever. How long do you estimate it will be before he/she launches another attack?" said Allan.

The profiler thought for a moment.

"Hard to say but in my opinion, it will probably be within the next day or two. They will want to keep their momentum going to feed a narcissistic personality. I would hazard a guess that you are dealing with one extremely dangerous individual who has one or more associates to help him achieve his goal or goals".

"That's extremely helpful. Thank you very much for coming in at such short notice" Allan said.

"Not at all. Good luck with finding these people. You have a difficult task on your hands, Detective Inspector. If I'm right, even if you get to know who they are, trying to gather the required evidence for a conviction is going to be tough. They will undoubtedly use all their considerable talent to avoid that happening".

"Yes, I think you're right there", replied Allan.

As the profiler got to the door, he turned.

"Tread carefully, Jack"

After the profiler had left, Allan looked thoughtful.

"Penny for them, sir," said Szymanski.

"I would lay money on Cunningham having something to do with this. He fits the profile to my mind, supercilious, cold, calculating and highly intelligent".

"But those characteristics don't necessarily mean he is a murderer," said Szymanski.

"No but seeing as these things are happening and he lives and works very close by, you know full well I don't believe in coincidences. We need to have a snoop around. First, we'll go to Misslethwaite Hall, wait until his lordship goes out, ring the bell and profess to the housekeeper we need to speak with him. When she says he is out we'll ask if we could wait which hopefully, she will agree to. Then one of us has to find the toilet and have a sneaky peek around. Followed by the other needing the convenience and doing likewise. It means an initial stake out, but hopefully it will pay dividends".

The next day, the two detectives were sitting for what seemed an age a few hundred yards from Misslethwaite Hall in a convenient lay-by when finally, the tall, imposing gates opened and out drove Freddie Cunningham in his splendid vehicle.

They gave it five minutes, during which it was agreed that Allan would poke around the garages and outside generally and Szymanski would head for the study. They then drove over to the entrance. Gaining admission without any difficulty, Allan asked for the toilet to which he was directed, while Szymanski kept the housekeeper occupied with inane conversation about how stunning the Hall was.

Allan quickly walked across the hall, past the cloakroom turning left down a corridor leading to French windows that led into the gardens. Putting on gloves he headed for the three double garages and tried each of them in turn without success. They were all locked. He threw his hands out in despair and wandered round the back of them. He was about to give up, go back and allow Szymanski to locate and snoop in the study when he noticed a piece of tarpaulin sticking out at the opposite side of the garages. Curious he gave it a tug. His eyes gleamed with satisfaction as before him was a pristine motorbike adorned with the distinctive helmet with the skull and crossbones that Mrs Bowman had described. This was indeed a find. He got out his mobile and took a picture.

“Oi what are you doing there?” a gruff voice asked at his shoulder.

“Oh sorry, I thought I heard a scream and obviously came out to investigate” Allan lied, displaying his warrant card and smiling broadly.

At that moment, before the gardener could say anything further, his mobile rang.

"Sorry, sir, but we've just heard on the television of another similar incident in the south of France just outside a place called Port Grimaud. Thought you should know. Really weird sir!" said Dev.

"Thanks Dev. I'll follow it up when I get back."

Allan, realising that he had been more than enough supposed time in the toilet beat it back to the lounge waving an apologetic hand at the gardener who was standing glaring at him with his hands on his hips.

"See what you can find in the study" he said quietly to Szymanski who was sitting on one of the sofas looking slightly on edge.

"I'll fill you in on my findings when we get back to the car" he added.

Szymanski found the study quite easily and put on gloves. As she suspected the desk drawers were locked as were the filing cabinets. She didn't have much hope of accessing information on the computer, but she opened the lid and turned it on just in case there was no password protection. She was correct in her supposition; a password was needed. As she had very limited time, she didn't waste it in trying to guess what the password was. Closing the lid, she moved the laptop slightly revealing a scrap of paper which had some sort of formula or code written on it. Stuffing it in her pocket she walked to the door. Someone was coming down the corridor. Looking around she dived behind one of the floor-to-ceiling thick brocade curtains and prayed she wouldn't sneeze. She heard the door open, and someone walk to the desk. She held her breath as the person stopped and there wasn't a sound for some moments. She remained motionless, scarcely breathing. Then the person walked back towards the door, opened and closed it softly. Hesitantly, she came out from her hiding place and ran to the door, slowly opening it. Peeping through the crack she couldn't see anyone. She walked quickly back to the lounge where she could hear voices.

"Ah here's Detective Sergeant Szymanski. Thank you very much for letting us stay" Allan was saying to the housekeeper.

"I think we'll leave now. Obviously, Mr Cunningham is going to be out for some time, and I've just had a call from the station clearing up the matter that I needed to talk to Mr Cunningham about so there is no need to bother him about our visit today. I'm sure he is a very busy man now that he is heading up the family business" and

Allan gave the woman one of his most disarming smiles.

Driving back to the station, Allan and Szymankski swapped their findings.

“We’re getting somewhere now, Julia” said Allan gleefully.

“Certainly, it would seem Cunningham is the man Mrs Bowman saw on the motorcycle, but it is circumstantial isn’t it, sir, I mean he could have been there quite by chance, or it could be that someone borrowed it?”.

“You’re right it wouldn’t get a conviction, but it has convinced me that we’re on the right track. I heard from Dev earlier and there appears to have been a similar incident in France. That’s thrown a spanner in the works. We know Cunningham has been in this country for the past week so if the mystery virus is to do with him, how has he managed to reproduce something in France?”.

“There must be others involved then, sir?”

“Yes. Unless we have the whole thing wrong, Cunningham doesn’t have anything to do with it, and this is a much bigger operation than we first thought”.

“Also, what is the meaning of the code that I found a scrap of paper hidden under the laptop on the desk in the study?” said Szymanski.

“We need to give the scrap of paper with that code or whatever it is to the NCA as soon as possible, Julia. It may hold the vital clue we need”.

Chapter Nine

Allan was looking forward to seeing Vanessa. As he drove home through the picturesque Cambridgeshire countryside, he sat back in the driving seat and tapped the button for her number on his car phone. It was a beautiful evening, and the sun was setting in front of him in all its pink and gold glory.

The phone rang and went to voicemail. He frowned slightly. That was odd. She wasn't on duty today; she'd rung earlier to say as much, and they had arranged to meet at his place at seven o'clock. He smiled to himself then. She was probably showering before coming over or at the supermarket selecting a bottle of wine. He must limit his alcohol intake. It was starting to get a too enjoyable habit at the end of a hard day – a large glass of chilled crisp white wine. It was just as well they didn't eat by any means regularly together due to the shifts; he reflected.

His thoughts wandered to his father and his alcoholism. He, too, had been a Detective Inspector but not in Cambridgeshire. Growing up in Wiltshire on the borders of Cranborne Chase and the West Wiltshire Downs in the picturesque village of Corton, his father had constantly been called out during family get-togethers, and outings were often postponed where duty had called. He thought about how many times he had seen him going straight to the drinks cabinet in their lounge and pouring himself a whisky and soda to contend with the stress. In the end he had died of cirrhosis of the liver. Jack had been badly affected by his father's death. It had come when he had been in his first year at university. His father had been only forty-eight when he died, and he had been so proud of his son for going up to Cambridge and it was during that year that he had decided to follow in his father's footsteps and make a career in the police. He grew to love Cambridgeshire while he was at university and in the event, he didn't go home after graduating but took up the position of DC in the Cambridgeshire Constabulary. He had a love-hate relationship with his work and now fully understood why his father had hit the bottle but absolutely refused to go the same way. This was why he kept rigidly to his workouts as much as possible as it helped with the stress and kept him in good shape, and why he ate healthily and only drank moderately.

His thoughts went to his mother. He pressed the dial tone for Warminster Hospital and asked to be connected to her.

"Hi, mum, how are you doing?" he asked in as cheery a voice as he could muster.

"Not too bad, son, not too bad" she said sounding breathless.

"I'm sorry I haven't been back; this case seems to be more complicated than it was to start with! As soon as it's finished, I'll come and visit you again, I promise" he said.

"Don't worry, Jack, I understand. Really. Goodness, I should understand about policework by now, if I didn't there would be something very wrong with me! More importantly how is the new girlfriend, Vanessa, I think you said her name is?".

"I should be seeing her this evening as it happens".

"Good! Well, I'm looking forward to meeting her. Perhaps when the case is over you could bring her over for lunch".

"Sounds great, mum. When do you think they will be discharging you?"

"Not for some time, I understand, unfortunately" she said morosely.

"Well, let me know and we can arrange for someone to be with you until Jane comes home.

In the meantime, promise me that you'll take care and most of all, rest! That's an order!"

"I promise" she said demurely with a hint of amusement in her voice.

He rang off and after ten more minutes he arrived home, taking a quick shower and changing into a kimono and loose trousers. Padding over barefoot to the kitchen he asked Alexa to put on one of his favourite jazz melodies. Raiding his fridge, he started to put together a scrumptious salad to go with the fillet steak and prawns he had bought yesterday. He laid the table with red candles, cutlery and serviettes. He wanted to make an impression tonight. It was Vanessa's birthday, and he had given her several options to be spoilt. She had chosen to stay over at his place, for him to cook a meal and to eat by candlelight. He had a bottle of Pouilly Fumé chilling in the fridge in case she had forgotten to bring the wine.

An hour later he was still waiting for the doorbell to ring. He looked at his watch, at the kitchen clock and rang her number again and again. At last, he went into the bedroom changed into his jeans and sweater, grabbed his jacket and keys. Closing the door, he pushed open the exit doors and took the stairs two at a time. He felt something was wrong and driving as fast as the speed limit would allow, he arrived at Vanessa's apartment block twenty minutes later.

He pushed the voice entry button with no response. When a resident exited a couple of minutes later, he took the opportunity of entering before the door shut behind them. He ran up the stairs and hammered on her door. An elderly man opened the door to the apartment opposite.

"Do you have to make that much noise, young man. Obviously, the young woman is out", he remonstrated in a rather frail, cracked voice.

"I'm sorry to have disturbed you, sir, but have you seen Miss Fenchurch recently".

"As a matter of fact, I have seen Vanessa. Only about an hour ago. I heard her door shut and then I heard her walk down the stairs".

"Oh, thank you very much for your help. I won't make any more noise, I assure you".

The man grunted and retreated inside.

Allan felt he had over-reacted. Probably because of the current investigations he was undertaking, he was beginning to see everything in a sinister light.

He fished a scrap of paper and a pen out of his pocket and scribbled a note. He pushed it under the door and drove back to his apartment. When he got back, he half expected to see Vanessa waiting for him. With no sign of her and no reply to his text messages he pushed his worries to the back of his mind and realising that he was ravenous, prepared a meal and a glass of wine for one.

After a restless night, he got up as usual to do his workout, first checking his mobile for any messages. None received, he gunned the rowing machine and treadmill. Having consumed a wonderfully revitalising smoothie he grabbed an apple and a banana together with a bar of dark chocolate and left for the station.

"Morning, boss. The DCI wants to see you ur………" said Dev as soon as he entered the main office.

"Yes, I know. Urgently" filled in Allan a sardonic smile spreading across his face.

He was on his way to Walters' office when his mobile buzzed. Looking at the screen, his heart leapt.

"So where is my mystery woman?" he asked, the relief sounding in his voice.

"Sorry to disappoint" said a voice that sounded tinny and distorted.

"Who is this? Where is Vanessa?" asked Allan standing still, his body tense.

"Calm down and listen very carefully Detective Inspector Allan. I suspect you are wondering why so many people have fallen sick suddenly and some very unfortunately have died. There is a package waiting for you at the reception desk at your station. Inside will be an explanation and what you are required to do to stop the situation from escalating beyond your wildest imaginings. You have twenty-four hours".

The line went dead.

Allan forgot about the summons by his DCI and raced downstairs to Reception.

"You have a package for me?" he said breathlessly to the on-duty sergeant.

“Yes, sir, here you are” she said, picking up the parcel that was sitting on the side of the desk behind her.

“Did you see who delivered it?”

“No, Simon brought it in” and she turned to call the constable.

“Si, did you see who brought this package in for DI Allan?”

Simon walked over to the plastic screen.

“No, sir, sorry, sir. The package was propped up at the side of the outside step to the station. I looked around but there was nobody about”.

“Okay. No worries. Sargeant, have a look at the cameras – see if we can identify the person who left the package from the footage. Let me know immediately if there is a clear image”.

“Yes, sir” she replied.

Allan looked at the large brown envelope. The label was typed. As it had been hand delivered there was no postmark to give a clue as to where it had come from. He felt sure there wouldn’t be any fingerprints. Gloves would have undoubtedly been worn. He walked to his office and shut the door. Sitting at his desk he opened the envelope.

Inside was a single sheet of typewritten paper. He was just about to read it when his mobile rang again. It was Vanessa's mobile.

"I haven't had a chance to read it yet so……………………." barked Allan.

"Read what?" asked Vanessa in a puzzled voice.

Allan hesitated.

"Read what?" asked Vanessa again.

"Vanessa, who is with you. Have they hurt you?"

"What are you talking about, Jack? No-one's with me and I'm not hurt".

"Where have you been? You were supposed to be coming round to dinner last night and you didn't show. I came round to find you and there was no answer at your apartment. Where have you been?"

"I must have fallen asleep. I've done so many shifts recently I think my body must have failed me. That's why I'm ringing to apologise for not coming round. I promise I won't do that again!"

"Vanessa, someone has just used your mobile and rung me".

"That's absurd, how can that be. I have my mobile here."

"One of your neighbours, the elderly gentleman who lives next door to you, I spoke to him, and he said he heard you leaving the building just before I arrived. So, you must have been somewhere. Where did you go?"

"I didn't go anywhere, I've been here. As I said, I was very tired from all the shifts I've been doing so I must have fallen asleep. My neighbour is suffering from dementia, so he probably dreamt that he heard me or heard someone else and thought it was me. Sometimes it's very difficult to know which door you heard open; sound carries in a strange way sometimes doesn't it?"

"Even if that were so, someone rang me on your mobile" said Jack disbelievingly.

"Who rang you on my mobile, Jack?"

"It's complicated, Vanessa. I can't go into that now. Did you find the note that I slipped under the door last night?"

"Just a minute I'll go and have a look".

There were a few moments silence and then she was back on the phone.

"Yes, I've found it! Sorry again, Jack. I'll make it up to you".

"Yes, you will! Anyway, I'm glad you are safe. I've got to go now. I'll call you!" and Allan clicked off.

He sat for a moment staring into space only coming to at the sound of a knock and Szymanski's head popping round the door.

"Come in, Julia" he said.

Julia came in and sat down in the chair in front of his desk.

He relayed to her all that had happened in the past hour.

"On the one hand, I'm so glad that Vanessa is okay but on the other I have to entertain the ugly possibility that she is in some way involved with recent events".

"Would it be wise to alert the DCI about conflict of interest, sir?"

"No, not for the minute. It could be that she did, indeed, fall asleep and it could be that the neighbour was wrong about her going out yesterday evening".

"But if you got a call from her mobile then she must have known that her mobile was being used. It's not as though she had lost her mobile somewhere, is it?" Szymanski commented.

"No, there must be an explanation but at the moment we need to read the contents of this envelope".

I expect you are wondering, Detective Inspector Allan, who I am and what I want. I suspect you are also trying to work out why there has been a sudden inexplicable virus affecting many people in your area and why children have gone missing only to return with no memory of what happened over the previous few hours. Hopefully, you will never know the answer to the latter mystery. If you do then those people, many of them children, will have unfortunately met a rather gruesome death. But on a more cheerful note, that need not be the case if you follow my instructions. Now is when I tell you what I want. One million pounds to be transferred to an account that I will text to you in the next twelve hours. The money will need to be transferred at a very specific time of which I will advise you. You are probably thinking two things. First, where do I get this money from? Secondly, why should you? Firstly, that's easy, just go to the local high street branch of a bank, I will tell you which one in due course, and ask them to oblige, leading on to the second question, the answer to which you can use to persuade the bank manager to act and that is if my demand is not met one of the children that went missing will die. A ransom note has already been sent to the bank and they are probably getting in touch with you at this very moment so it shouldn't be too hard to convince him of the sincerity of the, ummm ..... I won't say 'threat' because that's not a good word...let's say 'request'. You are probably now telling yourself that this isn't the normal way that such transactions proceed. Usually, the payer is approached and asked not to contact the police, but this way makes it so much simpler, doesn't it? The police have already been contacted and they are helping facilitate my demand. Neat, wouldn't you agree? Please, believe me, Detective Inspector, when I say that it will be on your head should a child meet a horrifying fate. To work then, Detective Inspector Allan and good luck!

Allan threw the paper onto his desk.

"Bastard!" he muttered.

"It's certainly chilling" replied Szymanski.

"He is taking delight from mocking the police. I need to see the DCI" he said, picking up the paper.

On his way his mobile rang, and he answered it curtly as usual.

"We've just had a call from the Manager of the local branch of the Countryside Bank. He says he needs to talk with you urgently" and the officer gave Allan the telephone number.

Allan got through straightaway and calmed the very agitated manager, assuring him that the situation was under control, and they would be in touch soon to discuss the next steps.

A few minutes later he knocked on the door of his superior.

"About bloody time, Allan. I asked to see you over an hour ago! Are we any further with the deciphering of the code on that scrap of paper and what's happening about the search for the atomizer at the village school?" Walters exploded.

"Sir, I'm sorry for the delay but there is a further development which I need to tell you about".

"On top of everything else, the French police have been totally unhelpful regarding the similar incident near Port Grimaud. They feel the people that collapsed were suffering from some sort of virus like Covid and has nothing to do with what happened here!" continued an irate Walters ignoring Allan.

Allan sat still while his boss expended his displeasure.

“Well, what development?” Walters finally demanded.

Allan handed Walters the note and sat there waiting for his response.

At length, seemingly having read the note twice, Walters removed his titanium rimmed glasses and stared at Allan.

“Obviously, we can’t oblige this maniac. Have we any idea who is behind this?”

“I found a motorbike with a distinctive helmet at the back of the garages at Misslethwaite Hall. The same helmet had been noticed by a Mrs. Bowman at the village green where she found the atomizer. So, it’s highly likely that Freddie Cunningham was the bike rider and could have left the bottle in the wastebin, sir”.

“’Highly likely’ ‘could have’ these are not words I want to hear, Allan”.

"Also, I’m not sure I believe the alibi from Manning for Cunningham on the night of the fire at the Hall. In my view, Cunningham is at the back of this but, at the end of the day, we have only twenty-four hours until the threat of a child's death may be carried out" Allan continued.

"This whole thing is a complete mess, Jack, and you say there are significant similarities between the fire at Rosedene Grange five years ago and the one at the Hall?" Walters had calmed down now and began to address Allan by his forename.

"Yes, sir, but as yet I don't know how that can be and why".

"Right, we don't have time to tarry, I will get you the necessary search warrant for Cunningham's property and, I would suggest, his office buildings and laboratories. We need some evidence to arrest and detain Cunningham to establish whether or not he is the perpetrator and if so, stop this nightmare. If not, we're up the creek without a paddle. In the meantime, get together a team of officers and by the time you are assembled I'll have your warrant".

"If we draw a blank, I think we have to act on the instructions of that letter and put a trace on where the funds go" added Allan as he got up to go.

"Let's hope it doesn't come to that but, yes, that would be a consideration. The parents in the village, especially those whose children went missing, should be put on alert. Organise that, Jack, will you".

"Sir".

Allan's mobile rang as he reached the door of the DCI's office.

"Allan"

"Sir, the atomizer was found discarded in one of the bushes around the green near the school. Do you want me to have it sent to forensics?"

"Yes, tell them it's very urgent. I want any results in two hours max and let's hope we find some prints. Get together the entire team back here will you, Dev?"

"On it" replied Dev.

"I don't know whether you picked up on that, sir……" began Allan.

"Dev's voice is so loud I'm surprised the whole station isn't up to date!"

Allan smiled and hurried out of Walters' office.

Before he could reach the main office, his mobile rang again.

Allan sighed and picked up.

“Hello Jack, I’ve managed to break the code. It isn’t a code as such” said Malcolm Pearson head of the NCA.

Allan sighed inaudibly; Malcolm’s pedantic style of speech was not appreciated with time so tight.

“Well, what does it mean exactly?”

“It’s a formula for some sort of substance but I’m damned if I know what it is”.

“Send it the Scientific Advisory Department as fast as you can, Malcolm. Say it is extremely urgent and to get back to me within two hours. Thanks” and he clicked off.

“Okay everyone” Allan called out as he strode into the outer office, immediately attracting his team’s attention. There was complete silence as everyone only had eyes for the boss.

“Right, we are about to be issued with search warrants for Misslethwaite Hall and Cunningham and Sons office building and laboratories. We’ll do all three simultaneously. We are under extreme pressure" and Allan relayed details of the note and why they were conducting the searches.

"Julia, arrange for uniform to help with the searches. As the three buildings will be searched at the same time, we need more bodies".

"Sir" Julia replied.

"Just one other thing" said Allan amidst the scraping back of chairs as everyone hurried to get into action.

"Needless-to-say with speed and time of the essence, all leave is cancelled for the immediate future".

Everyone nodded. They had all assumed that was the case.

Thirty minutes later Allan and his team arrived outside the Hall. Four police cars in total lined up on the sweeping gravel drive.

Allan got out of his car before it had completely stopped, strode up the wide steps and banged on the front door. After a few moments a very relaxed Freddie Cunningham appeared smiling smugly.

“To what do I owe the pleasure of the whole of the Detective Inspector’s team I presume, landing on my doorstep?”

“Stand aside, sir, we have a search warrant for these premises and for your firm and laboratories”.

Far too easily, without any remonstrance or questioning as to why the search was taking place, Freddie stood back waving his arm, ushering in the stampede of police officers.

“Search everything thoroughly!” commanded an irritated Allan. This man was too smug, he thought, and a creeping feeling of dread, emanating from his gut, told him that this search was unlikely to turn up anything of value. He glanced at his watch. He had already used up three valuable hours.

His fears came true when at the end of the search nothing was found, and he just hoped something would turn up with the other two.

As the team were exiting the establishment, filing past Cunningham who had an arrogant look on his face, Detective Constable Baddock, came rushing down the stairs, an excited expression on his face.

“Sorry for the delay, sir, I found this in one of the bedrooms upstairs!” he exclaimed breathlessly, brandishing a small atomizer.

“Well done, Constable!” grinned Allan and put the bottle in an evidence bag.

“We need to fast track this to forensics” he said handing the package to Patel “If it turns out that traces of the virus are found in this…………..” he trailed off as his mobile started to ring. He raced back to his car, Szymanski getting into the driving seat as Allan took the call.

“Detective Inspector, I would have thought you would have better things to do than annoy respectable members of the community,” said the metallic voice.

“I can’t speak now, I’m afraid. Call me at the station at, shall we say, an hour from now” and Allan clicked off.

“Make him sweat a bit!” said Allan.

"Fine line though, sir, isn't it? With the lives of children potentially at risk, I mean. We don't want to upset the bastard".

"Yes, there is an element of risk but if we rile him a little, he might start losing it and make that much wanted tiny error that will be what we need to catch him" said Allan, a grim expression on his face.

His mobile rang again, it was the Desk Sergeant. "No luck with the cameras I'm afraid, sir, the person's face was covered with some sort of joke mask.

"Okay, disappointing but I thought that would be the case. Thanks Sergeant" and he let out a deep sigh as he put his mobile away.

Back at the station, Allan organised a trace to be set up on the expected call which came spot on the hour.

"I expect you've put a trace on this call, Detective Inspector," said the distorted voice, "You're wasting precious time."

"Two minutes for the trace" Szymanski signalled, and Allan knew he had to keep him talking.

“If anything happens to any children you know we won’t stop until you’re caught when you’ll face..........”

The voice interrupted him.

“Good try Detective Inspector but you failed in your trace. The penalty, two children will die if I don’t get the money” and the line went dead.

Szymanski indicated that the trace had failed.

Heads were in hands; pens were thrown on desks in frustration by several officers.

Allan answered a call.

“Hello, you asked for us to establish the meaning of a formula. This formula is for the same virus that we recently found in an atomizer which we examined for you. We can’t identify it, as you know, but it is without doubt lethal in high enough quantities”.

“Thank you for your assistance” said Allan rubbing his hand across his brow.

“So, the fact that you found the note in Cunningham’s study means he is definitely involved if not the prime suspect we are looking for. However, we shouldn't have been in that study so in itself would be inadmissible evidence and it could be argued that someone else left it there. Nevertheless, it is another nail in Cunningham's coffin" he said to Szymanski.

"Indeed, sir. I've just heard that nothing of note was found at the offices, but forensics are at the laboratories together with officers and have taken samples of any suspicious substances. They are going to work on them immediately and should have the results to us within the hour" she said.

Chapter Ten

Allan was seated in front of DCI Walters' desk. He had just given an update to the senior officer.

"So why don't we arrest Cunningham. After all, an atomiser was found in his house and the bike and distinctive helmet were also found on his estate" Walters demanded tapping his pen on the table.

"We've yet to hear from forensics about the atomiser, sir, and the bike could have been used by someone else on the estate. We strongly suspect, but don't know for certain and we have no hard evidence, that Cunningham is behind all of this. However, it could be someone unidentified who is making these demands. If so, we could risk children being killed if we don't comply. It's not ideal but I think we must seriously consider paying the ransom and putting a tracker on the money" Allan suggested quietly.

"And what if the bank doesn't cooperate?"

"I think it will. I've already spoken to the manager who has received a ransom note and is very upset that children's lives are at stake. In addition, the bank couldn't risk all that bad publicity if the kids died because they wouldn't put up the money".

“The Super is not going to like this one bit. It’s against policy to give in to such demands. However, I agree if children’s lives are at risk, we have arguably a unique situation on our hands. Set it up Allan, and let’s pray we can trace this bastard”.

“Yes sir”.

Allan turned as he reached the door.

“I think we know who the bastard is, sir, it’s getting the evidence to arrest him and finding out who else is involved”.

Szymanski walked up to Allan as he reached his office.

“I took a call from forensics, sir, a few minutes ago. No luck with the atomizer found at Misslethwaite Hall. There is no trace of the virus or any other substance at all. The bottle doesn’t appear to have been used”.

Allan heard his mobile buzz alerting him to a new text message which he quickly read.

“We have the account number and the time” he looked at his watch.

“Eighteen hours’ time. Okay. Julia, you need to liaise with the bank to set up a transfer and trace to be done at the exact time, nine o’clock tomorrow morning”.

Szymanski left the room and Allan sat for a moment deep in thought. Then he got up and walked into the main office.

“Listen everyone, can I have your attention” he called authoritatively.

Complete silence reigned as all eyes focused on the boss.

“We have eighteen hours until the ransom must be paid to avoid unthinkable tragedy. In my opinion up until that time we have a window of opportunity to find where this, almost certainly manmade virus, is being manufactured by these murderers. Logically, it appears that Cunningham & Sons laboratory is connected and yet there is no evidence there. Therefore, it must be being processed at some building or buildings nearby and I would suggest a building that is isolated. There can’t be many such buildings with that capacity, isolated and close by”.

Someone got a local map, and they gathered round. Allan got a marker pen and drew a ring round the likely area.

“Everyone clear what we are looking for?” Allan asked looking round his team.

“Julia, round up some uniform to help us if you can”.

She nodded and walked off a little way to make a call.

“Right, we’ll meet at three o’ clock sharp at Misslethwaite village station car park.

There were general nods and grunts of agreement from his team.

Later, having made all necessary arrangements, the team grabbed their coats and mobiles and rapidly made their way to the station car park. They walked a couple of miles at a measured distance from each other, over open countryside and then through woodland.

The search had been underway for about thirty minutes when one of the officers gave a shout.

“Over here, I’ve found something!”

Everyone ran over to the spot where there was a clearing in a wooded area. A large building surrounded on three sides by trees but with a narrow, rough track to the remaining side appeared before them.

The team's elation was short-lived. Having wrenched open the doors, their reward was to face a huge and completely empty interior.

Allan phoned for forensics who arrived twenty minutes later. Everyone donned barrier clothing and the interior was searched methodically but after another hour and a half they had nothing to show for it except a cigarette packet for a particular brand of French cigarettes. With a gloved hand Allan picked it up and turned it over in his hands, looking thoughtful.

"What is it, sir?" asked Szymansky.

"I don't know but I wonder who smokes this brand of French cigarettes? They have a distinctive smell," he said, and something stirred in the back of his mind.

"Yes, probably not many people smoke them. I don't even know if many places sell them here in the UK. Shall I bag it, and we'll make a note to keep an eye out for someone smoking them. As you say, they do have a peculiar smell".

"Something else though. The French have reported a similar event of people suddenly falling sick. So, there's a potential connection here, maybe?" he asked rhetorically.

He popped the packet into the evidence bag proffered by Szymanski.

Allan waved to Stewart Strange.

"Have you noticed the fresh tyre tracks in the lane?"

"Yes, and we have taken samples".

"Good man. I should know by now nothing escapes your eagle eye, Stew!" and Allan placed a hand on Stew's shoulder giving it a pat.

"So, what now, sir?" asked Szymanski as they got in the car, Allan in the driving seat.

"Buggered if I know" replied Allan and then smashed his fist on the steering wheel in an uncharacteristic display of frustration.

"We always seem to be on the back foot. I'm as certain as I can be that makeshift building is where the substance was being manufactured. We only arranged to search the area today and yet it seems as though they had a heads up and cleared out without leaving virtually any trace. That indicates to me that they knew we were coming pretty much from the time of our meeting this morning. I'm wondering how they knew that?" asked Allan looking at Szymanski.

"I don't know, sir. Are you thinking what I think you're thinking?" she asked, her eyes wide with surprise.

"I'm thinking 'mole' but there's no-one that springs to mind as a possible".

"No, sir" she said hesitantly.

"What's on your mind Julia?"

"Nothing really, sir" she said evasively and looked out of the side window. Her face was flushed. She felt embarrassed.

"Out with it, Julia!" demanded Allan.

"Well, it's just that we were, you were, wondering about Vanessa after her unexplained disappearance. Did you by any chance tell her that you might be going to search that area, sir?"

"I see where you're going but no, I haven't spoken to her in the past two days, and I certainly haven't spoken to her this morning. I've avoided calling her for two reasons. The first is that there is an element of doubt, although I'm struggling to believe that she is in any way involved, but there is that remote possibility. The second is the conflict of interest. But no, I can't see that she was the culprit in this case if indeed, there is a culprit, but I am curious to know how that warehouse was cleaned out so thoroughly in such a short space of time and I'm fairly positive it was just before we got there because of the fresh tyre tracks".

They sat examining their own thoughts for a while then Szymansky broke the silence.

"So where do we go from here? I'm not sure forensics will come up with any damning evidence".

"We need to get back to the station and go through everything we have so far. We might have missed something".

Seven o'clock that evening they were no further forward.

Allan stood up. "There is nothing more we can do tonight so I suggest we call it a day and get back here at seven o' clock tomorrow morning to implement the transfer".

The following day, Allan, Szymanski and Patel needed to get to the bank early along with officers who would set up the transfer and tracking for nine o'clock.

"You're absolutely sure that we will be able to track the transfer?" asked Allan with an edge in his voice.

"Yes, boss, definitely".

"Great! Even if it ends up going to a Swiss Bank account with the sort of threats, we are dealing with I'm sure they will want to cooperate discreetly". Allan smoothed back his thick, dark hair which had flopped onto his forehead.

As nine o'clock drew near everyone in the room tensed and you could slice through the thick silence.

The transfer was made, and the tracker followed it to a bank in Venezuela but almost immediately the screen showed it moving from there. What followed caused a gasp and incredulous expressions crossed the onlookers' faces.

"It's been rejected, sir, the money has come back to us!" and the officer conducting the transaction looked up at Allan who just stared disbelievingly at the screen.

He stood upright and put both hands on his head, his mouth slightly open.

"What the devil.................." he began.

His mobile rang.

"Just two things. Firstly, don't try to be clever, Detective Inspector, because you have now caused the death of two children. I should really make it three as you have already made one mistake by going to a certain empty building. Really, I would have thought a man of your seniority and experience would not have displayed such utter stupidity. Secondly, this was never about just one million pounds. I will be in contact again shortly with my real demand. Take it seriously - but, of course, you will, won't you? I should concentrate in the meantime in trying to explain and console the parents of the children who, unfortunately, will now pay the price" said the robotic voice and the phone went dead.

Allan turned to Szymanski and Patel. Get in touch with all the families whose children went missing at the fête and at the school and tell them not to let their children out of their sight for a second.

Allan was in the middle of a call to one of the parents when Patel approached him. Patel signalled to Allan that he needed to take the call.

Finishing his current call as quickly as possible, he grabbed the phone from Patel's outstretched hand.

He could hear the sobbing on the phone even before he put the receiver to his ear.

"Detective Inspector Allan. Who am I speaking to?"

“Its .... its.... Mrs Swan, Timmy’s mum ...oh inspector its.... Timmy.... he’s .... he’s dead” and the woman’s voice wailed unintelligibly.

“I’m so sorry Mrs Swan. I’m so sorry. We will be with you shortly. We are coming over right now”.

He signalled to Szymanski who quickly finished her call and joined Allan who was updating Patel on the situation.

“Carry on with the calls, Dev, there will be at least one other child in danger”.

“Will do, sir”.

An ambulance and two police cars were outside the Swan’s house when Allan and Szymanski arrived five minutes or so later.

They walked up the path of the well-kept front garden. Timmy’s father opened the door looking distraught, with red rimmed eyes and ushered them in without waiting for their identification.

In the lounge, Timmy’s mother sat hunched up on the settee, fiddling with a handkerchief, looking down at her fingers, her hair sticking out in all directions, the tears flowing down her wan cheeks.

The two detectives sat down. Szymanski sat on the settee next to Susan Swan and put her hand on the woman's arm.

"We're so sorry for your loss, Mrs Swan. We are here to help but we need you to tell us what happened. Do you think you can do that for us?" Allan let Szymanski do the talking initially as had been agreed on the way over, both feeling that a woman's voice was softer and more likely to be calming at times of extreme distress.

There was a silence for a while and then Susan suddenly turned on her.

"You? Help? It's because of you police that Timmy is dead. It was something to do with when he went missing, and you still haven't found who took Timmy or the other children. It's your fault he's dead" and she burst into wracking sobs.

"We will catch whoever took Timmy and the other children, Susan, but we need your help" said Szymanski in a gentle, soothing voice that belied what she was feeling.

Susan just shook her head and continued to cry.

"I think my wife isn't in any fit state to continue, Detective," interrupted Stephen Swan.

"If you want to know what happened maybe if you come with me into the kitchen" and he indicated that the detectives should follow him.

"Would you like something to drink, a cup of tea maybe?" he asked.

Allan and Szymanski, both thanked him but shook their heads.

"Well, I will if you don't mind. It's better when I have something to do".

"Yes of course, we completely understand," said Allan.

"Susan, she doesn't mean it you know. She's just distraught and wants someone to blame" he said, busying himself with making a cup of tea.

"Completely understandable, Stephen. We are doing our very best to find out who is at the bottom of all this," Allan spoke in a reassuring voice.

Stephen nodded and sat down opposite them at the pine bench kitchen table.

He picked up his mug and took a sip of his tea and Allan noticed his left hand was shaking so much that some of the tea slopped onto the tablemat. He put the mug down.

"It was all very sudden and very strange" he said staring at the blank kitchen wall behind the two detectives.

"Timmy was playing on one of his computer games in the lounge and he suddenly stopped and seemed to go into a trance. He was staring straight ahead of him and nodded once or twice. Then he simply said 'Yes' as though he was talking to someone. This all took no more than a couple of minutes. Then he…he…" Stephen rubbed one of his shaking hands over his face and wiped away the tears that were beginning to fall.

"Take your time, Stephen" said Allan and Szymanski nodded her agreement.

"Then he fell to the floor and seemed to pass out but in a matter of seconds he was fitting and struggling to breathe. Then blood started coming out of his mouth and nose then more and more blood. He was choking, there was terror in his eyes. There was nothing I could do but hold him close. I felt so helpless. He was my son but there was nothing I could do. Then he died. It was all over in a few minutes" Stephen then just broke down in uncontrollable sobs.

"Is there someone we can call to be here for you both?" asked Szymanski putting a hand lightly on his arm.

He shook his head.

"No, we just want to be left alone with our grief" he managed to say.

"We'll go now then, Stephen. Thank you for your time and once again, we are very sorry for your loss," said Allan.

The front door closed behind them and once through the front gate they paused.

"That was awful, sir. I felt so sorry for them," said Szymanski.

"Yes, it was, and I do, but that won't get the baby bathed, will it? Being sorry, I mean. We've got work to do. First, we're going to visit the morgue. I want to know what they have found about the cause of death. I fear it will confirm that it was the virus but how did he ingest that? And why didn't the parents also ingest it? Then we have the question of Timmy's trance before death, what was that about? We seem to have more and more questions to answer".

Allan was about to get on the phone to find out Dev's progress when his mobile rang.

Szymanski looked at him questioningly raising one eyebrow. Allan finished the call.

"There's been another death. Little Mary Peters. This is a bloody awful fucking case, Julia. Let's go" he said curtly and strode over to the car.

Szymanski followed him quickly and the thought crossed her mind that the case was getting to Allan. In over five years working with him, she had never once heard him use the 'f' word.

An ambulance was outside the Peters' house together with several police vehicles when Allan and Szymanski arrived.

"What do you make of the cause of death?" asked Allan walking straight over to Stewart Strange who was bending over the body of the little girl.

"I can't say for sure, obviously, Jack, but it is pointing to asphyxiation caused by I know not what at the present time, although it could be the virus. There was a lot of blood which the little girl had spewed out, indicating maybe some sort of infection maybe from the virus. I'll let you know more after the autopsy".

"Thanks, Stew. Get back to me as quick as you can".

"Of course, I came here first as it was the nearest to my house but I'm off to examine little Timmy Swan now. Catch up with you later" said Strange.

The two detectives went in search of Mary's parents. The paramedics were resuscitating Mrs Peters while her husband stood looking bewildered, rubbing his head, his hands going backwards and forwards on his bald pate. He looked across at Allan and Szymanski as they entered the lounge.

"Wot the fuck is going on? My kid's dead and my wife's .... it's all your fault. You should have done somink!" his voice suddenly rising, he lunged at Allan.

Allan dodged the impending blow and helped him up from where he had stumbled on the floor.

"Sit down, Mr Peters, please. We understand how you feel, we really do, and we are very sorry for your loss; I assure you we are doing everything possible to get to the bottom of how your daughter died but we need to ask you some questions".

"It's too late in't it. My kid's dead" and he buried his head in his hands.

"Sadly, yes, it is too late for your daughter and we're so sorry for your loss. However, I'm sure you will feel the need for closure in knowing what exactly happened?" countered Allan.

Mr Peters didn't reply, as he sat shaking his bowed head.

"So, can you recount the events just before your daughter passed away, Mr Peters".

The paramedics interrupted.

"Excuse me, I'm sorry to but in. We are taking Mrs Peters to hospital. She has suffered a mild heart attack".

"Wot. An 'eart attack. No. She's only firty-five. She can't be 'aving an 'eart attack. There ain't no way!"

"We're taking her to Addenbrooke's Hospital now. If you would like to follow on as soon as the police have finished, just come to A&E and they will direct you. Okay?" asked the paramedic looking at Peters with a kindly expression on her face.

"I'm coming now! Are we done?" he hissed at Allan.

"No, sir, unfortunately we aren't. If you would just tell us about the events, then you can go and be with your wife".

Peters looked as though he was about to explode, then he thought better of it.

"Mary was dancing round the room with 'er doll, yer know, like little girls do. She was saying she was goin' to be a ballet dancer when she grew up and oh I dunno I weren't really listening. She went quiet all of a sudden like. I were texting on my mobile and I looked up at Mary. She were standing stock still like and staring at somefink. I looked in the direction she were looking but there was nofink there. I went over to her and waved my hand in front of her eyes but she just stared right through them. Then she said 'yes' as though someone was talking to her. It were really weird. Seconds later she wos on the floor, fitting. Struggling to breathe she was. Loads of blood coming out of her mouth and nose. It wos horrible. My wife screamed at me to ring for an ambulance, which I did. Then Mary didn't move anymore and my wife was crying and screaming. The paramedics came and yer know the rest. What was it that killed 'er?" and his voice wobbled.

"That's what we mean to find out, Mr Peters and we do appreciate your time. Once again, we are very sorry for your loss. We won't keep you any longer and let you get to the hospital to be with your wife," said Allan.

Back in the car, Allan turned to Szymanski.

"We need to call in the profiler again. We need to get into this maniac's mind. What exactly do they want? What are we dealing with? The press and the super will be on the DCI's back too. The pressure is rising to boiling point, Julia, two children dead and we are no further with our enquiries".

A couple of hours later the detectives were once again sitting across the table from the profiler who had just been brought up to date with the latest developments.

The profiler took off his specs and sucked on one of the arms.

"This person is, I have already suggested, a psychopath but in addition he is displaying his narcissistic tendencies. As I have already indicated he is highly intelligent and extremely dangerous. He is, in fact, playing with you. I have no doubt that you would have been unable to track the transfer of the monies into his account and therefore there was no need for rejection of funds. He did that purely for his own warped amusement. He is enjoying making you sweat and confounding the police. Equally, and chillingly, he enjoys killing and feels nothing, no guilt, and that extends to murdering innocent children. The only hope I can give you is that he slips up and you are thus able to gain the evidence you need".

After the profiler had left, Allan looked at his mobile that had been vibrating in his pocket while the profiler had been speaking. The message was from Strange. Very brief as usual just confirming what Allan already knew that traces of the virus had been found in both the children's blood streams which had turned into a fatal infection which in turn had caused death by asphyxiation, the victims unable to breathe from the flood of blood from their noses and mouths.

Patel knocked and poked his head round the door.

“Call from Mrs Swan on Line 2 sir”, he said.

“Hello, Mrs Swan, DI Allan speaking”.

“Detective I don’t know if it is of any interest to you or relevant but I’ve remembered something”.

“Let us be the judge of that, Mrs Swan” said Allan just a tad impatiently.

“Yes, well, it was about ten minutes before….before….”

“Yes, Mrs Swan”.

“Well before it happened, and Timmy had a call on his mobile”.

“Who phoned him?”

“Well, that’s it, Detective Inspector. He wouldn’t tell us. He said he didn’t know but we told him that couldn’t be. He must know who phoned!”

“And what did he say to that?” Allan thought “blood and stone”.

“He said he was telling the truth, and he didn’t know who it was. In the end we thought it must have been a wrong number and perhaps it was and I'm wasting your time" she said apologetically.

"On the contrary, you have been most helpful, thank you Mrs Swan. We will need Timmy's mobile and a uniform officer will be over to collect it shortly and if there is anything else you remember, please just call me at any time".

Allan replaced the receiver and having asked Patel to get someone to pick up Timmy's mobile, he located his notebook and found the telephone number he was looking for.

Picking up the receiver he input the number. It rang a couple of times and then a man's voice answered.

"Good afternoon, Mr Peters. Detective Inspector Allan here……" he began.

"Not you lot again! Can't you bloody leave us alone! I'm at the 'ospital with my wife".

"I'm afraid not, sir, not while there is a murder enquiry" and before Darren Peters could remonstrate further, he continued.

"Firstly, I hope your wife is feeling better?"

"Yeah, she is, no thanks to yer".

"I'm very glad to hear that, Mr Peters. Now I want you to cast your mind back to before Mary seemed to be in a trance. Did anything odd happen?" asked Allan ignoring Peters' unwarranted comment.

"I told yer already. I've answered your questions. No nofink 'appened okay?"

"Bear with me, sir, if you will. For example, did your daughter take a call on her mobile maybe a half-hour or an hour beforehand?"

There was a pause while Peters thought about it.

"Yeah, yeah there were summat. I fink she did 'ave a call. Yeah, yeah. Now I fink abou' it. I asked 'er who it was, and she said she didn't know. I said that was rubbish, that she must know. In the end I fort it were a wrong number, know wot I mean?"

"I will need Mary's phone. When will you be back home, sir?"

"I dunno".

"Mr Peters, may I remind you again that this is a murder enquiry. I need to know when you will be back home this afternoon" Allan said sternly.

"Okay, Okay, keep yer 'air on. I'll be back by five o'clock" he replied grudgingly.

"One of our uniform officers will be over to meet you at five o'clock. Thank you, Mr Peters you have been very helpful," and without waiting for a response Allan hung up.

Allan crossed quickly to the door of his office and signalled to Patel.

"Yes, sir" said Patel closing the door.

"Dev, I want you to get in contact with all the parents of children in the village and surrounding villages to a five-mile radius and ask them to take their children's phones and switch them off," Allan instructed.

"Sir?" queried Patel.

"Just do it, Dev and it's urgent!"

"On it, sir" and he rushed towards the door.

"Oh Dev, ask Julia to step in".

“Sir”

Szymanski shut the door behind her and sat down on the chair in front of Allan’s desk.

“Okay so we know how this maniac has murdered the children. Obviously, they were programmed in some way to die when instructed”.

“I’m not sure I understand, sir. How could a particular word induce death by asphyxiation?”

“I’m not sure but let’s suppose that a particular word activated the fatal effects of the virus. So, the virus that they were carrying was inactive until that word was heard by them. The question is how was the virus prevented from killing them until that word was spoken?”.

“It sounds a bit far-fetched sir, if you don’t mind me saying”.

“Yes, but the theory fits what happened. Let’s assume that I am right. As I see it, we need the children’s mobiles and my gut feeling is that we will find the calls were made from burner phones which indicates that they were the killer calls. Also, I think we can conclude that a relatively mild dosage of the virus was spread around the victims at the fête to create a distraction while the children were abducted. What we don't know is where the children were taken, what happened to them, who took them, how a virus was introduced into their bodies and how it could cause a fast acting and fatal reaction but kept 'on ice' until a certain word activated it.

Finally, with the rejection of the requested funds, what is the motive? Particularly, what was the motive in abducting children? Or indeed, is there a motive? Are we, as the profiler suggested, and the most chilling thought of all, dealing with a narcissistic psycho who is doing this purely for what they see as fun?"

Chapter Eleven

Jack was working up a sweat on the treadmill. Unusual for him to exercise at this time but he found it helped him to think. It was ten o'clock in the evening and he was already running hard when he heard his doorbell ring. Reaching for his towel he dried the sweat off his face and walking over to the door he peered through the spyhole.

"Vanessa!" he exclaimed as he opened the door wide.

"I couldn't sleep. I'm on early shift tomorrow but I hate to say I'm missing you. Sounds slushy, doesn't it? Before you put your fingers in your mouth to be sick…." she came up close and putting her arms around him she kissed him long and passionately. He pushed her up against the wall and bringing her legs up either side of his hips he entered her.

He woke up at a quarter past six and before opening his eyes remembered the evening before. He smiled and reached out to the other side of the bed, his hand patting the sheets. Then he opened his eyes and looked at the empty space. He listened to hear her moving about. Then he recalled that she had said she had an early shift.

Sighing he went into the kitchen to prepare his usual healthy start to the day.

While eating, he texted Vanessa.

“Fantastic last night; missing you loads this morning. Call me”.

He showered and dressed, grabbed some fruit, keys and jacket and made for the door.

Driving to the office he got a call from his DCI.

“Sir” he answered.

“Just had a call from Antoine Dumas, Inspecteur en Chef at Saint Tropez police station. It seems they now have suspicions that their sickness incident could be linked to ours. It would appear that they have found a small atomiser with a tiny amount of residue of an unidentified but potentially lethal virus”.

“So, this is now definitely an international affair then? Far bigger than we first thought. I’ll do some further digging into Cunningham. Then there is the fire at the Hall and the link to the cold case. What on earth is the connection there? I’m certain there is one. I don't believe in coincidences".

"Indeed. There may be a need to go to France but leave it to me", Walters rang off.

Ten minutes later Allan was back at the office and called out for Patel to come in.

"Good morning, Dev, I want you to find out if Cunningham owns or is renting any properties, businesses or warehouses in the vicinity of St Tropez".

"Sir".

"Oh, and Dev, that's within the hour!"

"Sir!" said Patel hurrying out of the office.

Barry knocked on his door a couple of minutes later.

"Sorry to disturb you, sir".

Allan waved a hand to beckon him in.

"I've just taken a call from Addenbrooke's Hospital. It seems that there are a significant number of casualties from the surrounding local area suffering from an unknown virus who have been admitted by A&E. They want to know if it has anything to do with the virus that was found at the fête and if so, do we know what it is?"

"Did they give any indication as to what they mean by 'significant'?"

"Yes, they said they had fifty in the space of an hour".

"Did they say whether these patients had been in the same place or were they from different locations?"

"They were from different areas, but all had been at the local sports centre a short time before, sir".

"Get on to the sports centre immediately and shut it down!" barked Allan.

After Barry had gone off to carry out his boss' instruction Allan bounded up the steps to the DCI's office two at a time.

"Excuse me, sir, I have some bad news" and he proceeded to relay information about the incident.

"I think we need to have a Press Conference before this gets out and also, we need to give an update on where we are with the deaths of Timmy Swan and Mary Peters" Allan finished speaking. "Agreed" said his superior.

The Press Conference was hastily arranged, and Allan and Walters faced a myriad of microphones virtually obliterating the faces of those who held them outstretched to avoid missing anything the policemen uttered. Behind the press were the cameras lined up ready to relay the news straight onto people's televisions.

"Good morning, everyone, thank you for being present today at this Press briefing. My name is Detective Chief Inspector John Walters and on my left is my colleague Detective Inspector Jack Allan from the Cambridgeshire Constabulary".

"My colleague will now relay the facts as we know them today regarding the multiple cases of sudden sickness and the deaths of two local children. After this, there will be a short time for any questions you may have". Walters then turned to the DI and looked expectantly at him.

Allan cleared his throat, sorted his papers and began.

"We were first aware that some members of the public were experiencing an onslaught of sudden sickness on 27 May when at a fête held by Mr and

Mrs Cunningham at their home, Misslethwaite Hall. After forensic examination we can confirm that the virus is currently not able to be categorised, but it is man-made and a team of scientists are looking further into it. We can also confirm that the two children died of a fatal reaction caused by that same virus. We are now actively seeking to apprehend those responsible for the murder of these children and for the murder of those adult victims who died at the fête on 27 May. We will, of course, update you as and when we have further information".

A chorus of voices started to ask questions.

Allan held up his hand.

"One at a time please" and he pointed to a reporter in the front row.

"When you say man-made virus, have you any leads as to who has produced this virus? Are we looking at an individual, a group or a country?" he asked.

"This is something that will need to be further clarified but for the moment from the evidence we currently have we are looking for an individual or a group of individuals" answered Allan and he pointed to a woman in the back row.

"If it is a virus why didn't more people catch it?"

“I’m unable to comment on that point at the present time”.

Before he could indicate another reporter, she continued.

“If it is a virus then how did the children suddenly catch it? I understand they were at home at the time”.

“That is unclear at this present time and as I have said the scientists are working on it” and he pointed to another questioner.

“If it is a virulent virus why did relatively few people at the fête catch it?”.

“Again, we are working on it” and he pointed to a guy on his left.

“Do you have suspects for these crimes?”

“I’m not at liberty to discuss that at this time”.

“Does that mean you do have a suspect?” the reporter persisted.

“You will be kept up-to-date as soon as there are any further developments”.

Walters got up and Allan followed suit.

“That’s it everyone. Thank you for your time” said Walters firmly.

They both rapidly walked away and through to the back of the curtained off area of the conference hall.

Allan's mobile rang and he answered it curtly.

"Sir, I'm sorry I haven't been able to get hold of you, I did leave a message on your mobile, but I expect you haven't had time to get back to me……."

"Get on with it, Dev for pity's sake, man" rasped an exasperated Allan.

"He has, I mean Cunningham has, a property or, in fact, two properties in the south of France. One is near Nice, and the other is outside St. Tropez near Port Grimaud!"

"Good work, Dev. Get the addresses and telephone numbers of both properties. I'm heading back to the office now".

When Allan arrived back at the station there was a large envelope waiting for him at Reception. He took the stairs two at a time, walked quickly to his office and closing the door he ripped open the envelope. There was a single sheet inside.

Hello again, Detective Inspector Allan. I keep turning up like a bad penny, don't I? I enjoyed your Press Conference. Very entertaining. Not very informative though, was it? You don't really have a clue, do you? Well, never mind. Perhaps this nightmare will end soon, and you can go back to your healthy, mundane life. However, before you can do that there's something I would like you to do for me. There now, that was very polite, wasn't it? I've made it a request when in actual fact you don't really have an option. I think I suggested to you that it wasn't about one million pounds, and I was telling you the truth. It isn't about the million, it's about twice that, two million. This time though don't make any mistakes. If you do, needless to say, more people and particularly children will die. Don't worry about Countryside Bank, they already know what is required of them. You need to collect the money this time, I require the money in cash - don't want to risk another wasted exercise with you trying to put a trace on the money, now do we? I would suggest you telephone the manager now and arrange to collect the cash. I will text you with further instructions in due course".

Allan immediately phoned the bank manager who informed him that the criminal had rung him yesterday morning and given him twenty-four hours to get together the required ransom without contacting the police or else his wife and children would be killed. The caller had also informed him that the police would be in contact with him.

Allan called the team together and relayed what had happened.

“As soon as I have the information on where this bastard wants the cash, we need to surround the area with officers, posing as refuse collectors and whatever else is appropriate for the area. My guess is that he will choose an area that is crowded and easy to blend in. He will be expecting that we will be posting officers around, so it is vital that we blend in with the crowd and catch this man to prevent further deaths. In the meantime, Julia and Dev drive behind me, Barry and Sophie you take another car and follow on too. It’s a lot of cash that I’m picking up and in case he is thinking of snatching the money at the bank we’ll be ready for him”.

Ten minutes later the small convoy drove out of the station and arrived at the bank a short while later.

The manager looked pale and nervous as he ushered Allan into his large office adorned with photographs of his wife and children.

“I do apologise for not telling you that this man had contacted me, but I was terrified that my family would be killed” he stuttered.

“No need to apologise, sir. I completely understand. Now where is the money? I’d very much like to get it back to the station and we can take it from there”.

Back in his office, Alllan stowed the money in a large suitcase under his desk. He and Szymanski impatiently awaited the text that the caller had promised. Allan was drumming his fingers on the desk and Szymanski kept pushing her hair back from her forehead and then clasping her two hands together, a sure sign that she was agitated.

Patel knocked on the door and Allan signalled for him to enter.

“I’ve got those addresses and info on the properties in France you wanted, sir” and he put a printed sheet on Allan’s desk.

“Thanks, Dev”. The DC nodded and left the room.

Allan looked at the information briefly and called upstairs to the DCI.

“As I said before you may need to take a trip to the south of France but first things first. Deal with the situation in hand and the trip may be unnecessary. Keep me informed" and Walters rang off.

They had to wait for two hours before Allan received the text telling him what the arrangements for handing over the money were.

"Right, we're on" said Allan as he strode out of his office and into the main area with Szymanski close on his heels, where the team were ostensibly busy with their tasks but in reality, were, like their seniors, impatient to hear where they were heading. The team turned their heads as Allan and Szymanski entered the room.

"Okay, everyone, we've heard, and it is as I suspected one of the most crowded places in the area tomorrow afternoon at two o'clock. I don't know why I didn't guess straightaway, Strawberry Fayre, of course. The ideal place for a perpetrator to hide. So, the text tells us to enter via the Victoria Bridge entrance. I should walk along the path until I reach a dilapidated blue Transit van decorated with pink flowers with a personalised number plate. The van will be unlocked, and I should put the money in the back and walk away. Now, there will be a lot of people milling around and we need different people to be mingling with the crowd. Two of us will be stationed some way away from the van in an unmarked vehicle. Barry, can you get in touch with the organisers. We need the use of one of the festival vans parked in an area taking in the van from a different angle. Meanwhile everyone else put on gear that will blend in with the event. I would suggest Amy and Peter, you act as a young couple with a baby in a pram, playing ball on the grass in the immediate vicinity of the suspect vehicle. Get hold of a pram and put a doll in it to add a bit of authenticity. Mike, you act as an amateur photographer just keep taking snaps from all angles but don't point the camera at the van. Barry, get hold of some leaflets for a bogus new restaurant and hand them out. The rest of you use your imaginations. Dev, can you organise firearms to be present but discreetly.".

"Yes, sir, what if you get another text tomorrow changing the plan and asking you to go somewhere else?" Mike asked.

"Obviously if I get a text from the suspect to go to another location, I will let you know over the comms and you can follow me at a safe distance".

"What if the suspect doesn't text you but grabs you and takes your comms before you can tell us where you are going?" asked Peter.

"Good point again. Could happen although I think it is unlikely. However, if so, you can track me through my mobile".

"What if the suspect takes your mobile or you drop it in a struggle?" asked Barry.

"Well, let's hope that doesn't happen. There is only so much you can anticipate and have a solution! Okay, so no more questions?".

Everyone shook their heads.

"Good luck everyone and let's hope this time we'll catch the bastard".

Everyone cheered as they turned to their tasks in hand.

The next day the sun shone brightly and there was a slight, warm breeze. The perfect day for the Strawberry Fayre which would start at midday.

Szymanski's phone rang at six o'clock. She looked at her mobile displaying the caller's name.

"Good morning, sir" she said stifling a yawn.

"Are you up and running?" he said with smile in his voice.

Quietly she got out of bed endeavouring not to awaken her partner and crept downstairs to the kitchen.

"Not quite, sir, but a strong cup of coffee should do the trick!" she replied.

"Julia, I think we should interview Cunningham this morning. If it is him at the back of this, then our visit may act to make him relax and then, with any luck, he'll make a mistake".

"I'm not following, sir, why would our visit make him relax?"

"If he thinks we are not using our time to catch him receiving the money, hopefully he will relax, become over-confident and slip up".

"Ummm. Maybe. What will our reason be for the visit?"

"We haven't yet followed up on finding the bike and helmet. That will serve as a good excuse".

"But we shouldn't really have been out in the grounds snooping around. We didn't have a warrant. Won't that play into his hands? He would have grounds for a complaint, and he does have some standing around here. Ostensibly he is a respectable businessman", Szymanski countered.

"We'll use the excuse that I used with the gardener when he challenged me. I thought I heard a scream, and I went to investigate. In so doing, I found the bike and helmet".

"Okay, sir. Do you want me to meet you there or shall I pick you up?"

"See you here in an hour. We should be there around eight o'clock. Time enough for him to be up and breakfasted".

On the way over to Misslethwaite Hall they were absorbed in their own ruminations for a while, then Szymanski broke the silence.

"So, sir, I hope you don't mind my asking, but have you had any further thoughts about Vanessa's potential involvement in all of this?"

"What makes you ask now particularly?"

"Nothing, really, sir" and she could feel Allan's eyes fixed on her.

"Well, I don't understand how she didn't hear you when you were banging on the door that evening and then the calls from her phone. How could that happen? Also, if she isn't and she hasn't somehow bugged your phone and/or your apartment, then someone in our team is very likely a 'mole' because how did the murderer know we were conducting a search of that warehouse? We never answered that did we?"

"No, you're right, we didn't, and it is something that we need to be aware of. However, I don't think Vanessa is involved. For one thing, from a practical perspective, I don't think she would have the time with her work as a hospital doctor with all those long shifts plus she didn't have the opportunity to gain the necessary information. I thought about it hard, and I know I didn't tell her anything of what was happening on the case. I very much doubt that she has cloned or bugged my mobile and from a purely personal point of view, it would be totally out of character. So, we do have a problem but it's not Vanessa" he said firmly but inside he was wondering why Vanessa hadn't answered the door that evening and how he had received phone calls from her phone if she didn't know anything about it and answered her phone a few minutes later. Szymanski broke into his thoughts.

"Okay, sir. I hope you didn't mind me bringing that up?"

"No, not at all, you should if you have worries of that kind".

They had just arrived outside the Hall where the door had already opened revealing the relaxed figure of Freddie Cunningham in an ornate gold smoking jacket, a supercilious smirk on his face.

The two detectives walked over to him their feet making scrunching sounds on the sandy coloured gravel.

"You just can't keep away can you, Detective Inspector. To what do I owe the pleasure this time?"

"Just a couple more questions to help with our enquiries, sir".

"Well, I'm not sure that I want to help any further, after all you caused me a great deal of embarrassment searching not only my business and laboratories but also invading my home with not a jot to show for it. So, detectives, can you give me one good reason why I should oblige?"

"I do apologise for any inconvenience caused, sir, but this is a murder enquiry and as such we would expect that an upstanding member of the community such as yourself would be willing to help find the perpetrators".

Cunningham didn't move or reply for some moments, then inclining his head he ushered them in.

Once seated, Cunningham ordered tea for three and then looked at Allan expectantly.

"As I said sir, just a couple of questions. Firstly, can you tell me how long you have been in possession of the motorbike which is parked behind your garages?"

"Motorbike?"

"Yes, sir, the motorbike and helmet behind your garages?"

"I don't know what you think you have seen but I don't know of any motorbike. I certainly haven't ever possessed one. So, I can't help you, Jack. Unless, of course, my gardener or other member of staff owns it. I would suggest you show me where it is".

They went out through the French windows and walked over to where Allan had seen the bike.

"Nothing but overgrown ivy and weeds, as you can see. I would be very surprised to have seen anything else. Maybe you saw a bike somewhere else and thought it was here?" he asked with a patronising air.

Allan wasn't fazed.

"The motorbike has obviously been moved" he said resolutely.

"Can we now ask your gardener whether he owns the bike" Allan continued.

"Of course, that isn't a problem. Oh, I've just remembered Arthur is off today, but I will ask him and get back to you".

"No, I will need to speak to him myself. I will need his telephone number".

Cunningham hesitated for a fraction of a second then he inclined his head.

They walked back to the lounge where tea was waiting on a silver tray which had been placed on the coffee table between the settees.

Cunningham poured the tea and handed the bone china cups and saucers to each of the detectives before serving himself and sitting back in his chair.

"So, Jack, you said there were a couple of things?"

Allan put his cup and saucer back on the coffee table secretly thinking that he could have done with a good, large mug of tea instead of a tiny, fancy porcelain cup.

"Ah, yes, sir, just one other question. Can you tell me, your movements on the thirtieth of May?"

"The thirtieth of May. That was shortly after the demise of my poor parents" he said, shaking his head, a sorrowful expression spreading over his face.

"Yes, that's right, sir".

"Well, Inspector, as you can imagine I was still overwhelmed with grief, so I don't exactly remember what I was doing but I would hazard a guess that I was right here at the Hall trying to come to terms with my loss and concerned with making funeral arrangements. You will understand?"

"And would someone be able to vouch for you. A member of staff perhaps?"

"This sounds like I need an alibi?"

"If you could just answer the question, sir".

"Yes, I think so, for most of the time but there again, the staff aren't sitting with me in the same room for the duration so perhaps not. I'm sorry, detective, I can't be more helpful than that, I'm afraid".

"Do you have the number for your gardener?"

"Just a moment, I will get it from my study" and Cunningham got up and went out of the room.

"He's lying about the bike, sir. I'm sure of it," Szymanski started to say in a hushed voice but stopped as Cunningham walked back in brandishing a small, white piece of paper.

Allan took the paper and got out his mobile.

"Oh, are you going to ring him now? I thought you would call him at the station" asked Cunningham for the first time looking wrong footed.

“No time like the present” replied Allan.

After three rings, a voice answered.

“Hello, Arthur, this is Detective Inspector Allan here, Cambridgeshire Constabulary. I have a question for you, and I need you to answer honestly as this is a murder investigation and obviously if you don’t answer totally truthfully you could be facing a perjury charge. Is that clear, Arthur?”

“Yes, I understand” he replied in a rather sulky voice.

“Now, Arthur, behind the garages at the Hall a motorbike was recently parked there together with a distinctive helmet. Do you remember it?”

“Yes, I remember it. You uncovered it and were looking at it the other day”.

“Whose is the motorbike, Arthur?”

“I dunno. It was covered up and I never saw it before you did”.

“Okay, Arthur, thank you for your time”.

Allan clicked off and looked at Cunningham.

“Can we gather all the staff together, sir”.

“What now?”

"Yes, sir, now, if you would".

The staff filed in at Cunningham's request but when questioned no-one admitted knowing anything about the bike. Disappointingly, the housekeeper confirmed Cunningham had been in the house all day on the thirtieth.

The staff having gone back to their duties, Szymanski now questioned Cunningham.

"Here's the thing, sir, we are having difficulty understanding why a motorbike would be on your land, covered up without you knowing anything about it".

"What is the importance of this infernal bike?" asked Cunningham.

"Unfortunately, sir, it was seen at a location connected with the recent events which we are currently investigating. So, it is very important that you tell us now, what you know about this bike which was found on your land".

"I'm sorry, Jack, I don't know anything at all about the motorbike and if that's all?" he said standing up.

"That's all for now, sir, but if we have any further questions, we will be in touch" Allan said.

“I don’t know about our visit relaxing him but we certainly rattled his cage, sir” commented Szymanski once they were back in the car.

“Yes, we did but it also made him think that we are getting close and are focussed on this line of enquiry. He will probably surmise, wrongly, that we don’t have the additional resource to stake out this afternoon at the Fayre which hopefully will cause him to relax, become less alert and watchful which is the window we need to catch him”.

Allan clicked on ‘Dev’ on his mobile.

‘Dev, you and Soph stake out here at the Hall. Be discreet and if he leaves this afternoon, I want you to follow him to the Fayre. We know then we are looking for him although no doubt he will be disguised”.

“We’re on it, sir”.

Chapter Twelve

Allan and his team arrived separately via the Victoria Bridge entrance. The band playing music could be heard and the crowds of merrymakers made it relatively easy for the police officers to blend in dressed as they were in casual summery outfits. They took up their positions near to the Transit van as they had discussed earlier.

Amy and Peter pushed a pram with a lifelike doll in it to a space on the grass with a clear view of the van but far enough back not to cause suspicion if the suspect was watching. They proceeded to spread a blanket on the ground and Amy bent over the pram and adjusted the canopy to shield the supposed occupant from the sun.

Barry turned up in a black hat with various badges pinned on and took up his position to afford a different angle on the van. He had two piles of leaflets either side of him and with an inane smile handed them out to whoever would take one. Luckily not many were interested which meant he wouldn't run out very soon.

Amy and Peter started playing ball, laughing and generally acting as though they were out for a lovely summer afternoon.

Meanwhile Mike moved around with his camera, taking an odd shot here and there, pretending from time to time to be interested in adjusting his camera or looking at his shots.

Szymanski sat in a deck chair on the far side. She was facing the van, had sunglasses on and appeared to be totally absorbed in her book.

At two o'clock Allan appeared as arranged pulling a very large suitcase. He walked to the back of the van, opened the doors which revealed a completely empty interior and using all his strength dumped the case inside. He then closed the doors firmly, took a quick look around and walking back to Victoria Bridge, seemingly disappeared.

The whole team was alert. Allan radioed to the police van parked discreetly in a nearby side road that the drop had been made and to be ready.

Tension was mounting in every member of the team. Amy and Peter had sat down for a rest and, after checking on the 'baby', they were munching some crisps. Barry was beginning to experience face-ache from grinning so much and Mike was sitting down leaning against a trunk of an oak tree drinking from a bottle of water.

When three o'clock came and went and the money hadn't been taken, they felt a sense of disappointment. There was a distinct possibility that there was going to be a no show.

Allan's mobile rang. It was Dev.

"No movement from the Hall, sir. How's it going?" asked Dev.

"Cunningham is not action man; he may be behind this or involved but he is not doing the dirty work".

"Looks like it, sir. What do you want us to do now?"

Allan was about to answer when he heard a cacophony of screaming sirens heading in his direction.

He hesitated and dropped his arm by his side looking all round him.

"Sir.....sir?" Dev's voice sounded like a squeak coming from where the mobile was in Allan's hand.

Allan raised the phone back to his ear.

"Sorry, Dev, I'll call you back". Clicking off, he ran in to Midsummer Common. The music had stopped and there was only the sound now of screams and crying. He found himself surrounded by people running to see what the commotion was about. He stopped short as he stared at people who had fallen on the ground. He started to shout for people to move back. He held out his badge and heard his colleagues doing the same. They managed to move the crowd back and he radioed for help from backup parked outside. Soon a tape was put round the area where the people were being attended to by medics.

“Hello Stew, we need your team at Midsummer Common now, we’ve got another potential incident of this damned virus causing casualties. I need confirmation”.

“Coming right now, Jack”.

He ran at full speed back up the path towards Victoria Bridge, which was virtually empty now, the crowds having dispersed although there were still quite a few onlookers.

Reaching the van, he noticed there was an envelope attached to the windscreen. Tearing it off, he raced round the back and opened the van’s rear doors. The suitcase had gone.

Venting his pent-up anger, he slammed the doors shut. He ripped open the envelope.

It was no surprise that it contained a single A4 sheet of type written paper.

He leaned against the back of the van, one foot crossing the other and read.

Tut, tut, Detective Inspector. You really are easy to give the run around, aren't you? So now, not only have you lost two million pounds, but you also have further casualties. You don't seem to be doing a very good job, do you? Although I did think it ingenious to have Amy and Peter playing mummy and daddy to a doll in a pram, very good! And Barry handing out very realistic adverts, ingenious! Your team are quite talented; perhaps they should change career and take up acting! But it all came to nothing, didn't it, Detective Inspector and to cap it all you haven't experienced the worst of it yet. Because, Detective Inspector Allan, I have a further demand, but I'll let you know about that in due course. Au revoir.

Back at the station, Allan called Szymanski into his office.

"Before I face the DCI, who will undoubtedly have been pressured into yet another Press Conference and where I will almost certainly be subjected to a right royal bollocking, we need to find out who the 'mole' is in the team". He decided to mention the contents of the latest demand to Szymansky later when he had had time to consider it himself.

“I can’t believe any one of us would be a ‘mole’!”

“It makes me sick to the stomach to think that but nevertheless you can’t argue with the facts. This bastard knew the names of the team and who they were posing as. He knew he wouldn’t be able to get the money unless he created a diversion and by knowing who the team was, he organised the diversion some way away”.

“I suppose the only way to find out who it is, is to lay a trap. Feed some false information and see who rises to the bait” suggested Szymanski looking very uncomfortable.

“Exactly and we need to do it now. Get your thinking cap on while I go and see the DCI”.

Szymanski stayed in Allan’s office thinking hard about all her colleagues. She couldn’t believe that one of them had betrayed the team. She knew all of them so well or at least she thought she did. They had all been round to her place shortly after Sally had given birth to their baby son, to whet the baby’s head. It was just horrible to think that one of them was giving information to a criminal. Deep down she knew it was probably one of two people. It was unthinkable but each could have a possible motive for their actions but how could she tell Jack? She would feel like a rat, a snitch, an informer but, on the other hand it was her duty, wasn't it, if she had suspicions? Or could she just let it ride and it would sort itself out. But suppose it didn't and she was guilty indirectly of more deaths?

Her dark thoughts were broken into by a knock on the door.

"Come in" she called.

Patel poked his head round the door.

"Where's the boss? An interesting discovery has come to light".

"Oh good! What is it?" Szymanski sat upright in her chair eager to hear what Patel had to say.

"Well, did you know, sadly two more children died at the Fayre, but it turns out that those children had gone missing at the village school on the day they were hit by this mysterious poisoning. Stewart Strange is of the opinion that they died in the same way as Timmy Swan and Mary Peters".

"The exact same format then but why? He had the money, why kill the children and assuming that it was some activation by a previous recent phone call that caused their death, why do it after he had collected the money?"

While she and Dev were sitting at the meeting table at one end of Allan's office, Allan had walked in quietly.

"Because he is playing with us. As he said this is not just about money. He will go on killing I suspect because he enjoys it. He does it for the most part for the sake of it. There is a bigger plan, though and we have either yet to divine what it is or to hear what it is from the suspect" he said startling Szymanski and Patel who turned round to face him.

Patel filled Allan in with the latest development at which Allan was not surprised.

"Thanks, Dev. I just want a few words with Szymanski, if that's okay" he said without indicating a question.

Patel got up and quietly left the room.

"The DCI is fuming and if I don't solve this satisfactorily soon, I am facing an enquiry which might cost me, at best, my rank, at worst, my career! Now let's get on with matters in hand" he said with a grim look on his face.

"Sir, I don't want to appear a snitch, but I have been thinking about the 'mole' business" she faltered.

“This is no time for acting Snow White, Julia, if you know something that could help, spill, we have to have a team that is one hundred per cent loyal to the law” and his penetrating gaze fixed on her.

She met his unblinking stare.

“There are two members of the team that I think we should consider. Mike and Amy. The reason that Mike may be the ‘mole’ is financial. I know he is in considerable debt, and I know he hasn’t told his wife. He is a secret gambler, and he is getting desperate. Amy is also a possibility. As you know she has been rejected yet again for promotion to DS. It’s the third time and I am aware, I think everyone is, that she is very angry and feels she has been targeted and discriminated against. She is threatening to ‘jack it all in’; her words, angrily said”.

“Yes, I am aware on both counts, Julia, but thank you for bringing them to my attention”.

“Oh, I didn’t realise you already knew, sir. I mean not that……” she faltered. She was visibly taken aback, and her face flushed red as she realised her remark might seem to indicate that he didn’t know what was going on in his team.

Allan smiled.

“Nothing much gets past me, Julia, but thank you again for letting me know. What puzzles me is why the hell doesn’t Amy take it up through the complaints channel if she feels like this? As you say, she could be the ‘mole’”.

“It’s my guess that she doesn’t really believe that she has been discriminated against; she knows deep down that she just doesn’t cut it for promotion at the moment but refuses to accept that and try again. Of the two, though, sir, in my opinion, I would go for Mike, if I had to choose. He is truly in a bad way and on the brink of disaster”.

“Even though I was already aware, thank you for this information, Julia, I know how hard it can be feeling you are betraying your colleagues but believe me you have no choice. So, the next thing is to set a trap. Here’s what we do”.

“But suppose we’re wrong, and information is getting out in some other way or maybe it’s someone else on the team?”

“Yes, you’re absolutely right, which is why I am going to spread the net”.

Allan walked out into the main area, Szymanski following close behind him.

“Okay everyone, gather round. We now know the whereabouts of our mystery criminal and we have sufficient evidence to make an arrest. Tomorrow we will assemble here at nine o’clock sharp and I’ll outline the details of the operation then. In the meantime, go home and get some rest. Any questions?”

After Allan had answered one or two queries, he turned to Szymanski while everyone was still around, and spoke in a voice he knew would be loud enough to be heard by the rest of the team.

“Julia, I’m going to put the evidence in the third drawer down in my desk, together with details of this bastard’s whereabouts so should anything prevent me from being here tomorrow, you will know to go ahead without me” he said.

“Oh! Is it likely that you won’t be here then, sir?”

“Well, I hope to be, but I have one or two personal problems that I need to sort out and I need to head off now. I suggest you do too. It’s probably going to be a long day tomorrow!”

“That goes for everyone else too! Home time!” he called out.

It was midnight and the office was totally silent. The light from the streetlamps outside created an eerily empty atmosphere while the wall clock marked time noiselessly. The door to the main office creaked as it slowly opened, and a figure clad all in black entered. The figure moved stealthily across the floor and went into the DI's office. It moved quickly to the desk and went to the third drawer down, got out the contents and shone its torch on the information. Suddenly, the fluorescent tubing in the office and the outer office lit up the floor. Allan and Szymanski walked in.

"Stop right where you are!" yelled Allan.

The figure stood still as though transfixed, and the mobile dropped to the floor. Szymanski moved forward to pick it up while Allan tore off the balaclava that the figure had over its face.

The contorted features of Amy stood before them. She was clasping her neck, struggling for breath. She fell to the floor, her body convulsing and thrashing around.

Allan rang for an ambulance.

Amy lay inert on the floor where she had fallen. Allan rushed over and tried to resuscitate her to no avail. When the paramedics arrived, they pronounced her dead explaining to Allan and Szymanski that the probable cause of death was brought on by a sudden asthmatic attack.

After the ambulance had taken the body away, the two detectives sat in silence in the otherwise empty offices.

“You think you know someone, don’t you? Then it turns out you don’t. Right up to the minute her mask came off, I truly believed that we had to be wrong and there was some other way the information had got out to the suspect” said Szymanski finally breaking the silence.

“It’s certainly going to be a shock to the rest of the team. I’m not looking forward to breaking the news tomorrow. She was well liked, despite her moaning, and they are going to miss her even though they will feel let down and disappointed in her actions. Speaking of which, surely she didn’t jeopardise her career just because she had been passed over a couple of times. It seems to me an exaggerated reaction” he said turning to look at his colleague.

“Maybe it was just that, she felt she didn’t have a career and had nothing to lose. She fancied the money she was almost certainly offered, and just took the wrong path”.

“Yes, maybe. Anyway, we had better call it a day. We’ll be busy tomorrow and on the bright side our murderer won’t have an advantage over us”.

Driving back home, Allan rang Vanessa without success. He wasn't really expecting an answer. He knew she was on late shifts this week and only rang on the off chance it had been changed at the last minute.

The next morning, the team assembled at Allan's bidding, and he relayed the events of the previous evening. Everyone was incredulous and Barry was disbelieving.

"Amy was such a nice person. I know she was miserable about being passed over and she did bang on about it sometimes but that was understandable in a way, anyone would feel bad about that. I can't believe it, I really can't" he said shaking his head.

The others murmured their agreement.

"I know it's a shock for everyone, but we have to move on quickly, we have a murder enquiry to conduct and a culprit to convict fast. From a practical perspective we are a man down on the team and I am going to ask Maxine García to join us. I think you all know Maxine and are aware of her abilities. I want you to welcome her when she joins us later today".

There were uneasy looks and hushed comments among the team, but nothing was audible. Maxine or Max as she liked to be called, had a reputation for being efficient, very good at her job, but without a shred of a sense of humour and not the best of team players. She definitely wasn't the easiest of people to work with.

"Good. I'm off to see the DCI to give him an update then we'll consider our next move".

While he was gone, Mike's mobile rang. He looked at the screen 'unknown caller'. He let it ring and eventually it stopped.

"Another sales call" he muttered raising his eyes to the skies.

His phone rang again, rang off and rang again.

"I don't want whatever it is you're selling so piss off" he said angrily. The rest of the team grinned but they all donned curious expressions as Mike went completely silent listening to the caller. He then walked out of the room and out of hearing.

The others looked at each other and then Barry shrugged his shoulders, Dev turned round to his screen and Soph took a call.

Mike returned to the main office a few minutes later with an unreadable expression on his face. He sat down and seemingly got busy.

Allan entered the main office thirty minutes later.

"That went well.... not" he said to Szymanski.

"I'll bet!" she mocked.

Mike came over.

"Can I have a quick word, boss" he said.

"Yes, sure".

They went into Allan's office.

"I've been approached by the suspect, sir" Mike began.

"What! So, he is trying to acquire another 'mole'. What exactly did he say?"

"He offered me fifty thousand pounds for regular information on the team's movements and plans".

"I take it your answer was negative or you wouldn't be telling me about it".

"Well, no. Actually, I didn't refuse, I said I would think about it. I wanted to make sure you didn't want me to string him along, sir".

"Ummm. You did the right thing, Mike. Well done! I'll give it some thought and let you know the way forward".

"Sir" and Mike left Allan's office.

Allan remained for a few moments. Two completely different reactions to the same situation by two different people who each had problems that personal financial gain would have helped to solve. He wished all such people would be as honest and upright as Mike.

Something was bugging him about the most recent letter from the murderer. He pulled the paper out of his drawer and re-read it.

“Of course,” he suddenly muttered under his breath, grabbing his coat and car keys.

“Szymanski, you’re with me. Bring your passport!” he called as he strode out of his office without stopping to close the door. Julia grabbed her coat and followed.

“Where are we going, sir?”

“To France” he said getting in the driver’s seat of his car.

“Au revoir!” he added looking jubilant.

“You mean Bonjour, don’t you? We’re going there! Not coming back!” she retorted.

“No, I mean Au Revoir! That was the clue in the letter; it finished off Au Revoir. If I’m reading this right, it means Cunningham’s next play will be in France and I’m willing to bet it will be somewhere near his property. Get on to Dev and tell him to take Soph to Misslethwaite Hall. He can think of some pretext for the call should Cunningham be there though I strongly suspect that he won't need any. Get him to call us immediately as to whether he is there or not".

"Yes, sir," said Szymanski.

Meanwhile Allan rang Walters.

"Sir, you suggested that perhaps the way forward was for me to go to the south of France now that the French police have identified traces of the virus in the atomizer found at the scene of a similar incident to the one over here. I have taken the liberty of heading towards the airport. I am certain that the next attack will take place in the St Tropez area near to Cunningham's property. Patel has so far found that he owns two properties but the other one is located just outside Nice in a busy area which I doubt would be suitable for his purposes. I would suggest we work outside the box on this one, sir. The murderer is devilish clever. Do I have your permission to proceed, sir?"

"I don't want to know how you are working outside the box, Allan, but I do authorise your visit to France, and I will get in touch with my counterpart, Antoine Dumas, over there to alert him of your arrival. Let's see it's coming up to ten thirty. What time do you expect to be at the airport? Which airport are you flying from?"

Allan looked across at Szymanski who nodded and mouthed the destination airport and the time of the flight she had just booked for them.

"Szymanski has just booked us on the twelve-thirty to Marseilles from Stansted which arrives their time fifteen thirty. I'm currently on the M11 and about twenty minutes away".

"Good. I'll leave you to it, Allan. Keep me updated" and the DCI rang off.

Arriving at the airport and slinging his car into the short-term car park the two detectives made their way to check in. Once through security they split up to do a little shopping for necessities before the flight. Thankfully there were no delays or cancellations, and they boarded the plane on time.

The flight time was just a fraction over two hours. They refrained from talking about work in a public place and after finishing her coffee and pack of chocolate fingers Szymanski looked across at her boss who was swirling round the remains of his coffee in the bottom of his cardboard cup.

“Look, I feel awful about questioning whether Vanessa might be involved with this case. I shouldn’t have mentioned my concerns, sir”.

“Really don’t worry, Julia. After all, I had to take that thought into consideration and there is no harm done. You should always bring anything like that to my attention. You are, first and foremost, a police officer”.

“Thank you, sir. So how are you and Vanessa getting on?” she asked.

“Yeah, good thanks” he replied still looking at the bottom of his cup.

“I tried to get hold of her yesterday, but you know what it’s like with her shifts and my shifts, come to that. I guess that’s why it works, we both understand the demands of our jobs”.

“Ummm”

“And how are you and Sally now?” he asked, having eaten a banana, he was now scrunching a Red Delicious apple.

“Okay, I think we’re working through it. She is a lot happier now that we have Polly coming in to do the chores. I think she’d still like me to have a desk job, but she knows that’s never going to happen and I guess and hope she has just accepted that nothing is ever perfect" and she let out a deep sigh.

"By the way, how is your mother?"

"Oh, you know, she's determinedly independent in her mind still, but physically, she is deteriorating" and he bit another chunk out of his apple looking pensive.

"I'm sorry to hear that, Jack, about your mum deteriorating, I mean. Is it something more than just getting older?" she asked sensing he was holding something back.

"The house has been way too big for her now that dad's gone, and Jane and I flew the nest years ago. She gets a gardener in to help and has someone to clean the house once a week" he put the apple core in the waste bag provided by the airline. He took a deep breath, sighed and turned slightly towards Julia.

"Yes, you're right, it is something more than old age. You remember when I took sudden leave because mum had had a fall,well, it was more than just a fall. She has Parkinsons, Julia".

"I'm so sorry, Jack" said Julia her eyes misting up.

"But that's not the worst of it. They did comprehensive tests and found that she has Stage 4 lung cancer. She hasn't got long, just weeks according to the consultant. You wouldn't think so to speak to her. She tries to shrug it off and tells me that she's alright. She wouldn't have it that I stay with her while there's an important case to solve but as soon as this is in the bag, I'll take some more of the leave owed to me" and he looked away to mask wiping a tear from his cheek.

Szymanski was silent for several minutes.

"You come from Wiltshire, don't you?" she said at last.

"Yes, that's right".

"It's a pretty village, isn't it? Corton if I remember correctly? Whatever made you want to leave, it's a nice area and you must have had friends over there?" asked Szymanski.

"Yes, and yes to the first two questions. And yes again, I did have friends there, although sadly I haven't kept up with them. It is a nice area but so is Cambridgeshire and since I went to Cambridge University, I guess my friends are here now" he said putting the core of his second apple in the paper bag provided for rubbish.

Szymanski felt guilty as she finished the second packet of chocolate fingers.

"How do you function on just fruit and health foods" she asked wiping away the excess chocolate round her mouth with a tissue.

Allan grinned broadly.

"Oh, I manage somehow! It's not as gruelling as you think. I have plenty of fish, cheese and egg dishes. I've always liked fruit and vegetables and never liked sweet stuff much, so it isn't a hardship. I enjoy a glass or two of wine as much as the next man, but I won't make it a habit. I just don't want to end up like my father. Don't get me wrong he was a good cop but in the end the stress was too much. I deal with stress in a different way".

"Through pounding the treadmill, you mean?" and Szymanski raised an eyebrow.

"Something like that" he said but turned away and looked out of the window, a sad expression on his face.

Szymanski knew he was thinking of his dad.

The flight over, as they had no baggage, they were the first to step off the plane into the brilliant, Mediterranean sunshine.

Chapter Thirteen

As soon as they alighted, two Frenchmen in creaseless cream suits, discreet ties and wearing expensive aviator sunglasses, approached them.

"Welcome to France, my name is Inspecteur Pierre Rochefort, Commissaire de Police, and this is my colleague Lieutenant Jean Thomas. We hope you had a pleasant flight?" he said in heavily accented English.

"Thank you for meeting us. Detective Inspector Jack Allan and my colleague, Detective Sergeant Julia Szymanski".

They all shook hands and walked through the airport exchanging pleasantries.

Once in the car, Rochefort who was in the driving seat, began to talk business.

Hardly had he started, when Allan's mobile rang.

"Sorry, I have to take this" he apologised when he saw Patel's name come up on his screen.

"We're at Misslethwaite Hall, sir. We've been here a couple of hours, rung the bell and walked all the way round the house. There's no sign of anyone and no movement in or out of the gates".

"Okay, that's what I expected. So, here's what I want you and Soph to do" and he went on to give his instructions.

"Is that clear, Dev. Any questions?" he asked when he had finished.

There was a pregnant pause.

"Er…sir….do you think……" and he stopped mid-sentence.

"Dev, that is an order but are there any questions regarding my instructions?".

"No, sir".

"Right so, you know what to do, let me know the outcome as soon as. And Dev I will take full responsibility" he said firmly.

"Sir" and the line went dead.

"Sorry about that Pierre. I do have to make another call then we can talk. Okay?" he said apologetically.

"No worries, Jack" the French detective replied.

"Hi Barry, I need you, Mike and Max to check out flights to the south of France, start with flights to Marseilles from Stansted and Luton from yesterday morning. You are looking for

Cunningham or anyone resembling him under a different name. It's urgent so get cracking".

"On it, sir" he replied.

"OK, Pierre, I'm all yours" grinned Jack displaying his perfectly even, white teeth.

"Don't take this as an affront, Jack, but I'm not sure why you are here. Yes, we have a total of three atomizers now from where the incident took place, and they did contain traces of the same virus as those found near the incident at Misslethwaite but what do you hope to gain by coming here?"

"I need an unmarked vehicle for a start. This perpetrator is not the usual criminal. He is a highly intelligent, psychopathic, narcissitic individual with a lot of money at his disposal and that makes him extremely dangerous. His motive for his actions is unclear. I'm guessing it isn't just about the money. We have to stop him before further murders happen. He is not on the radar with Interpol or any other criminal agency. That has been checked. We have established that he has two properties, one being in the Nice area and another one just outside Port Grimaud. I've already discounted the property near Nice as it is located in a very busy area and in addition, as the incident happened a few miles from Saint Tropez,

I think it is fair to assume that his house here may yield some evidence of his wrongdoing".

"So how can we help you?" asked Thomas who had hitherto remained silent.

"Okay, so to catch this bugger we need to bend procedures a little. I understand that you may not feel you can officially support us, but we won't implicate you if this operation turns sour".

Rochefort shrugged his shoulders and briefly turned round in his driver's seat raising his eyebrow questioningly at Allan.

"First, we need to establish whether anyone is present at Cunningham's property. If not, I suspect his alarm system is wired to the police in the event of a burglary. If that is so, we need you to disable it and give my colleague and I the entry code. We will need an unmarked car. At around midnight tonight we will enter the building and search it".

"You are asking us to ignore the need for a warrant" Thomas asked.

"We don't have enough evidence, I fear, to obtain a warrant. This is the only way and if I'm right we may be able to stop any further incidents and catch this bastard".

"But even if you find anything, how are you going to explain how you came by the evidence?"

"Because then we will get a search warrant of the entire house".

"On what grounds?" Rochefort asked.

"Don't worry, I'm banking on that being revealed after the search," replied Jack grim faced.

Rochefort nodded.

There was no more conversation for the rest of the journey and Allan looked out of the window at the passing French countryside.

They arrived at the St. Tropez police station sometime later where Rochefort organised an unmarked pool car and Allan made a note of the entry code to Cunningham's villa.

"You realise you are on your own at the property, don't you. We have to deny all knowledge of the break in. We will simply explain that you hacked our system, broke into the station and stole the code.

"Understood" replied Allan.

He and Szymanski checked in at a small, unassuming hotel in one of the charming, cobbled side streets in Saint Tropez and each went to their rooms for a freshen up.

Allan had just stepped out of the shower when his mobile rang.

****

Vanessa picked up Allan's call after her shift finished at one o'clock when, unbeknown to her, he was mid-flight to Marseilles. She tried calling him, but it went to voicemail. She continued walking, still in her scrubs, towards the changing room. Donning her home gear, she thought about Jack. She had always shied away from anything permanent, preferring the non-commitment of maximum one-month relationships or one-night stands but there was something about Jack. Yes, he was handsome with his chiselled chin, thick dark hair, perfect teeth and no-fat muscular physique but it wasn't just that. He was sensitive without being sloppy and a tender and passionate lover and her stomach did a flip when she saw him. He seemed to affect her far more than any other lover. She admired his determined and independent streak too. She had to admit this was the closest she had ever been to falling in love, if she hadn't already.

Another medic entered as she gave out a huge sigh.

"Oh dear! It can't be that bad!" said the medic rolling her eyes to the skies.

Vanessa laughed.

"No, no, just the end of another long day. Double shift for me! Can't wait to hit the sack".

"Yeah, I know the feeling! Short straws seem to have taken a shine to me lately as well!"

Vanessa smiled and picked up her bag, heading for the exit.

It was a lovely balmy evening as she walked out of the side entrance. She fished for the car keys in her rucksack oblivious to her surroundings. Walking over to her car she pressed the zapper and felt a little surprised when it indicated that the car was already open. She shrugged her shoulders; she must have forgotten to lock it. Getting in she fastened her seat belt and started the ignition. Closing the door, she put the car in first gear and drove off. There was a queue for the exit to the car park and she had to wait five minutes before she was able to turn onto the main road. She lived in an apartment around twenty minutes' drive away; it would have been quicker if it hadn't been for the constant traffic.

Suddenly, her heart skipped a beat as a black hooded head appeared behind her and she could feel something pushing against the back of her seat.

"Do as I say, or you'll die, do you understand?", a man's voice asked menacingly, as he pushed something hard against the back of her seat.

Vanessa was shaking with fear and failed to answer.

"Do you understand?" he said emphasising each word and pushing into her back even harder.

"Yes, I understand" she whispered, and she could feel her body heating up with tension. Her hands were becoming sweaty, and she gripped the steering wheel firmly to ensure she kept control.

"At the next junction, turn right onto A3107" the man instructed.

Vanessa didn't know how she managed to stop her legs shaking enough to stay steady on the foot pedals and obey the instructions but somehow, she did.

They were just coming up to Wandlebury Country Park and she was plucking up the courage to ask what this was all about when he issued his next command.

"Turn here into the park!"

She dutifully did so and drove slowly at the required ten miles an hour along the entrance road. When they reached the car park he spoke again.

“Park over there to the right”.

She drove over to where there were no cars, and some trees screened them off from anyone walking on the grass in front of them.

“Get out of the car slowly and don’t think of running”.

They both got out of the car and with his gun trained on her, he opened the boot and indicated for her to get in it.

She shook her head at first, but he cocked his gun and with tears streaming down her face and shaking violently she walked to the boot of the car. He pushed her roughly and she got in. The lid closed and she was in total darkness. She heard the car start and felt it move. She tried to breathe deeply and slowly to calm herself down. She started to try to work out why this was happening until finally lulled by the movement of the car, worn out from a double shift at work and the ordeal that had followed, she fell asleep.

******

Wrapping a towel round his waist, Allan padded over to the lamp table where he had left his phone and picked it up.

“Hello, sir, it’s Dev. You were right, sir, there is a cellar. It took us ages to find it. The entrance is under a very expensive looking rug in the dining room and a large dining table and chairs had been placed over it”.

“Okay Dev, good but have you managed to access it?”

“Yes, sir. It looks like it’s where they are producing this virus, judging by the apparatus that’s down there. What do you want us to do, sir?”

“Where are you now?”

“Back at the station. We’ve left everything exactly as it was, sir”.

“Good and very well done to you and Soph. Now I want you to arrange for round the clock surveillance on the Hall. Get a search warrant for the premises but don’t go in unless Cunningham appears. If he does, then use it and open up the cellar. Then arrest him on the suspicion of intent to harm with a potentially lethal virus etc. etc. I have to say I doubt he will turn up but if I’m wrong, and he does, we have our man”.

“On it, sir” replied Dev.

Dressing quickly, he walked along the corridor to Szymanski’s room and knocked on the door. She answered swiftly and let him in.

“We should eat while we can, Julia. I suggest we keep a low profile and eat here in the hotel. In fact, here in your room would be good if that’s okay with you?”

“Yes, of course, good idea, sir”.

While they were waiting, they discussed Dev’s information and the plan for that night.

“So, it would seem then that Cunningham wanted to keep on using the pharmaceutical company as a front whilst using its facilities to produce this lethal virus. The exact main motive has yet to be confirmed. His father, Piers Cunningham didn’t want anything to do with it, confirmed by the argument that father and son were having the night before the fête, and at the fête itself; so Cunningham killed his father himself or had his father killed and his mother was collateral damage maybe. Then knowing that he may come under suspicion, he concealed his lab under the floor. He calculated that if he was investigated by the police, they would assume that the drugs company would be manufacturing this virus at their laboratories, when in fact they would be found to be squeaky clean which would deflect police attention from himself, who would protest annoyance at such treatment. Thus, the police would feel that they had made a mistake in mistrusting him. As we already know we are dealing with a very clever individual and this confirms it".

"So why don't we nail him now?" Szymanski asked.

"Because I think we will find that he isn't in the UK at the moment and is using one of his properties here to create another incident. We've always been one step behind him but now we stand to be one step ahead of him after tonight".

"What makes you think that?"

"Because I'm pretty certain I know that he is manufacturing the substance here as well as in the Hall. He is using the basements of both properties which are extremely hard to discover even if the houses were searched. Tonight, I think we will find a similar basement when we search the house. If I'm right, we need the help of the French police to put surveillance on the property for when he returns to collect the atomiser containing the virus. I've instructed Dev to put a surveillance on the Hall in case I am wrong and this is a wild goose chase, so that we have all our basis points covered. We're going to get this guy, Julia".

"But what if he is at home tonight?"

"Pierre rang me earlier and confirmed that there has been no activity at the house so it's a go. If he comes back unexpectedly, we'll have to think on our feet. Let's hope that doesn't happen".

At that moment there was a knock on the door and simultaneously Allan's mobile rang.

Szymanski went to the door to let room service bring in their dinner.

"Hold on a moment, Barry" said Allan and waited until the waiter left the room closing the door behind him.

"Okay Barry, I've put you on loudspeaker so Julia can hear".

"The team did as you requested, sir, and we've been in touch with the Port Authorities and Airport security, and no-one has had sight of any individual resembling our Mr Cunningham. I'm sorry for the disappointment, sir".

"Yes, so am I, Barry, but a thank you to you and the others for the speedy work. Barry, have you had any more approaches to work as a spy for the suspect?"

"No, sir, not yet".

"Right, well, if and when you do, refuse, okay? We're closing in and I don't think we will need the facility to feed this monster false information".

"Right you are, sir" said Barry and Allan ended the call.

They both sat down and started their meal. After a few mouthfuls, Szymanski put down her knife and fork.

"Sir, isn't it possible that the virus is being spread by a number of hired hands, or devoted members of some sort of sect he is running who are doing his bidding, and he has disappeared somewhere remote while they do the dirty work for him?"

"Yes, that would seem logical, but I have a hunch that the profiler's description of him fits more of a serial killer, someone who enjoys inflicting pain and suffering himself. He is not averse to obtaining lots of money but only because with money he can buy people and money brings power which enables him to enjoy his 'hobby', if you like, that is killing people, and the foreplay is foxing the police".

"One hell of a strange guy!" commented Szymanski as she cut into her steak.

“Indeed, and a very dangerous one too!” said Allan, his mouth set in a grim line.

At a quarter to midnight, Allan and Szymanski, dressed completely in black with their balaclavas stuffed in trouser pockets and carrying large sports bags, ran lightly down the fire escape stairs located at the back of the building, quickly got in their car and drove off. It was a clear night with a velvet black star-studded sky. The drive took about twenty-five minutes, and they were silent throughout, both in their own separate worlds.

Finally, they arrived and parked in a country car park a little way up the road. Putting on their balaclavas and night vision goggles, they walked along the road to the long private drive which led to Cunningham’s beautiful, detached ultra-modern villa commanding stunning views of the Cote d’Azur. There were no cars visible, so they walked stealthily across the gravel drive and up the black marble steps to the glass and steel front door. Allan punched in the entry code and hearing a click, pulled on the vertical full length steel handle, relieved that the door opened without any alarms sounding off. Pierre had worked his magic. Inside the imposing hall boasting black marble walls, floor and ceiling, Allan and Szymanski got their bearings and Szymanski pointed to a corridor which seemed to lead to the rear area. Swiftly they moved along opening doors as they went until they reached the dining room. With great difficulty they managed to move the huge dining table little by little to one side and rolled up the rug on which it had been standing.

"No, it's not possible. Damn, damn, damn. I was so certain the villa would be the same design as the Hall but there's no handle. This looks like a solid floor. Shit, shit, shit!" he ran the fingers of both hands through his hair and stared uncomprehendingly at the floor. They both went down on their knees and felt over the whole area to see if there was a crack or crevice that would indicate that there was an opening but to no avail.

"Maybe there is a secret room somewhere behind a bookcase for example or some kind of mechanism that when activated will reveal a room?"

"Possibly. Let's feel and tap along the walls" said Allan rallying himself quickly from his disappointment.

Szymanski was beginning to feel despondent and privately began to wonder if they were in the wrong place altogether. She had examined nearly all of her side of the vast dining room and all that remained was to take a painting off the wall in the vain hope that what they were looking for was behind it. She caught her breath and whispered loudly to Allan to come over though she did wonder why she was being so cautious, after all there was no-one there to hear them. A lever in a horizontal slot had been revealed and after looking at it for a moment, Allan pulled the lever along the slot. As he did so, they heard a grinding sound. Walking back over to the area on which the dining table had stood, they watched the floor first drop down and then move to the side to reveal a gaping hole and some steps leading down.

The room below floor level was huge and furnished as a laboratory. There was scientific equipment in abundance.

"Over here, sir" called Szymanski. She was standing looking in an eye-level cupboard which was stacked with atomizers. She took one out.

"This is one of them, isn't it, sir? This is like one of the atomizers we found, and the French found" and she handed it to Allan to examine.

"I'm willing to bet on it. We need to take one for analysis to be sure, but we don't really need confirmation" he said looking at it closely as he turned it around in his gloved fingers.

Szymanski pulled out an evidence bag. Allan handed her the atomizer, then he walked to the other side of the lab where he tried the drawers of some filing cabinets.

How it happened neither of them ever knew but somehow the atomizer came apart in Szymanski's hand as she was putting it in the evidence bag.

"Jack, I……." she called and something in her voice made him turn at once and race over to where she was standing, her entire body was trembling.

"We have to get you out of here, Julia. Do you feel faint?" asked Jack as the shock realization of what had happened hit him.

"No, I feel okay, boss. Maybe it's not what it seems. Maybe the phials just contain some sort of harmless liquid?" she asked recovering from her initial fright.

"I shouldn't think so but you're still standing so that's a good sign. Let's get out of here and get you to the hospital!"

Having pushed the lever to close the floor, replaced the picture and pulled the table and chairs back into place, they both headed for the exit.

Suddenly, they heard a noise coming from the hall. Allan glanced at Szymanski and put a finger to his lips. They quickly and silently stole down the corridor, opened a door to what seemed to be a large storeroom and waited.

Footsteps approached. They hardly dared to breathe. Then the footsteps stopped the other side of the door. They kept completely still. They heard him tap a number into his mobile. The person spoke in French. The detectives both knew enough of the language to understand that he was questioning someone as to why the alarm had not activated when he entered. Seemingly, he accepted the explanation as his tone was courteous at the end of the conversation. Then the footsteps moved on and up the stairs to the next level probably to the main bedroom. Slowly they opened the door and crept out. They headed for the entry door and then bending double they moved swiftly through the woodland next to the long drive to their car.

Once in the car, Allan phoned Rochefort.

“Thanks for all your help, Pierre. It was worth the risk although it was a bit hairy when Cunningham turned up. Nevertheless, we have established that here is where the virus is manufactured in France. So, if you could arrange surveillance of the villa hopefully, we will catch the bastard with the atomizer before any more deaths occur?”.

“Did you see that it was Cunningham, may I ask?”

“No, we didn’t but who else could it be? I think you said that he lived alone there when he visits as far as you are aware?”

“Yes, yes, I just wondered if you could confirm that it was him tonight but as you say, who else could it be?”

Chapter Fourteen

Allan had tried hard to make Szymanski see reason and go straight to hospital for assessment, but she was adamant that she was feeling fine and so, against his better judgement he yielded to her pleas.

Apart from Allan and Szymanski's car there were two others discreetly parked in the road leading to the entrance to Cunningham's villa. The night was clear and the stars bright. There was a full moon, so the entrance was clearly lit up. The villa backed on to the fields that led down to the cliffs that offered a sheer drop to the shore below. Several police had been stationed around the edge of the grounds at the back just in case Cunningham somehow became aware of the stake out and made a run for it.

Everyone's eyes were trained on the area they were watching.

"Do you want to get some shut-eye, Julia. I'll take first watch if you want".

"Yes, thanks, that would be good" and yawning involuntarily, she propped her head against the door.

Three o'clock came and went and there was no movement. Three-thirty and then four o'clock and still not a sign of movement.

"Anything, sir?" asked Julia waking up.

"No, nothing. Something's off. I'm sure he would have made a move by now".

"He usually strikes during the day though, doesn't he, sir? I mean at the fête, the school, the festival, all in broad daylight".

"True. We just have to be patient I suppose. Slowly, slowly catchy monkey".

At that moment he received a call over the walky-talky.

"Not a sign this end. How long should we wait?" a heavily accented voice asked.

"He will make a move at some point today. We wait" answered Allan.

It was eleven o'clock in the morning when the call came through on Allan's phone. It was Rochefort.

"I'm recalling the officers on stake-out. There's been an incident at a supermarket just outside the town. Several people have been taken ill. According to eyewitnesses they appeared to be fine and then just fell to the ground suddenly. You might want to come along. It smacks of similarity to the other cases under investigation and if Cunningham hasn't left the villa, then a person or persons unknown are doing his bidding".

"I think it is important that we go in now and arrest Cunningham".

"We can't. The only reason you know where he is manufacturing this virus is by illegal entry into his villa. It's inadmissible evidence. You should know that. That's why we had the stake out to catch him with the atomizer or atomizers on his person. That hasn't happened and I have to withdraw my manpower to attend to this latest development. I'm sorry" and having given Allan the details of where the incident had happened, he rang off.

"Damn, damn, damn" and Allan hit the steering wheel so hard that Szymanski was convinced it would break.

"There's nothing we can do here, sir. Do you want to get over to the supermarket and see if that throws up something?"

Thirty minutes later they arrived at a scene of mayhem. Ambulances were there in droves, police cars too. People were crying and screaming everywhere.

Rochefort approached.

“It is an exact repeat of the other incidents. We have four deaths so far. Most people have survived and are receiving treatment. Three children are missing. No-one saw anything suspicious. Finding the children, of course, is our priority but while the surrounding area is combed for them, atomizers are also being looked for. I cannot let you interview anyone officially but if you want to wander around unofficially and chat to those affected, please feel free to do so”.

Nothing fresh turned up as a result of Allan and Szymanski’s chats and so they walked back to their car in silence.

Allan’s mobile buzzed indicating there was a new text.

“Perhaps a visit to your hotel might be in order, Detective Inspector Allan” it read.

Allan accelerated fast as they left the incident site and they made it to their hotel a short while later.

They ran up the steps and into the foyer.

“Any messages for me?” asked Allan breathlessly.

The receptionist smiled politely and walked over to a set of numbered pigeonholes.

“Just this” she said smiling politely again and handing him a large A4 envelope.

“Did you happen to see who delivered this?” he asked.

“Just a moment, sir, I will enquire of my colleagues” again the professional smile from the receptionist.

A few moments later she returned.

“I’m sorry, sir, it appears no-one saw who left the envelope. It was found on the counter”.

“Thank you” he said snatching the envelope and running to the elevators.

Once in Allan’s room, Szymanski closed the door behind them and joined her boss who had pulled out a single piece of A4 paper which he was avidly reading.

"Dear, dear, Detective Inspector, have you nothing better to do than break into a perfectly respectable establishment? Correction, though, you didn't break in did you. You sent your poor underling to do you dirty work. Of course you would, because if it all went wrong you would be in the clear and deny all knowledge of such a thing. If you would only realise that you are not going to win it would be so much better for you. Not only you though, so much better for your loved ones. Your mother for instance is safely tucked up in hospital under expert care although unfortunately I understand is not long for this world. Whereas your girlfriend, Vanessa, I believe her name is, no, actually I know her name is, hasn't been so lucky. I expect at this moment you are going red in the face with fury. Well, that's understandable. Presently, I am holding your beautiful girlfriend. Unfortunately, she is one frightened young lady but maybe you can save her from a fate worse than death. I'll leave you to think about that for a while but don't worry, I'll be in touch with you shortly with one final request. In the meantime, you will have to hope that poor, sweet, Vanessa will hold out. Yours ever".

Allan was indeed red in the face, but his eyes were wet. Szymanski had been reading the letter over his shoulder.

"Jack are you ok?" she asked.

"Fucking psycho. Fucking bastard" he shouted.

He walked over to the fridge and took out two miniature whiskeys. He downed each in one gulp and shook his head as the alcohol stung his gullet. Then he tossed both bottles in the nearby bin.

He picked up the letter, sat down on the edge of the bed and re-read it while Szymanski sat opposite him on a chair and looked at him with a concerned expression.

“One thing this does tell us”.

“What’s that?”

“He now no longer knows everything we are up to. He merely mentions Dev breaking into the Hall but not that Dev discovered the basement. We need to maintain that advantage and we need to find Vanessa fast. I’m thinking that we ask Rochefort to get a warrant to search his villa on the basis that he was suspected to be involved in an incident in Britain. Once in, we know where the switch to the basement is and that the atomizers are there”.

“Yes, I agree, that sounds a very good idea. So, if we do a thorough search and happen to find the switch to the basement, we don’t have to mention that we have already been down there. If it came out though through DNA that we had been down there before that would probably get the case thrown out. Supposing Rochefort doesn't want to take that chance?"

"Well, I do. It's the only way otherwise Vanessa is going to die. We are dealing with a sadist. We have to stop him and now. I'm not going to let anything happen to Vanessa".

Szymanski followed him out of the room.

****

Vanessa awoke to the sound of the car boot being opened. She had lost all track of time and her body ached from being in a cramped position. She blinked at the bright light unable to focus for a few seconds. Something was glinting in the strong sunshine. Then she saw the gun aimed at her head.

"Get out and don't try anything" a man's voice said. His face was covered with a black balaclava.

She got out slowly and with difficulty, her limbs reluctant to obey her wishes. Her legs didn't feel strong enough to support her as she stood up. A second man appeared, his face also covered and pulled her arms roughly behind her back and bound her hands together so that the rope cut into her wrists. She yelped with pain. Then he blindfolded and gagged her.

“Walk!” he commanded, pushing her roughly in the back.

“I can’t see where I am going” she said.

“That’s the idea sweetheart. Now walk!” and the first man gave her another shove with something hard which made her stumble and almost lose her balance. She moved cautiously along, the man every so often pushing her hard with his gun. Eventually, she heard a door opening and they went inside. The building had a musty, stale smell as though it hadn’t been used for ages. They walked across a wide area and then through another door and then another.

“Okay stop here!” the second man said and turning her round, he pushed her down onto a seat and removed the gag.

“Please, please, what is this about? What do you want? Please don’t hurt me!” she pleaded.

The blow the man struck across her face caused her lip to burst and she felt the warm trickle of blood run down her chin onto her neck. She started to cry as she felt each of her ankles and wrists being tied roughly with thick, strong rope.

Her blindfold was removed, and the men walked to the door.

“No, no don’t go, don’t leave me here!” she shrieked.

The first man turned and walked back to her. He lifted his arm in a fraction of a second and before Vanessa could react, he hit her across the other side of her face.

“Don’t make a sound, if you do or try to escape you will wish we had killed you” he said in a voice that sent a chill through her body.

The men left and Vanessa looked around her. Apart from the wooden bench she was sitting on there was no other furniture. A small amount of dim light was afforded by the tiny, glazed window just below the ceiling but otherwise the room was in darkness. She felt fear like she had never felt before. She started to cry again and then all cried out she began to think. Why was she here? Who were these people? What did they want? She tried to remember if there was anything that could have led to this happening to her.

****

Allan rang Rochefort for back up to search Cunningham’s villa in connection with an incident that occurred in Britain for which he was under suspicion. Rochefort reluctantly agreed with the proviso that Allan took responsibility for the search and conducted it himself. An hour later found Allan and Szymanski arriving together with two French police backup cars.

They tried the intercom three times before a maid came to the door. Both detectives flourished their identity cards to which the maid gave a cursory glance before inviting them in.

“Do you speak English?” Allan asked the maid.

“Yes” she replied.

“We are here to see Mr. Cunningham. Is he at home?” Allan asked.

“Yes, I believe so” she replied without moving.

“Can you let him know we are here, please and that we would like to speak with him” Allan said, not without a hint of irritation.

“Of course,” and the maid went upstairs.

A blood curdling scream resounded round the house a few minutes later.

Allan and Szymanski took the stairs two at a time and headed up the corridor to where the maid was standing at a doorway, her hands clasped over her mouth.

Allan was first in the room.

On the floor of the bedroom lay Freddie Cunningham. He lay on his back, his hands clasped at his throat, his eyes open, staring at the ceiling. His mobile lay a few feet away where it could be assumed to have fallen from his hand.

Without touching anything, Allan looked at the body, took in the position of the phone and noted that nothing seemed to have been overturned or broken in the room. So, no signs of a struggle.

He turned towards the doorway.

"Julia, take the maid downstairs and call in one of the French detectives to arrange for a car to drive her to the police station to take her statement. Get them to put a cordon round the entire house".

He then got out his mobile and rang Rochefort.

"Cunningham is dead. I strongly suspect that he died the same way the children died. A phone call and then death by asphyxiation. We need your forensic guys down here now. I need to know the cause and time of death".

Szymanski joined him a couple of minutes later.

"The time of death is all important".

"Because he was the one that came in when we were here?"

"No, Julia, because if he died before the incident at the supermarket then he either had an accomplice or hired someone else to do it. That means it's unlikely he was doing this merely for self-gratification, enjoying killing for killing's sake, and there must be others involved. Again, if he died before I was sent that last letter, chances are, even if he was involved, he is only part of it and not the orchestrator. The most interesting part, though, is that his mobile phone was on the floor, only a short distance away from where he fell, which indicates that he probably received a fatal phone call. This smacks of a body of people and not some psychopath. This is getting more and more unclear as we go on. Are we looking for several killers. Was the profiler wrong?"

"I don't know, sir. Where do we go from here?"

"Firstly, we shut this villa down and the lab underneath, so the person or persons unknown don't have access to them. The virus must be safely removed and kept as evidence. Then we wait for the French forensic report on the details of Cunningham's death. I'll phone Patel to organise the closure of the Hall together with that laboratory cutting off access to the virus there. Whoever wrote that letter, presupposing it is not Cunningham, will be contacting me again with their demands. We need to make sure we meet those demands in exchange for Vanessa. We need to get back to the UK".

"Sir" said Szymanski hesitantly.

Allan turned to face her.

"Sir……I know you don't want to hear this, but might it not be a good idea to let the DCI know about your involvement with Vanessa?"

"No. I know you feel I shouldn't be working this case because of personal involvement but I must. I need to be the one to free Vanessa because if it hadn't been for her relationship with me none of this would have happened to her and she would be safe and well".

Szymanski nodded her head sympathetically.

They drove back to their hotel, Szymanski at the wheel while Allan phoned first Patel and then his DCI to bring him up to date with the recent events. He mentioned that he had been informed by the suspect that Dr Vanessa Fenchurch had been kidnapped but omitted to mention his personal involvement with her.

"So now we have a hostage to boot" exclaimed an irate Walters.

"Yes, sir, and time is of the essence. We now know that Cunningham was involved but is not the sole psycho perpetrator. We are probably dealing with a group who will continue without him. However, we are in the process of shutting down the operation at Cunningham's villa here and confiscating everything in the laboratory. I have given Patel the order to shut down the Hall and arrange for the virus there to be safely removed and kept as evidence. That may drive those involved to make a move or, alternatively, when we receive the demand by letter as the writer has indicated we will, we capitulate and draw them out that way".

"Except that last time, we lost two million pounds if you recall and got nothing in return! We are still none the wiser as to who is behind this, and I doubt that the Super will authorise another two million! You have to find out who is behind this, Allan, and fast" the line went dead.

"That went well then!" said Szymanski turning to him, a weak smile on her face.

"Unfortunately, he is right though, Julia. We have to find out who it is. Unless it is some sort of co-operative there must be a leader of the gang. The question is who" and he stared out of the side window absorbed in his own thoughts.

Back at the hotel, Allan fell on the bed and slept for three hours. He then took a shower and as he was wrapping the towel around his waist his mobile rang.

“Allan” he barked.

“It’s Pierre, Jack. We’ve had the forensic report back. Cunningham died of asphyxiation which is interesting but even more of interest is the time of death which was approximately twenty-four hours ago. What is also of note is that he received a call on his mobile twenty-six hours ago from a burner number suggesting that it was a self-destruct instruction as with the other victims”.

“So that would indicate then, to my way of thinking, that we are getting too close, and that Cunningham is……sorry, was a liability”.

“I would tend to agree, Jack. What is your next move?”

“We are returning to Britain on the next available flight. Thank you, Pierre, for all your help. I know you stuck your neck out for us, and I appreciate it! It’s paid dividends!”

“I take it ‘stuck your neck out for us’ is one of your nonsensical expressions, Jack” he said laughing.

“Yep”.

“Pleasure to help” Pierre said in a serious tone.

The next flight to Stansted airport was at eleven-thirty that evening, and Pierre dropped them off in good time. Having shaken hands, the Frenchman wished them a good flight. They walked through the departure hall, checked in, and consulted the flight information board.

“No delays or cancellations. Good to know” muttered Allan.

“Do you want anything from the shop?” Szymanski asked.

“Yes, a couple of bottles of still water”.

“I’ll be a few minutes, sir”.

“No hurry, we’ve got over an hour to wait. While you’re there can you pick me up a newspaper. Telegraph or Times will do”.

She smiled and walked off.

Allan found an empty seat in a reasonably quiet area and reflected on the case. He felt he had been left wanting so far, being convinced that Cunningham was behind it all and that the profile would seem to fit. Now he was dead and coupled with that Cunningham had the perfect alibi for the latest incident – he had been dead at the time, and not only that, had been murdered. It could be the work of a group but...............

He was awoken from his thoughts by a buzz indicating that he had a new message on his mobile. He clicked on the video he had been sent and viewing it he suddenly felt violently sick and ran blindly to the gents, rushed into a cubicle, locked the door and vomited into the toilet pan. When there was no more to come up, he flushed the toilet, put down the seat and loosening his tie he sat down. The sweat was pouring down his face. He brushed his hand down from his forehead over his nose, mouth and chin. He clicked on his phone again and watched the video for any clues as to where this might have been taken but reluctantly decided he would have to wait for the techie boys back at the station to analyse it.

Finally, he got up on shaky legs and walked back to where he had been sitting. Szymanski had arrived back with newspapers, bottles of water and two coffees. She looked up.

“You look terrible, sir! What’s happened?” she asked, an alarmed expression on her face as she stood up.

He simply handed her his mobile and slumped into the empty seat next to hers. She sat down, looked at the phone in her hand, hesitating for a second and then clicked it on.

As she watched, she clapped her other hand over her mouth and gasped.

The video started with a slide saying,

"Just a little reminder for a favourable reception of the demand you will shortly be receiving".

The slide then disappeared, and Vanessa was revealed sitting in front of a grey, concrete wall. She was in her underwear with her ankles tightly tied with rope to each front leg of a wooden chair. Her arms were outstretched, and her wrists were tied with rope to wall rings. She was gagged and she wore a terrified expression, her eyes wide with horror. She let out a scream partially strangled in her throat because of the gag. A hooded, masked figure came into view holding two lit cigarettes. The figure bent over Vanessa and put out one cigarette under her arm. She screamed and screwed up her eyes. The figure crossed to the other side of his victim and put out the other cigarette. The figure disappeared again and suddenly a bucket of water was thrown over her and her whole body shook as she choked trying to get her breath. She had barely recovered when another bucket was thrown over her. She was now shaking uncontrollably.

Another slide came up "This is just the start of a beautiful relationship with the lovely Vanessa. Nothing like a bucket or two of icy water to start things off. There's so much more to come unless you stop it, and you know how to do that. I'll just leave you with one more morsel of food for thought".

The figure raised his arm and brought the full force of the back of his hand across the left side of her face which flopped to one side, the blood streaming down from her cut lip and the bruise already spreading over her cheek. She was crying and screaming with pain. He then walked to the other side and executed the same torture. Her body was contorting, her face lolling to the right. He grabbed the hair on top of her head and forced her to face the camera, her eyes staring wildly. The screen went black.

Szymanski swallowed hard.

"We're going to get this bastard, sir. We will. Vanessa's alive and she's a survivor" and she managed to sound more convinced than she actually was.

"Yes, we are, and she is" he had been holding his head in his hands and now he sat up straight, a look of determination on his face.

“God help him when I get my hands on him” he said.

“I didn’t hear that, sir” she said.

“It does confirm what I had concluded sitting here thinking while you were in the shop”.

“And what’s that, sir?” she asked, a questioning frown on her brow.

“That we had it wrong. This isn’t the work of a group; it is as we concluded in the first place the work of one person. A narcissistic psychopath, just as the profiler said, working either alone or with one or two others maximum. It’s Manning”.

The flight indicator board displayed a ‘boarding’ sign. Allan and Szymanski proceeded to Gate 20.

Chapter Fifteen

Vanessa had passed out after her last ordeal. She came round slowly unsure at first where she was. Then she felt the pain in her jaw and her ankles sent searing bolts of pain up her legs if she moved them even slightly. Her arms were now bound behind her back and her underarms felt like they were on fire from the cigarette burns.

She looked around the room in the gloomy light and started to cry but then shook her head and thrust her chin up defying her fear. She had to get out of here. There must be a way. She looked around searching the corners of the room for inspiration. Despair started to well up from her stomach, but she squashed it down. Her nose started to run so she turned to her shoulder trying to wipe the drip away. That was when she saw something that she hadn't noticed before. By the side of her was a small table with some sharp instruments on, knives with sharp blades, a whip, a pincer like tool, a saw and some others that she didn't recognise. Fear gripped her as she realised that this was a tray of torture tools.

She used all her strength and agility to move the chair a little towards the table. Inch by inch she moved closer and turned the back of the chair to face the table. Managing to get hold of the saw she moved the chair inch by inch back to its original spot. Fear gripped her again when she heard a door shut in the distance and footsteps approaching. She kept very still with her eyes closed. The footsteps became louder and louder. Her heart was thumping so hard she was convinced that it was going to explode. The door creaked open, and the black clothed man strode in. He had a small bottle of water in his hand. He bent over Vanessa, pulled out the ball of cloth stuffed in her mouth and gripped her nose between his finger and thumb forcing her to open her mouth to breathe. He then poured the water down her throat, releasing his grip on her nose, while she coughed and spluttered trying to catch her breath. Barely had she done so than he stuffed the cloth back into her mouth. He left without saying a word closing the door behind him.

She listened intently to the fading footsteps until she was sure she was quite alone. Then she set about sawing the rope that was binding her hands. It was a long, slow and very difficult process and she caught her skin a few times causing her to wince and cry out in pain.

Finally, her hands were free, and she removed the cloth from her mouth. Next, she set about sawing the ropes off each of her ankles. Getting up slowly from the chair she felt wobbly on her legs partly from being kept in the same position for so long and partly because she had had no food since she had been kidnapped. She walked round and round the room several times as the blood started to flow faster, and she began to feel stronger. As she walked past the tray with the torture implements on, she noticed a couple of long threads that looked like they had come from an item of clothing. She picked them up and tied them round one of her fingers. She tried the door to see if it was locked although she knew the answer even before it was confirmed. The window was too far up the wall and inaccessible, so she picked up one of the longest, sharpest knives and took up her position behind the door.

Hours later she was still waiting, and she began to wonder if she had been left to die there but if that was so, why did he give her some water? What if something had happened to him though and no-one knew she was here? She quickly put that thought aside and concentrated on what she had to do when he reappeared.

At last, the footsteps returned, and the door creaked open. She moved swiftly and stabbed him in the leg. He howled with pain and fell over on the floor. Running faster than the wind she flew down the corridor, through the next door and the next. She could hear him coming now with an uneven tread. She was fit and she knew she could outrun him for a while, but she needed to hide. She glanced all around looking for inspiration. There was nothing but a vast warehouse with no nooks or crannies that afforded cover. She could hear him louder now; he was gaining on her. She never knew where she got that extra surge of energy, but a good dose of adrenalin was probably the answer. She burst out of the warehouse and blinked in the blinding sunlight. Quickly adjusting to the light, she saw a Range Rover parked a few feet away. She raced towards it and got in the driver's seat. She fumbled at the glove compartment, looked in the holders in the centre, no keys. He had come out of the warehouse now and was limping over to the car, his face frighteningly contorted with rage.

She pulled down the sun visor. The keys dropped in her lap. She couldn't get the keys in the ignition her hands were shaking so much. He was nearly at the door now. She pressed the lock button and heard the reassuring click. Her hands stopped shaking enough to allow her to get the keys in the ignition. The car roared into life just as he got to the car. She put her foot down and the car surged ahead leaving her assailant stumbling forward onto the ground.

Vanessa drove on and on down the winding lane, glancing in her rear mirror from time to time, her heart in her mouth praying that she wouldn't be followed until she came to the highway. Taking a deep breath, she waited for a break in the oncoming traffic and turned left, heading towards Cambridge. Half an hour later she turned into the warehouse car park and rushed out of the car running towards the outer door leading to Jack's flat. She punched in the code to the security box and took out the front door key. Her hands were shaking so much she had difficulty getting the key in the lock but finally she managed it and stepped inside.

Tearing her underwear off as she walked to the bathroom, all her pent-up emotion came out and, crying, she entered the shower cubicle. Then she remembered the threads and untying them from her finger she put them on the bathroom stool. Stepping back into the shower cubicle she turned on the shower. She stood still, her head tilted back allowing the hot water to cascade over her face, down over her shoulders and body. Gradually she stopped sobbing and massaged her eyebrows, eyes and face with her hands. Reaching for the shampoo she thoroughly cleansed her hair, face and body. Enfolding herself in the thick, fluffy towelling robe she began to feel more human and walked over to the bathroom mirror to examine the damage done by her captor. Both sides of her face were badly bruised, and the cigarette burns were still sore although not quite as painful as they had been.

Her ankles and wrists were red and chafed. She took some lotion from the shelf over the bath and applied cream soothing her wounds.

Sauntering out into the hall she picked up her discarded and soiled underwear and put them in the wastebin. Realising she was starving she searched Jack's fridge, found some eggs and cheese and made an omelette.

She must have fallen asleep on the couch in the lounge area, the dirty plate, knife and fork on the table in front of her because the next thing she saw when she opened her eyes was Jack's concerned face looking intently at her. He raised his hand, which she noticed was trembling slightly and stroked her bruised face and then her hair. They locked together and kissed passionately. He took off his shirt and trousers and then gently took off her robe. They fell back on the couch, and he ran his fingers up her leg.

When they woke up it was four in the morning, and they made love again.

"I'll make our breakfast while you run your essential three-minute mile!" she laughed.

"Cheeky! Then tell me everything you can remember. We need to catch this bastard!" he replied smiling and kissing her gently but firmly on the lips.

While they were eating breakfast, she told Jack everything that had happened and how she had escaped. Jack's mobile rang. He clicked to answer and before he could say anything his ear was blasted by a raging female voice.

"You bastard. I knew something like this would happen. It's all your fault and now we could lose everything because of what.... what? Just because you want promotion! Why don't you just give in to this monster? Why can't you just let it go!?" and the voice cracked, and a wracked sobbing sound followed.

Jack knew that it was Szymanski's mobile, but the voice wasn't hers.

"Is this Sally?" he asked in a soft voice.

"Yes" came an indistinct answer muffled by sniffles.

"Okay, so tell me what has happened. Is Julia alright?"

"What do you care?"

"I do care believe it or not. She is a valued colleague. Please tell me what has happened".

"She just collapsed, and she couldn't breathe".

“Where is she now?” asked Jack praying that Julia was still alive.

“I rang for an ambulance, and they have taken her to hospital. I have to take the baby down to the hospital to be checked out in case our son has been affected. The paramedics think it is some sort of virus. If they die, I’ll hold you personally responsible”.

“Sally I’m so sorry and I promise I will do all in my power to stop this from happening to anyone else. I’ll come and see Julia shortly and I think it would be a good idea for you to be checked out too”.

Sally ended the call.

“Vanessa, we need to get you to the station to make a formal statement” he said as he put down his glass of spinach and kale smoothie.

“I have to get back to work, Jack, the hospital needs me” she said running her fingers through her hair.

“Sorry, it’s non-negotiable”.

“I haven’t got my mobile obviously, so can I use yours. I need to ring in to work” she asked.

“Yes, sure it’s on my bedside table” he called from the bathroom.

"There is another thing, Jack, that I had forgotten" she said as she walked over to get his mobile.

He turned and looked at her, his head on one side.

"I found some thread on the torture tray which looked as though it was from a garment".

"Where is it now. Do you have it?" he asked.

"Yes, it's on the bathroom stool".

"Great! He rushed into the bathroom, produced an evidence bag and popped the threads in.

Allan then went for a shower. While the hot water cascaded over him, he thought about the torture tray with its array of terrifying equipment that Vanessa had mentioned and shuddered at the thought of what might have been.

As he started to get dressed, he heard Vanessa's reassurances to whoever she was talking to at the hospital that she was fine and looking forward to coming back to work. He heard her then dive into the shower and within thirty minutes or so, they were in the car heading for the station.

The team cheered as she entered the main office, and she felt herself redden with all the attention. Vanessa went off to the interview room to be debriefed and make a statement while Allan got together the team for an update but first, he spoke to Patel.

He then addressed the team.

“First, an update on Julia Szymanksi. We are all, I’m sure, very concerned to hear that she is battling with this horrific virus, coming into contact with it while carrying out her duties. We all know that she is an outstanding officer and I’m sure you will all want me to wish her a speedy recovery when I visit her this afternoon” and he looked round the team who nodded solemnly. He paused, looking down at the floor for a few seconds and then continued.

“I’ve just spoken to Dev Patel who will be my acting DS while DS Szymanski recovers. Obviously, it’s very good news that Dr Vanessa Fenchurch managed to escape and is virtually unharmed, a few bruises but nothing that won’t clear up in a relatively short space of time. Another piece of good news is that she managed to obtain a couple of threads from one of the perpetrator’s garments. I’ve sent it off for forensics to look at but if it matches Manning’s DNA, and I would be surprised if it didn’t, then we have our murderer. Dev has it been established whether Manning was out of the country at the time of the French incident?

“No there’s no evidence that he was” Dev answered looking round at the rest of the team who were all shaking their heads.

“Okay. So, it looks like Manning fits the profile but doesn’t work alone. While he was here enjoying his sadism with Vanessa, he also killed one of his accomplices, Cunningham, by phone, probably because he was becoming a liability. My thinking is that he is as mad as a hatter. His motive is to cause as much suffering and mayhem as possible. This isn’t entirely about the money unless it helps further his sadistic aims and his thirst for power. After confirmation that the DNA on the threads is a match with Manning’s, we’ll bring him in for questioning”.

He waited for a moment and then continued.

“Any questions?”

No-one spoke.

“In that case I’m going to the hospital and will update as soon as I hear from forensics.

He strode out of the main office just as Vanessa was walking by from the interview room.

“I’ve got to go to the hospital and find out what caused Julia to collapse. I’ll drop you off at yours on the way and you must stay there and don’t let anyone in. Not anyone, do you understand?”

"I have to get back to work, Jack. I can't stay in hiding. People need me at the hospital. So, thanks for giving me a lift but if it's only on condition I stay at home then I can't promise that. Okay?"

"No, I absolutely forbid that you go to work. He could kidnap you a second time. I could lose you again and this time it could be permanent!"

"I'm sorry, Jack, but that's the way it is. You know that. You can't stop doing your job just because it all gets a bit hairy from time to time. Well, I can't stop doing mine either. We are short staffed as it is. My presence will have been missed. I owe it to my colleagues and patients" and she stretched her hand out and stroked Jack's forearm.

"Now if you could drop me off at the hospital that would be really good, Jack" she said quietly.

He stared at her for a moment, and they hugged each other tightly.

Arriving at the hospital, Vanessa bumped into a colleague who was clearly overjoyed to see her, and arms round each other they walked off leaving Jack to head for the ward where Szymankski had been taken.

When he walked into the ward where she lay hooked up to machines that bleeped and flashed occasionally, he couldn't equate the pale version of his colleague to the lively, fit person he spent most of his days with.

She lifted her oxygen mask as he came in and whispered.

"Hello sir".

He went over to the bedside and sat down on a chair that would have been better suited to a child at junior school size-wise.

"How are you feeling, Julia" he asked putting his hand over hers.

"I've felt better, sir, but on the bright side it seems that it is the infection not the virus itself that causes death. My understanding is that my exposure was thankfully small, and the infection can be treated with normal antibiotics. If greater exposure or strength of the virus had caused a more serious infection much stronger antibiotics peculiar to this type of infection would be needed which they don't have," she said smiling weakly.

"That's terrific news, Julia, that you are on the mend, and everyone on the team is willing you to get better quickly. We all miss you. I certainly do. Dev will do a good job but he's not you and doesn't have your experience. So selfishly I want you out of here as soon as possible. That said I don't want you jeopardising your health, so you are under doctor's orders at the moment and not mine!"

He proceeded to update her. She was delighted to hear that Vanessa was safe but again suggested he need tell the DCI of his personal involvement.

Allan had just left his colleague when his mobile rang.

"Stew here, Jack. Good news! The DNA on the threads is a match for Manning's DNA."

Jack was thankful that they had persuaded Manning to allow them to take a sample of his DNA to eliminate him from their enquiries when he had attended for interview.

"Fantastic, Stew. Thanks".

"Thought it would brighten you day!"

Allan made a phone call and hurried out to his car. Driving with his blues on and siren wailing, he stopped by the station to pick up Dev. Then he, one other car and a van containing a number of armed police took off at speed, their blues and sirens on, heading for Manning's apartment block.

The police got out of their cars and armed police jumped out of their vehicle. Allan looked up at

Manning's flat and thought he saw a slight movement. It could have been a reflection of a bird or a cloud, but he saw something. Arriving outside the door the police shouted.

"Armed police open the door. Armed police open the door".

At no response they battered the door until it yielded and shouting again and again, they scoured the whole flat.

"All clear, sir" said the one in charge to Allan who immediately went in. He looked in every room of the luxurious pad and then went to the balcony where he saw below a man running across the car park.

Chapter Sixteen

Allan dashed back through the lounge calling as he went.

“He’s getting away. He’s across the car park”.

Police officers and the armed response unit followed but lagged far behind him as he pelted down the stairs jumping down five steps at the end of each flight. His superb physical fitness enabled him to make the end of the car park in a matter of seconds.

There was a long drive at the side of the apartment blocks and when Allan turned the corner, the figure was still in the distance running hard. Allan raced on and started to gain on the runner. Reaching the end of the drive he looked right and then left catching sight of Manning turning a corner. Allan raced after him, across a busy road, dodging traffic and causing cars to make emergency stops. Both pursuer and pursued pushing people out of their way, one lady landing face down on the ground, the contents of her shopping scattering over the pavement. On and on they went through the covered market area where it was refuse collection day. The hooded figure pulling down bins to slow down his pursuer. Allan jumped some and went round others and was almost on him when someone tripped him up thinking he was the villain. He got up cursing and showing his identification but had now lost ground. He raced on and across another road catching sight of Manning again who was just rounding a corner. He avoided being mown down by a car which screeched to a halt narrowly missing hitting him. Getting to the corner he saw that an area was fenced off a short way down the alley and the gate closed and padlocked. The figure had just scaled the fence and was running across the concourse to some large, parked trucks. Allan scaled the fence and jumped lightly on the ground. He ran over to where the trucks were when the shot rang out. It narrowly missed him, and he dived for cover. He had no gun to defend his position, so he stayed where he was and phoned the armed response team leader identifying where he was and the situation. Allan threw a coin which landed a little way away from where he was, and the response was a bullet shot in the coin's direction. He knew then that Manning was still there and if the team came soon, it would be over for him.

A second later there was a scuffling sound and Allan knew that Manning was on the move again. He cautiously peered around the truck and saw Manning disappearing towards the exit. Getting up he pursued as noiselessly as possible to avoid being shot at. It was at that moment the armed response unit and police officers arrived, but Allan held his hand up behind him as he entered into a busy thoroughfare. Suddenly, he heard the roar of a powerful motorbike and just had time to dodge out of the way as did passers-by. The bike roared onto the road and away.

“Right, I want twenty-four-hour surveillance on Manning’s flat in case he returns there” barked Allan into his mobile.

Next, he phoned Pierre Rochefort.

“Pierre, Jack Allan here. Have the missing children returned and have there been any more deaths?”

“Yes, all the children have returned home just like the other incidents. There have been fatalities. In total, twenty-three, all adults. It would seem either the victims were in some way more susceptible, or my best guess is the virus was more potent. Further tests are being carried out to discern the exact level of potency”.

“Do me a favour, Pierre, can you have the children examined to find out if there are any unexplained needle punctures or marks of any kind on them or anything unusual on their bodies?”

“What’s your line of thinking, Jack” the Frenchman asked.

“Could you just do it. It’s just a hunch and if it comes off, I’ll reveal all!”

“Okay, not a problem. I’ll let you know soonest”.

“Oh, and Pierre, gather up all the children’s mobiles. They must not be able to take any calls”.

A text pinged its arrival.

You will find an envelope awaiting you at the station, Detective Inspector Allan.

Allan ran all the way back to his car parked outside Manning’s apartment block and putting his blues and twos on he sped back to the station.

Picking up the large envelope at Reception he tore it open and read.

That was quite the marathon, Jack. I didn't think you had it in you but there again we all make mistakes, don't we? Now, Jack, to more serious matters. You are never going to catch me; you know that don't you? You're probably thinking that I'm making another mistake in underestimating you. Not at all. You're a very good cop, just not brilliant dare I say, like myself. You are also probably thinking that I no longer have anything to bargain with now that the lovely and, it must be said, brave Vanessa has escaped my hospitalities, and you have managed to shut down my little labs. but you would be wrong. Oh, so wrong, Detective Inspector Allan. Consider this, the strength of the virus has been increased. You know that to be true because of the increased fatalities in the French incident. You also know that more children were taken and at the click of a button they will die. Soon children taken in similar circumstances will not only die themselves but will turn into transmitters of the virus. Think about that tenfold or a hundredfold and so on. You see, Detective Inspector Allan you have no idea what resources I have at my disposal both in devoted followers or in available properties where my work can be carried out and perfected. It is a risk you can't take. So, to my final demand. I need a private jet and fifteen million sterling. Obviously, there will be no police presence and I will be cleared to fly wherever I want. I don't require a pilot; I can fly it myself with people I trust coming with me. If by any chance my demands aren't met, you will have a fatal virus spreading faster than you can imagine with dire consequences for this country and the world. You have experienced a small version of the havoc I can wreak, the power that I have. Don't be foolhardy and let it extend to uncontrollable, devastating events for which you and you alone will be responsible. I will contact you again shortly to let you know the exact location and conditions for delivery of my demands. Yours ever.

Allan ran two at a time up the stairs to his DCI's office.

"Come" shouted Walters in answer to Allan's knock on the door.

"Sir, I need to talk with you urgently".

His boss looked up over his titanium rimmed spectacles and nodded to the chair in front of his desk.

"Hopefully you are the bearer of good news? And before you start, Allan, I heard from the Super this morning. You've got forty-eight hours to put this to bed. After that it will be taken out of our hands and pushed up the ladder" he said.

Allan ran through the recent events.

“We have to supply what he wants and when he runs for the aircraft, we take him”.

“Fifteen bloody million. We can’t do that. And a private jet into the bargain. No way. Have you taken leave of your senses?”.

“What alternative do we have, sir, as Manning said, we can’t take the risk. This is escalating into a potential worldwide threat”.

“He could take the money and jet, fly into the blue and still wreak the havoc that he is threatening. We need a foolproof plan”.

“I’ve given some thought to that, sir, and I am certain that Manning has produced an antibiotic so should we demand that from him in exchange for the money and the jet?”.

“He could give you a whole load of rubbish while he flies off with the dosh. In any case if he had produced one, surely Cunningham would have been injected”.

“Not if Manning kept if for himself. Sir, what if we ask him to send us the antibiotic and say if it works, he can have his money sent to any account he specifies. In the meantime, we tell him he can have the private jet and fly off to wherever he likes to await payment which, of course, will never happen. This plan alleviates the need to rustle up fifteen million!".

"Do you think he will buy that. He would seem to hold all the cards".

"I don't know, sir, but we have to try and as you say, if we transfer the money to his account we stand to lose the money and the murderer. He must be aware that this is his only chance of escape. We know who he is, and his days are numbered. We will be watching and waiting at the appointed place. This time we will catch him".

Walters stroked his moustache and looked at Allan considering his subordinate's idea. Finally, he sat back in his chair his hands steepled.

"Okay, Allan. As you say, we have little choice, and this is probably the last time we will have the chance of catching Manning. Apprehend him we must for the sake of millions of people".

"Thank you, sir" was Allan's reply, getting up from his chair.

Allan ignored his mobile trying to grab his attention and ran down the stairs to the main office.

"Okay can I have everyone's attention" he said loudly.

The team immediately stopped what they were doing and turned to listen.

"I've spoken to the DCI about a development that has occurred in the last few hours. Another communication has come in from Manning. He has threatened to increase the potency of the virus to inflict mass deaths unless we meet his demands for a private jet and fifteen million pounds".

There were gasps and heads turned to each other.

"Okay. So that's not going to happen, but Manning is going to believe it is. We are waiting to hear the requested location for the jet and then we'll give him an ultimatum; the fifteen million will be transferred to an account to be named by him in exchange for the antibiotic after we have tested it. That negates immediate transfer of the money, and we have one chance to catch him at the airfield he names. We need to lay out infallible plans to catch him before he gets on the jet. So, I'll let you know as soon as. Any questions?"

"Yes, as I understood it antibiotics won't kill a virus?" asked Barry with a puzzled expression.

"No, you're absolutely right, Barry, but it isn't the virus that is killing people it is the lethal infection that this particular virus causes if the virus is strong enough. Remember, this virus is man-made, and its strength is controlled by the producer".

"Got yer!" said Barry and the others were nodding that that they now understood something that they had been wondering too.

There were no more questions and Allan walked into his office and closed the door. Taking out his mobile he saw that the missed call was from Szymanski.

"Hi Julia ...."

"We have some terrible news, sir" and Allan could hear her swallow hard but not before a sob escaped.

"It's our baby, Leo, he's contracted the virus. He is struggling to breathe, and the medics don't have anything to help him. They say he needs a strength of antibiotic that they don't have for the infection that's taking hold. It's a particular type of infection that they haven't come across before; they don't really know what it is. It's like the one I had but much, much worse and it can't be treated by normal antibiotics. They say that there is nothing they can do. He has an oxygen mask" she managed to say in a strangled voice".

Allan put the thumb and forefinger of his left hand on the inner corners of his eyes to stop his tears, still holding the mobile in his right hand.

“Listen, Julia, we are going to demand an antibiotic from Manning in return for fulfilling the demands I received from him today. We hope to have the antibiotic and him in custody by the end of tomorrow latest. So, you and Sally hang on in there and I’m certain everything is going to be okay”, he managed to say without a stumble or a catch in his throat.

“Thank you, sir. It’s just that he is so little and frail. His eyes wide with innocence staring at me, so trusting and his little hand clasping my finger. I feel so helpless. There’s nothing I can do”.

She sounded so vulnerable and hopeless, a stark contrast from the usual assertive and positive person she was.

“Leo will be alright, Julia, just be there for him while we work on getting hold of this antibiotic” he said reassuringly.

“I must take this call, Julia. Hang on in there” he said.

“Allan” his voice was more subdued that usual.

“Jack, it’s Pierre, you okay my friend?”

"Yeah, yeah, not too bad" he answered rubbing the fingers of one hand across his furrowed brow.

"Good, good. You were right to examine the children. We found the tiniest of capsules hidden under the nail of the big toe of each child which could easily have been missed. The capsules were empty but there was enough residue left to establish that they contained the virus. So, it would seem that when the children received a trigger phone call, they had been conditioned somehow during the time they were abducted, to press their toenail, which would release the virus into their system thus causing their death".

"At least we have saved those children. Have you collected all the children's mobiles? You will need to monitor them and hopefully the perpetrator will call which could give us vital information".

"Yes, of course. How are things going there?"

"Progressing. Thanks for the update".

"You're welcome, Jack. I'll let you know if we receive the phone call".

Allan drove home that evening, oblivious of the stop, start traffic. Normally, he would be getting impatient but today he was on automatic pilot and consumed by his thoughts on the case. They were so close to apprehending this monster and yet he had a horrible feeling that he was still not in control of the situation. This guy was slippery and undeniably brilliant. He couldn't rule out the unexpected. They would be ready, he and his team, yes, but would readiness be enough to catch him. If they didn't succeed the consequences were unthinkable. This bastard delighted in inflicting pain and exerting power, in fact, more than anything, it was this thirst that he wanted to quench, and that sort of madness combined with brilliance was a tough challenge to beat.

At last, he arrived home. He opened the door to a delicious smell of cooking.

"Hi Jack, just follow the aroma and you'll find me in a totally for me very unusual place, but actually, I have to admit, I'm quite enjoying myself" Vanessa turned as he entered, her broad grin disappeared instantly on seeing his expression.

She ran over to him and put her arms round him. He sagged against her and slowly brought his arms up around her too. They stayed hugging each other tightly for some minutes. Looking into his eyes she saw the frustration, anger and sadness. Turning for a second to switch off the hob she then pulled him over to the couch and sat beside him stroking his thick, dark hair.

"Tell me what has happened" she whispered.

He told her about Leo and they both wiped tears from their eyes. Then he told her the good news about the French children, and their sadness turned to smiles. They held hands and then kissed. She got up from the couch not letting go of his hand and pulled him up gently leading him to the bedroom.

It was around two o'clock and they woke up starving. The dinner was ruined but they feasted on a pasta and nut dish with cinnamon and herbs. When they had finished Vanessa went back to bed while Jack washed up and then started his routine gruelling work out.

When he arrived in the office that morning, Allan called the team together.

"I've just heard from Szymanski. Bad news I'm afraid. Her and Sally's little boy, Leo has the virus which has turned into an extremely bad infection. I'm assuming, at present, that he contracted the virus from an atomiser deliberately sprayed at him. Obviously, Julia and Sally are devastated which makes it all the more important that the deal we are going to offer does in fact work.

I've also heard from Rochefort confirming that, as we suspected, the phone call just prior to the children's deaths did indeed serve as a trigger for them to press and burst the tiny capsule hidden in their toenails thus causing the fatalities. The good news is that having found the deadly capsule, the affected French children have had them removed. They are now safe and out of harm's way. Their mobiles are being monitored for the trigger call which may provide more evidence. The bad news is that I am still waiting for the communication from Manning but hopefully it won't be too long now".

"So, it's a waiting game at the moment, sir?" asked Patel.

At that moment, his phone rang, and he signalled to Patel to accompany him to his office. Allan sat down as he picked up the call indicating Patel should sit on the chair opposite him.

"Hello, is this Detective Inspector Allan?" said the deep, rich, well-educated voice.

"It is".

"Good then listen very carefully to your instructions...."

Allan cut in before the caller could go any further.

"Before you proceed with your demands, I need to let you know that I have spoken to my superiors, and they have agreed to supply a private jet and the fifteen million pounds. However, there is one thing that is non-negotiable and that is, undoubtedly you must have an antibiotic for this viral infection, and we must be in possession of this if we are to transfer the fifteen million. Therefore, we will need time to satisfy ourselves that the antibiotic is authentic. So, we propose that you give us the antibiotic before you embark on the jet and fly to wherever you are going. When we are sure that you haven't tried to trick us the fifteen million will be transferred".

The line went dead.

"Shit" exclaimed Patel an agonized expression in his eyes as he looked at his boss. He was surprised to see a smile on Allan's face.

"He will ring back. Don't worry. To get this far he knows it will be more and more difficult to escape arrest and therefore he will be unable to quench his sadistic thirst. He knows we know who he is, hence he has given up on the mechanical voice he used to use. This is his best chance of getting away and he knows it. He can't hide forever".

At that moment Allan's mobile rang again. He let it ring a few times before he pressed answer but remained silent.

"Detective Inspector Allan?"

"Yes" said Allan calmly.

"You have a deal. Now this is what is going to happen".

Chapter Seventeen

The call ended and Allan strode out of his office closely followed by Patel.

"Okay team, we're on and the fun begins. Manning has just made contact. He has accepted the deal after consideration. It didn't take long for him to decide to agree to it, he hasn't got much option which is a plus point for us and gives us the much-needed advantage of not having to raise the money. The time agreed is five o'clock tomorrow evening. I emphasised it couldn't be sooner as it would take that time to organise a private jet and have the money ready for transfer as soon as the antibiotic is proven to be the real thing. Begrudgingly he accepted that. That's the good news. The bad news is that if he sees anyone near the jet, he will activate a mass killing of hundreds of civilians in an unnamed town or village in Cambridgeshire. We have no way of knowing whether his threat is a bluff or not, but we have to take it that it isn't. So, it is imperative that we do not show ourselves before he does and when he does it is equally vital that we arrest and handcuff him before he can do any more harm. He has asked for me to be totally alone to receive the box of antibiotic that he says he will have with him to conclude the deal. Now to the location.

He has picked the disused Bourn airport. It's wide open, as a lot of you probably know, with very little cover. However, from memory it does have extensive areas of long grass and gorse bushes and it has a hangar. I suspect Manning will examine the hangar so probably not a good idea to use that. There is only one entry and exit road so the best way to approach the airfield is on foot.

Soph, can you print off a large map of Bourn airport. Mike, can you liaise with Cambridge Airport about the loan of a private jet. Explain that it is a national emergency, and that the loan is not a request. Max, call Toby Jones at Cambridge TA and request loan of camouflage gear. Dev pull together a team of twenty armed police for one o'clock tomorrow and let them know they will be dressed in camouflage gear. They will need to be here for a briefing at five o'clock sharp today. Thanks everyone. Let's get to it".

Allan went into his office picked up his phone and hurried out. As he got in the car, the passenger door opened, and Szymanski got in. Her face was puffy from all the crying, but her eyes were dry and focused. She looked straight at Allan.

"Don't even think about saying I shouldn't be here, sir. I need to work. I have to have my mind on anything other than Leo and Sally. I'm ready and willing, sir" she said in her usual determined manner.

"My first thought is to do exactly that, Julia, send you back to your family but I have to admit you seem virtually your old self, although I know deep down you are very not. I'm glad to have you on board again, Julia, but if at any time you don't feel up to it, it is your duty to tell me and equally if I see that you are struggling, I will exercise my authority. Are we clear?"

"Yes, sir, absolutely" replied Julia and with her chin up, she fixed an unfaltering stare on Allan's eyes.

"Okay, we're going to do a recon of Bourn Airport" and he proceeded to fill her in on recent developments.

They drove through the pleasant arable countryside along the A428 to Bourn Airport arriving there twenty-five minutes later.

Allan parked the car and they both stepped out.

"This is as exposed as you can wish for if you were in Manning's shoes" he said shielding his eyes from the sun as he looked around. Consulting the map on his phone he looked up and down as he got his bearings.

"Looks like Cambourne is to the west. To the north is the A428. An approach from Crow End to the south or Highfields to the east would be the best bet. Agreed?" he said looking at Szymanski.

"Highfields, perhaps, would be the favourite. It's nearer and across country from the airfield so less likely that he will check in that direction".

"Yes, I think you're right and there is some sort of building, I think it is part of a farm over that way, but it isn't anything to do with the airport and too far away for Manning to bother or probably have time to check".

"But with binoculars the distance from the building to the airfield won't be a problem for us, sir".

They walked around surveying the whole area and mapping out exactly where was the best place for the approach. The edge of the airfield did provide good cover from a mass of gorse bushes and long grass as Allan had correctly remembered. They strolled over to the farm building and looked inside. It was totally empty and suitable perhaps for use by the team.

An hour later, having taken photographs, they were satisfied they had sufficient information to plan their strategy.

When Szymanski walked into the main office, the team one by one gave her a hug and welcomed her back.

At five o'clock the armed response unit joined the team. Allan emerged from his office and the briefing began.

"Soph, have you got an enlarged map, yes, great!" he took the map from Soph's outstretched hand and put it on the whiteboard.

"Okay Szymanski and I have visited Bourn Airport" he said picking up a wooden stick to point out the various pertinent positions.

"Firstly, you will note that there is very little cover around the airport which is the reason Manning has chosen it. However, if we approach the airfield from the east, it is unlikely that Manning will look in that area partly because there would not seem to be anywhere to hide. Also, there is a farm building that could afford some cover. We will need to contact the farmer to get his permission to use it although that will be a formality. At thirteen thirty tomorrow the armed response unit dressed in camouflage gear will be dropped off just outside Highfields. Advancing across the fields slowly in military fashion shielded by the gorse bushes and long grass the unit should take up their positions at eight hundred metres from the airfield. Julia, Dev,

Sophie, Max, Mike, Barry, and Peter will take cover in the barn having also approached from Highfields. I will be standing a few feet the other side of the jet shielded from view behind the only line of trees in the area. Max, how did you get on with Tony Jones?" he asked looking at Max.

"He was a bit taken aback at first but when I explained fully, he agreed, and he is organising delivery of the camouflage gear as we speak" she answered in a crisp matter-of-fact voice.

"That's great, thanks Max. Mike, you spoke to Cambridge Airport?"

"Yes, they put me on to a Wings and Company Limited who hire out private jets. They are happy to comply with our request. I said I would let them know the time for delivery as soon as possible".

"Fantastic, thanks, Mike. So, we'll have a delivery time of midday tomorrow. Perhaps you could let them know that the pilot should leave the area immediately after delivery".

"Sir" replied Mike making an entry in his notebook.

"Thanks, Dev, for getting together the armed response team and welcome to them" he said nodding at the team who smiled and one or two raised their hands in acknowledgement.

"So, any questions from you" Allan addressed the armed response team.

"Yes, sir, at what point do you want us to make a move?" asked Brian Peabody, the team leader.

"As soon as you see the suspect walking towards the plane then move forward cautiously but quickly and I'm sure you don't need me to say this but ensuring you are shielded by the long grass and gorse bushes, listen to instructions from me but in the event that our communication went down break cover and make yourselves known when you see me walking towards him. He will be expecting me to collect the antibiotic. He may well be armed and take a shot at me, but I will have a bullet proof vest on. As soon as he surrenders, I will arrest him".

"Understood" replied the officer.

"Any questions, team?" he turned to his own team.

"Do you think this is going to work, sir, I mean is there any way this could fail?" asked Mike.

"In my experience, Mike, nothing is ever foolproof, but this is as near as we're going to get".

Allan turned to the map again.

“So, everyone is clear that no cars will approach the airfield. We will all be dropped off discreetly just outside Highfields and all of us will approach from the fields. My team will also be in camouflage, but we will be hidden at first in the farm building. The long grass and gorse will disguise any movements. I doubt when we move into our positions that anyone will be watching as we will be there several hours before the suspect will think of getting there”.

Allan walked into his office still holding his stick which he threw on his desk, going round to his chair and slumping down in it. Szymanski and Patel had followed him in and sat down in the chairs in front of his desk.

“This is our last chance to get this bastard. The DCI has said we have until tomorrow evening to get a result, so it is cutting it fine to say the least. I bloody hope it works” and he absent mindedly got an apple out of his drawer and bit hard into it.

“It will work, sir, it has to,” said Patel.

Szymanski didn’t say anything.

Allan was restless that night. He couldn’t sleep and got up at one thirty. He rummaged around in the fridge for something to eat and ended up drinking a pint of goat’s milk. Something was bugging him. Things still didn’t sit right but he couldn't put his finger on what it was. There was something that didn't quite fit. What was it? Damn! He fervently hoped it wasn't going to upset tomorrow. It was imperative they caught this guy, he thought, as he ran faster and faster on the treadmill. He stepped off the machine and bent over, his hands on his knees, his head hanging down, catching his breath. Finally, standing up and towelling off the sweat, he drank some cold water. Then he continued with his regime as though his life depended on it.

Later he was eating his usual healthy breakfast and wishing Vanessa were there instead of on shift, when he got a call on his mobile. He glanced at the caller which was flashing 'DCI'.

"Morning, sir" Allan said glancing at his watch. It was six o'clock; he wondered what could be so important to ring him this early.

"An update please, Allan" Walters had obviously thought it was surplus to needs to start with pleasantries.

"Certainly, sir" Allan replied and proceeded to relay the current situation.

"Humph! Well, good luck, Jack, I have a feeling you are going to need more than luck with this customer. Keep me updated and, Jack, be careful" he said uncharacteristically. The line went dead.

"I didn't know you cared" Allan muttered under his breath.

There was a buzz in the air when he got to the station an hour and a half later.

By midday Allan's team were dressed in camouflage gear.

The team assembled in the main office.

"Okay. Everyone knows the plan. Good luck!"

They trooped downstairs and got into the two waiting vans for the thirty-minute drive.

When they arrived, everyone descended quickly with as little fuss as possible in a layby just outside the village. Slowly they moved forward behind the bushes, through the long grass. It was a cloudy somewhat dull day which made for poor visibility. The weather was on their side. So, anyone to the west of them would have trouble seeing them. The jet had not yet arrived. It was now a waiting game.

When the jet arrived and the pilot had quickly disappeared, as arranged, there was no further discernible movement. A slight breeze had got up and rustled the leaves in the trees at the perimeter of the airfield to the east of them. Behind the trees, camouflaged, a police van waited to take away the culprit.

"Ten o'clock" whispered one of the armed police into his mouthpiece.

All attention was focused on that direction and sure enough a figure dressed in black appeared looking all around cautiously making its way towards the jet. Equally cautiously and timing their movements to coincide when the figure looked away from them, the team moved forward, keeping low using the bushes and the long grass as a screen.

The figure reached the jet and opened the door ready to climb in. Allan had appeared and was advancing towards the jet.

"Go, go, go" shouted the leader of the armed police.

They rushed forward and within seconds they were on the figure and had their arms secured behind their back. The figure was roughly turned round to face Allan who moved forward to remove the black face mask.

Allan stepped back and took a second to take in the person standing before him.

Cunningham's housekeeper had a defiant smirk on her face.

"Not what you were expecting, Detective Inspector?" she spat at him.

"What is your name?"

"Fran Cooper" she answered after a moment's hesitation.

"Fran Cooper, I am arresting you on suspicion of aiding and abetting a criminal to escape, you do not have to say anything but, it may harm your defence if you do not mention when questioned something which you later rely on in court. Anything you do say may be given in evidence".

At that moment a car started up and drove off at speed. After a second's hesitation Allan called to Szymanski as he ran full pelt towards the police van. Allan ordered the driver to follow the car that they could see in the distance heading for the A428. Szymanski put in a call to control for back up and with their blue lights flashing the van sped down on the road closing in on the Range Rover in front which had switched to the inside lane. Coming to the junction the car hung a left onto the A14 heading towards Bar Hill. The van did the same and they stayed in the middle lane until a slower moving vehicle in front and a car in the fast lane caused the Range Rover to move to the slow lane. The van narrowly missed a car that attempted to come out of the fast lane into the middle lane and swerved behind the Range Rover and then they were both in the middle lane again. The countryside was speeding by as the Range Rover refused to acknowledge the police van and stop.

“Where the hell is he heading?” Allan muttered the rhetorical question.

“Not sure sir, maybe Huntingdon?” Szymanski suggested.

“Why would he go to bloody Huntingdon?”

“No idea. Do you want me to try to find a connection?”

“No let’s see where he ends up”.

The Range Rover had moved to the fast lane again. The police van’s sirens were blazing and the blue lights flashing as it came alongside making signs through the window indicating that the driver should stop.

The driver wasn’t wearing a mask.

“It’s Manning!” Allan said triumphantly.

The Range Rover pulled ahead and swerved in front of the van. They were both now in the middle lane but just before the next left hand turn the car suddenly pulled to the left and at the junction turned left on the A1.

“He’s turning left back down towards the south. Where the hell is he going?” Allan exclaimed.

“He’s heading for Buckden first but no.... where’s he going now?” cried Szymanski.

Manning had swerved to avoid a car coming from the opposite direction as he turned right up a country road.

The van was held up for a few minutes while a stream of traffic passed by.

Ahead was Grafham Water. The Range Rover had disappeared completely from view. A few minutes later they arrived at the Water but there was still no sight of the car. The driver stopped and Allan and Szymanski got out. There was an eerie silence.

“Where did it go?” Allan muttered.

The back up in the shape of three police cars arrived on the scene and Allan filled them in on the situation.

“Okay, we need to search this area. He could be hiding somewhere......”

“Sir, look here!” called Szymanski.

Allan went over to where his colleague was pointing excitedly. He bent over to examine the tyre tracks.

“These are fresh and look as though they could have been made by a Range Rover” he remarked as he stood up and shielded his eyes against the evening sun that had made an appearance burning through the earlier cloud. He was looking at the Water.

“Surely he couldn’t have driven over the top into the Water, could he?”

“Perhaps he realised he had nowhere to run and committed suicide?” volunteered Szymanski.

“I don’t buy that. Why would he have got his housekeeper who was obviously his accomplice, to act as bait so he could see if there was any trap if he didn’t have an escape plan?”

“Possibly he didn’t have an escape plan as such, sir. Maybe he just didn’t want to spend the rest of his life in jail, so he decided, if it was a trap, his last chance of freedom had gone and there was no alternative”.

“Ummmm. Well let’s get the divers in and see what turns up” said Allan looking at his mobile and keying in the relevant number.

The light was failing fast when the divers came up.

“The Range Rover is down there, sir, but somewhat damaged. There’s no sign of a body and no sign of anything in the car that resembles an antibiotic”.

“Damn” exclaimed Allan and Szymanski wiped away the tears streaming down her face.

“Listen, Julia, we are going to find the antibiotic. We are! Do you hear me?” and he grabbed her by the shoulders and squeezed them tight.

Szymanski nodded and gulped.

“Thank you, sir” she whispered and then shook her head and putting her chin in the air she gave him a wobbly smile.

Chapter Eighteen

Blue lights flashing, sirens wailing two police cars sped along towards Cambridge. Cars moved to the side of the road to let them through.

Symanski was on the phone to the hospital.

"How is he, Sal?"

Allan heard the sound of crying.

"Don't cry. It's going to be alright. We're on our way to get the antibiotic. Just keep stroking his hair and telling him we love him very much and he's going to be well again soon" she said unable to stifle the sob in her throat.

Sally said something else that Allan couldn't hear. She sounded as though she was still tearful, and the words came out muffled.

"I know, I know but it will be okay, Sal. We both love Leo, and he is going to pull through. We're all going to get through this. Love you Sal" and she hung up, wiping her hand over her face as she did so.

They arrived outside Manning's block of apartments in just over twenty minutes. Allan and Szymanski together with the other officers raced up the stairs and after several attempts one of the officers broke open the front door of Manning's apartment.

"Search everything and everywhere. You all know what you are looking for and how urgent it is" shouted Allan as they trooped into the hallway.

Drawers were pulled out and the contents rummaged as were the contents of cupboards, wardrobes, the washing bin. Two bathrooms, cisterns, behind toilets, tops of kitchen cupboards as well as the cupboards themselves were thoroughly examined. Carpets were ripped up and skirting boards ripped off. The six officers, Allan and Szymanski literally pulled the place to pieces. Hope was fading fast.

"Perhaps he hid the antibiotic at Misslethwaite Manor? Maybe we're in the wrong place? Remember the lab there. The antibiotics are somewhere there I'm sure of it" suggested a despairing Szymanski.

"Yes, you might be right, although it was searched thoroughly, and nothing was found but it's not here so we'll get over there as fast as we can. Maybe it's somewhere else in the house. Listen everyone, we're going to M……"

"Sir, I think we've found something!" interrupted one of the officers.

They all ran to the lounge where two of the officers were standing over an exposed area of floorboards.

“These boards are lighter in colour than the rest. Something is under here”.

After some effort the boards were prised up revealing a large metal box in the cavity.

It was heavy and it took two of them to lift it out. The box was in fact a safe with a combination lock.

“We need a safe engineer for this” said Allan already on his phone.

“No, we need him now, okay, this is an emergency and a matter of life and death, so I don’t want to hear probably. He has to be here yesterday!”

While they were waiting, Allan took another look in the cavity. He shone the torch into the dark interior and tugged at some plastic covering.

“My god. It’s the two million pounds! We’d have to count it, but my bet is it’s all there!” cried Allan.

Twenty minutes later the safe engineer arrived. Everyone was completely silent as he undertook his work. Finally, he succeeded.

Inside the safe were ampoules in strips of six by six. On top of these was a bizarre drawing. Two faces had been drawn. One was depicted as in pain and the other holding the ampoule to its face and smiling.

“Totally weird!” commented one officer.

“This is what we need. Let’s go!” responded Allan.

Allan drove while Szymanski held the precious box on her knees and phoned ahead to alert the hospital staff that they had the antibiotic. The car sped along and on reaching the hospital, they pounded along the corridors to where baby Leo was struggling to stay alive. He had just stopped breathing, and a nurse was doing CPR. Sally was crying with her hands over her mouth, a horrified expression in her eyes.

“Here’s the antibiotic” said Allan as they burst into the room.

A doctor turned.

“How sure are you that this is the antibiotic and not some other substance?” he said calmly.

“I’m as sure as I bloody can be! Now can you inject this into Leo, please?”

“I’m afraid that unless you are totally sure that this is what you think it is, then I cannot inject him. I’m sure you understand that?”

“No…………” began an irritated and irate Allan

At that moment, Szymanski whipped over to a trolley standing at the side and picked up a syringe. She spun round before anyone could react and took an ampoule from the box.

“You can’t do this. I know you think you are doing the right thing, but I cannot allow this”.

The nurse stopped doing CPR and turned round to face everyone, tears in her eyes.

“I’m so sorry” she said focussing on Sally and Sally let out a heart wrenching howl and fell to the floor on her knees, sobs wracking her whole body.

Everyone’s attention focussed on Sally.

Szymanski held her nerve and drew the liquid into the syringe tapping it to remove any air. She moved swiftly over to her son and taking one of his little arms she injected the liquid.

The little boy lay inert, and tears started to stream down Szymanski’s face. Allan could feel a lump in his throat.

"I'm so sorry for your loss Mrs and Mrs Szymanski ……." began the doctor.

Just then the little boy moved his head. Then the fingers of his left hand twitched. He opened his eyes and smiled.

Szymanski bent over Leo and kissed his forehead. Sally walked unsteadily to his bedside and kissed his hand.

"Hello my beautiful boy," said Sally.

"Hello, my son, you're better now. Your mummies are here, and everything is going to be wonderful" and she kissed his forehead again.

Everyone else moved out of the room to allow the three of them to enjoy this special time.

Allan took a moment in the car to compose himself. He didn't think he could ever be that emotional but clearly, he had misread the power of his own feelings.

He sent a text to Szymanski insisting she take a couple of days off to be with her family and saying he was looking forward to seeing her back after that.

As he drove back to the station, he smiled to himself re-living the moment when Leo opened his eyes. He visualised the absolute joy that had spread over Julia's face. She and Sally had been so happy, and he was very glad that they had been able to get the antibiotic in time to save the little boy's life. Then he frowned as he got himself back into gear for the interview with Fran Cooper. Who would have thought that the attractive, friendly housekeeper would end up being Manning and Cunningham's accomplice although he had thought she was a curious candidate for the position. He shook his head as he turned into the station car park.

At reception, he asked that the package be sent to relevant laboratories where quantities of antibiotic would be manufactured.

Walking into the main office he called for Patel to follow him.

"Close the door" Allan said.

"Right, which room is Fran Cooper being held in?"

"I believe it's Interview Room 3" Patel replied.

Allan looked up.

"You can do better than that, Dev. I don't want belief I want a definite answer. I'll ask you again, in which room is Fran Cooper?"

Patel's face reddened.

“Sorry sir, Fran Cooper is in Interview Room 3” he said his hands clasping and unclasping behind is back.

“Good. Let’s find out where Manning is likely to be, what part Cunningham played in all this, how many more disciples did Manning have and what part Cooper played”.

Armed with papers they walked down two flights of stairs and entered the interview room. Facing them seated was Fran Cooper. She had a mocking smile on her face. Her long, straight blonde hair was dishevelled but did nothing to detract from her good looks. Allan remembered the intelligent, piercing green eyes.

“Good evening, Ms Cooper” Allan said, and Patel nodded.

Fran Cooper said nothing but met Allan’s gaze.

Allan turned on the tape and recorded the required information.

Both Allan and Patel having introduced themselves, Allan indicated that Cooper should follow suit. She kept them waiting for a few minutes then decided to oblige.

“Ms Fran Cooper” she said finally, looking straight at Allan.

Allan looked through his papers and kept Cooper waiting, returning the compliment.

"Would you like a solicitor to be present, Ms Cooper?"

"I don't have a solicitor" she replied.

"A duty solicitor can be arranged, if you would like?"

"No, thank you".

"So, Ms Cooper I would like you to describe your movements and who you have been with over the past week, please",

"I went to the Bahamas, came back for a short visit and then had to fly back hence the private jet".

"You do realise, Ms Cooper, that this is a murder enquiry and as such it is a criminal offence to mislead the police?"

Fran Cooper seemed to reflect.

"If I tell you what you want to know, can I cut a deal?"

"We don't do deals, Ms Cooper, but your cooperation could stand you in good stead for a more lenient sentence" and he met her gaze.

She nodded once or twice with her head down, looking at the table, then she looked up suddenly seemingly coming to a decision.

"Okay, fire away" she said simply.

"As I said I would like you to describe your movements over the past week, please," said Allan.

"I spent most of it at my flat in Cambridge. I got a call from Roland on Monday saying that he wanted me to fly him somewhere today and that there would be a private jet at Bourn airport at five o'clock. To be dressed in black and to wait there for him".

"What else did he tell you?" asked Patel.

"Nothing" she replied.

"So, you didn't know where you were going?"

"No".

"Weren't you curious?"

"Not really. He was like that. He rarely explained much".

Patel gave way then to Allan to question.

"In the past couple of weeks what had Manning asked you to do?"

Fran fidgeted uncomfortably on her seat.

“Okay so he asked me to go to a fête and mingle amongst the guests”.

“Was this the fête at Misslethwaite Manor?” Allan interrupted.

“Yes, that was it. Then I was to take an aerosol and spray it around certain spots”.

“Did he say what was in the spray can?” asked Patel.

“No”.

“Did you ask what was in it?”

“No. I just did what he asked”.

“Why?”

“Why what?”

“Why did you blindly do what he asked?”

“You have no idea, do you? I was scared. He threatened me. He said he would find me and my family wherever we went, and he would kill us all. I had no choice. He paid me well but there was no escape”.

“Why didn’t you come to us. We could protect you”.

The smirk came back.

“I don’t think so” she said.

“So do you know what Cunningham had to do with it all?” asked Allan.

“Cunningham was the face of respectability, and he was in awe of Manning. His pharmaceutical firm legitimately took deliveries of substances that Manning required for his own purposes and at first the laboratories were used at the firm. I think he created a lab somewhere else when you lot became suspicious of Cunningham”.

“Yes, we’ve found the labs. What else has he asked you to do?”

“I had to drop an atomizer in a bin on the village green near Misslethwaite Hall” she said sullenly.

“Were you in a car, walking, how did you get to the green?”

“I was on a motorbike, why?”

“And did you hide the motorbike behind the garages at Misslethwaite Hall?” asked Allan, ignoring her query.

“Yes” she replied.

“Continue, please” Allan said looking at her sternly.

“I had to travel to Port Grimaud in France and use the atomizer there to spray in a certain area. Then I flew back”.

“You must have heard that people fell sick where you had sprayed these atomizers?” Patel asked.

“No, I don’t listen to the news” she said.

“So, let’s be clear. At no time did you ask what was in the atomizer or why you had to spray it in particular places,” said Allan

“No”.

“Okay so anything else?”

“No, that was it but okay I did eavesdrop once onto a conversation they were having, and it seemed that Manning wanted absolute power over everyone and everything. He told Cunningham that they would rule the world one day but wasn’t it fun giving you lot, the police, the run around and there was a satisfaction in being instrumental in causing suffering. He said he had always found that fun”.

“Okay so where do you think Manning is now?” Allan asked

“Now? What now he’s dead!”

“How do you know that?”

“Because of the last thing I heard him say when I was eavesdropping, before I couldn’t hear anymore because he, I mean Manning, moved towards the door where I was, so I scrammed pretty quick”.

“So, what did he say?” asked Patel.

“He said that if he knew there was no escape, that the police would take him, then he would commit suicide rather than go to prison”.

“So, you think that Manning has killed himself?” Allan asked.

“With Cunningham dead, me in custody and the police able to identify him, yes, I think he has” she said defiantly.

“So, what sort of a deal am I getting for being cooperative?” she asked meeting Allan’s gaze with her piercing green eyes.

“As I said before, we don’t do deals so it is for the judge to decide the severity of the sentence, Ms Cooper, but we will be entering a note on your file confirming your cooperation. Just one further question. Do you know if Manning ever got hold of Dr Vanessa Fenchurch’s mobile?”

Fran Cooper stared at Allan for a moment.

"If you are referring to the evening when you went to her flat and couldn't find Dr Fenchurch then, yes, he drugged the doctor and cloned her phone."

"I thought as much. Interview terminated at 8.03 p.m." announced Allan for the tape and switched it off.

Gathering their papers, they left the room while Fran Cooper was led away by the officer who had remained unmoving by the door while the interview was conducted.

Allan and Patel walked back to the main office.

"Well, that pretty much covers everything, sir" Patel said.

"It would seem so, Dev. It would seem so" replied Allan but still something was nagging at him, but he just couldn't quite home in on what was causing his disquiet.

Reaching the main office, silence descended on the team as Allan stood before the whiteboard that had numerous yellow stickies and lines drawn on it; evidence of the enquiry.

"Well done everyone. We have a result and although we don't at present know the whereabouts of Manning's body, I think it is safe to say that he won't be bothering us again.

Having interviewed Fran Cooper, from her evidence Manning has almost certainly committed suicide and with Cunningham gone and Fran Cooper about to serve a very long sentence if justice prevails, which I'm certain it will, there is no further threat from the life-threatening infection caused by this virus. In addition, we have the antibiotic. So, well done again everyone, very good work and I can see from Dev waving madly at me that the DCI wants a word." Allan nodded acknowledgement to Dev, made his way out of the office and bounding up the stairs he quickly reached Walters' office. He knocked on the door.

"Come" summoned the DCI.

Walters stood up as Allan entered.

"Congratulations Jack – well done!" Walters had been standing behind the observation glass of the room where Cooper had been interviewed so was already aware of the outcome.

"Thank you, sir, but I couldn't have done it without my excellent team" replied Allan with a smile.

"Well, that's as maybe and well done to them, of course, but you led the team, Jack" and Walters extended a hand towards one of the two chairs in front of his desk indicating that he should take a seat.

"Thank you, sir. Sir, there is just one thing that concerns me. We didn't ever discover what the link was between the fire at the Grange and the fire at the Hall. So, for me, the case is not completely closed," said Allan.

"Jack, you are seeing things where they are not. Much though we, detectives, don't like to admit that there are such things as coincidences, there are! This is one of them. If I were you, I would celebrate this evening with your team. You have all done an excellent job, as I said. Put it to bed, Jack!"

Jack smiled and nodded but he knew the puzzle would be on his mind for some time to come.

The DCI continued.

"Obviously, we have a Press Conference first thing in the morning at nine o'clock and we need to prepare. I will give a brief introduction, but I want you to take the lead on this one".

"Of course, sir".

"Before we get on with that though, there is something else I need to tell you".

Allan nodded but remained silent wondering what was coming.

"I will be retiring at the end of the month, Jack. I have been thinking about it for a while now and submitted my request for retirement a couple of months ago which was granted. I'm sorry to spring this on you but we have had a lot going on and when someone who has been in my position for a long time, and hopefully has the full respect of his subordinates, announces retirement it sometimes causes those subordinates to become unsettled and not able to fully concentrate on their tasks at hand. I would like to say that of all the DI's that report to me you rank as one of the best, if not the best, Jack. Your father was a credit to the Force, and he would have been extremely proud of you today. My replacement has been chosen and he will start at the beginning of next month. I would have, without a doubt, recommended you for the position but I know from previous conversations with you that you prefer to remain at DI level because, as I understand it, you don't want a desk job and to progress to DCI and remain involved at that level would necessitate you moving Constabulary and therefore relocate. Is that correct, Jack?"

"Yes, you are correct, but I very much appreciate, sir, your confidence in my abilities".

"Well deserved, Jack, but I'm sorry I haven't witnessed your further progression in rank before I retire, and I am certain that that will happen in time. For my part I will miss the Force at first but I'm also sure that the golf course and my wife will soon take over my life, not necessarily in that order!" Walters laughed.

Allan laughed too, but his eyes bore a serious expression.

"I will be very sorry to see you go, sir, and thank you again for your praise. It has been an honour to serve under you".

Walters smiled and made to get up.

"Before I go to prepare for the Press Conference, may I ask you one question, sir" Allan said without moving.

"Yes, of course, Jack, what is it?" replied the DCI sitting down again.

"Who will your replacement be?"

"Detective Inspector Tom Clarkson".

Allan's face dropped.

"I know you two haven't seen eye to eye in the past, but this is a new beginning, Jack, so try to make the best of it. For what it's worth I didn't suggest him, and he wouldn't be my first choice, but it is what it is" and Walters got up and walked to the door holding it open which was the signal to Allan that the conversation was at an end.

Nine o'clock the next day saw Walters and Allan seated in front of a formidable army of press reporters and cameras which were ready to film.

"Good morning, everyone. Thank you for attending this Press Conference. We are here today in connection with the deaths and life-threatening illness caused by a hitherto unknown manmade virus. I am handing you over to my colleague DI Jack Allan who will appraise you of our progress," and Walters extended a hand to Allan.

Allan then proceeded to elaborate on the investigation and how they had come to their conclusions. The suspects involved were Roland Manning who is presumed dead, Freddie Cunningham whose death had been confirmed and Fran Cooper who was remanded in custody pending trial. He then went on to praise his team for all the hard, painstaking work they had undertaken to get this result.

Walters then asked for any questions from the Press.

"Will this virus still spread even though the perpetrators are dead or locked up?" asked a lady with reddish coloured hair styled in a sharp, geometric cut.

"No, it won't. The virologists advise us that by treating everyone that has come in contact with the virus or is suffering from the virus itself, where the antibiotic will be used, if necessary, this will be enough to stop its spread. Next question" said Allan pointing to a tall, blonde guy who was waving his hand to get attention.

"Yes, thank you. I would like to know how you can be certain that this Manning chap is dead if you haven't found the body?".

"We have good reason to believe he is dead from the evidence we have collected, so there is no need for any concern for public safety" Allan pointed to a tall, dark-haired man.

"Why were the children kidnapped? What was the purpose of that?" he asked.

"As far as we can establish, Manning and Cunningham were testing whether they could cause a death in a human being who had previously had a 'sleeper' ampoule containing the virus placed in their body by using a trigger that would release the infection from the virus into the body within a matter of minutes. They would phone the victim and say a certain phrase which would cause the victim to press the ampoule which released the viral infection. By using children, they instilled the worst fear factor to underline the power they could wield, should they desire. Next question – the lady in the red suit".

"Hi, yes, thanks. If you hadn't stopped these maniacs could this have been the start of potential world control by them?"

"Well, er, we wouldn't like to speculate on that" Walters came in before Allan had time to answer.

After three more questions, Walters stood up.

"Thank you everyone for coming today. That's it" and Allan got up and followed the DCI out of the conference room.

That evening the whole team and the armed response unit met in the local Dog and Mouse pub. Everyone was elated that the case had been successfully wrapped up and the two million pounds recovered. Walters came and joined them. Allan was due to join after he had completed the last necessary bits of paperwork, and he was expected any time now.

Barry was suggesting that they all go for a curry at the Delhi Curry House just up the High Street.

"Why do you always have to choose curry? You know I absolutely hate it! It's disgusting!" complained Dev.

“Okay, sorry, I forgot” said Barry “Anyone for Chinese?”

There were several roars of approval not least from Dev.

Allan had his hand on the door of the pub when his mobile rang.

“Hello, sir,” said Szymanski.

“Hi Julia. Is everything okay with Leo and yourselves? And by the way, I know you have always liked to call me ‘sir’ but unless formality is required, please call me Jack”.

“Thank you, Jack, I will do my level best! Yes, we are all fine. I just wanted to apologise again for suggesting that Vanessa might be involved with the criminals and …….”

“Julia, we are nothing if not detectives and all detectives are suspicious beings. It’s in their nature. As I said before, there is absolutely no harm done and even I had to take on board that possibility although I was confident that Vanessa was totally innocent. You must remember, though, that I had the advantage – I know her very well. Please don’t worry any further. I had better go and join the others for the team celebration. You and Sally are welcome to join us later. I could text you where we are going for a meal?”

"No, thank you, Jack. We want to be with Leo all the time at the moment. I'll let you go now. Have a great time and say hello to the team for me".

"Will do. Take care. See you soon".

Once more, Jack had his hand on the door handle when his mobile rang again.

At first, he couldn't make out what the woman at the end of the phone was saying. It was unintelligible at first because of the intense sobbing.

"It's mum, Jack. She's…she's passed away" Jane finally managed to get the words out.

Allan stood stock still for a moment. He had been planning not to drink this evening so that he was fresh to start out first thing in the morning for Corton. He had been looking forward to seeing his mother.

He turned round and headed for his car, still on the phone to his sister, holding back the tears.

Chapter Nineteen - Six Months Later

Driving from the station to his flat Allan was feeling good. Better than he had felt in a long time. Physically he always felt on form but mentally he had felt bruised, but the habitual strenuous exercise helped. The main reason for his harsh regime had been the fate of his father but also it had helped him mend. Then six months ago the death of his mother. After the funeral, where the church had been filled with friends from her church and Bridge Club, he and his sister had both worked through their grief, reliving their childhood, looking through family photos, laughing, crying, remembering. Then they had come to terms with their loss and after a generous two week's compassionate leave he had returned to work. Now his mind went back over his failed marriage. He would never forget that day although the pain had got less and less over the two years since the divorce.

Theirs had been the fairytale marriage. They had known each other, he and Poppy since childhood. He was tall and dark; she was petite and blonde. They both liked sports and despite her seeming fragility she was a formidable squash opponent. It had always been assumed by friends and family that they would end up together and so it was that they married at the picturesque St Peter's Church near Corton where they had both grown up. Even a period of time away from each other at different universities had done nothing to diminish their love for each other. It was a white wedding with all the trimmings. She had arrived in a horse and carriage with her father, and he remembered coming out in a cold sweat because she had been ten minutes late, wondering whether she had changed her mind. The lychgate had been decorated with dark and pale pink contrasting roses interweaved with green foliage. He remembered her radiant smile as she looked up at him standing in front of the altar.

Married life was idyllic. After a wonderful honeymoon in the Seychelles, they had moved into the small semi-detached house in Cambridgeshire which they had managed to buy with money given to them from both sets of adoring parents and by taking on an affordable mortgage.

Poppy was a primary school teacher at the local village school, and he had gone into the police force at DC level. Then Poppy had fallen pregnant; they and all the family had been overjoyed but six months after the birth of their baby son, Daniel, tragedy struck. His was a cot death. After that Poppy and he had struggled with their relationship, and he should have seen it coming but somehow, he didn't. That fateful Tuesday he had come home unexpectedly. He recalled vividly as though it was yesterday putting the key in the latch, opening and shutting the door quietly as he always did. He sensed immediately that something was wrong and to this day he still didn't know what it was that made him tread very quietly upstairs, an unreal, indescribably horrible feeling rising in the pit of his stomach. He walked across the landing to their bedroom door and turned the handle. She was on top of him, completely naked, moving backwards and forwards, strangled ecstatic noises coming from her throat. He had felt sick as he saw his colleague and friend fondling his wife's breasts. It was Craig who first realised that he and Poppy were not alone.

"It's not what you think, Jack" Craig had said pathetically in a panicky voice pushing Poppy off him who stared wildly at Jack, shock making her speechless. Then she seemed to pull herself together and got off the bed and rushed towards Jack.

"I'm sorry, darling, I'm so sorry" she exclaimed.

He stared at her and detached himself from her arms which she had thrown round his neck. He remembered he hadn't said anything. He was too shocked himself. He walked unsteadily down the stairs and out of the front door. He never spoke to her or his colleague again. The divorce proceedings had gone entirely through their solicitors.

Then he thought of that day when Vanessa's shopping had scattered all over the pavement. Their eyes had met, it was corny, yes, but it was true, his heart had skipped a beat and later, when they had kissed, her lips had seemed to give him an electric shock. He had taken all of five months to realise that he was in love with her, but she was one independent lady, and he didn't want to frighten her away but………"

It was almost as though she knew he was thinking about her as his car phone rang.

"Hi, it's me. Are you in tonight and if so, could I interest you in a meal with oysters as an hors d'oeuvre, sex as the main meal and again as dessert? Maybe tonight? I'm off shift in three hours and starving, in fact so hungry that maybe we could skip the starter" she said with a grin in her voice.

"Can I wait until tonight? I suppose I'll have to! Listen, I have been due holiday for ages so today I asked to take it. I've got the next two weeks off. Any chance you could swing it your end? I know it's very short notice but……" he trailed off to give her a chance to answer.

"Well, I'll try but I'm not hopeful".

"Want you! Perhaps we could fast forward to tonight! In the meantime, I'll book a table at Le Jardin de Paris at nine o'clock".

"If only! See you at six!" and she hung up.

Three hours. That would just give him time!

Allan did it in two hours thirty and arrived back just in time to shower and put fresh clothes on before Vanessa arrived.

He opened the door. She came in and kicking the door shut with her foot she threw her arms round his neck and then started to undress him and herself at the same time. They didn't make it to the bedroom, and he took her against the fridge-freezer and then again on the island in the middle of the kitchen. They eventually got to the bedroom. When they were both satisfied and exhausted, they fell asleep in each other's arms.

It was seven-thirty in the evening when they awoke. Allan turned to Vanessa and gently woke her.

"Hello, gorgeous", he said. Smiling she turned towards him, and they kissed.

"I suppose we should get up or we're going to miss enjoying a delicious meal at that wonderful restaurant you have booked" she said kissing him again before he could answer.

“I suppose you’re right” he said reluctantly, and they both got out of bed.

“So how are you getting along with Tom Clarkson?” Vanessa asked.

In reply, he grimaced, glancing at Vanessa in the mirror who was tying a Windsor knot for him.

“Oh! Not bad news, is it?”

“Well, you know we go way back and not well. I won’t bore you with the details now but suffice it to say he’s not my favourite man”.

“I’m sure it will get better” she said while expertly finishing the knot.

“No probably worse but I’ll manage” he replied smiling and admiring Vanessa’s work.

“The main thing is that the murderers of that last major case we worked on are dead or locked up” he said.

“But there’s still something worrying you?” she asked noticing a lack of finality in his voice.

“No, not really”.

“What do you mean, ‘not really’”, she asked, her head on one side.

“It’s nothing tangible. Just a feeling” he said thoughtfully. “But it is just that, it’s only a feeling with no foundation at all. Taking into account Fran Cooper’s knowledge that Manning said he would rather die than go into custody, he has undoubtedly slunk off like a wounded animal and killed himself. Cunningham is dead and Cooper is locked up. The case is closed, I’m talking gibberish. I’m sure tomorrow, unfortunately, there will be another murder case to work on, so let’s go enjoy a hopefully wonderful meal while we are both not on shift!”

They arrived at the restaurant twenty minutes later and were ushered to a quiet corner table for two.

The waiter approached the table for the pre-dinner drinks order.

“Champagne?” asked Allan looking at Vanessa.

“What are we celebrating?” she asked.

“Anything you can think of as an excuse to have a superb evening!” he said smiling.

“I’d love champagne, and I’ll think of an excuse in a minute” she answered grinning.

“A bottle of Moet then, please” he said to the waiter.

"By the way did you manage to get the next two weeks off?" he asked after they had toasted each other and taken a sip of champagne.

Her eyes sparkled.

"We do have an excuse for this extravagance, if we need one of course! Yes, to my amazement it was agreed without any trouble at all. I do have a lot of leave left to take. I don't think I have taken more than a day or two in two years!"

"That's fabulous! Especially as ……." and he showed his mobile screen to her.

"Oh wow! That looks amazing! Where is it? Are you……going on holiday?" she faltered and then started to smile.

"We are going on holiday. To Dubai!"

"Ah but you are going to allow me to pay for my half?" she said suddenly deadly serious.

"Yes, of course, but we can talk about that later. No worries! I just wanted to surprise you. I know you said you wanted to go to Dubai. Normally, I would have discussed it with you but…."

"That's fine! That's great! Thank you for remembering! I can't wait!" she said reaching across the table for his hand.

“What would you have done if I hadn’t been able to get the leave?” she asked a mischievous glint in her eye.

“What do you think? I would have gone on my own and found a ravishing blonde to grant me my every wish” he laughed with an equally naughty look.

She mock smacked him across the face and they both giggled.

They enjoyed a delicious meal of prawn and crab for starter and lobster pasta to follow washed down with a bottle of Pouilly Fuissé.

“I’ve been wanting to tell you, Vanessa, how much you have turned my life around, but I just haven’t found the right moment,” he twiddled the stem of his wine glass looking at it, studiously avoiding Vanessa’s questioning look.

“I never thought I would be able to....to feel anything again for anyone, for any woman, after Poppy. I felt there must be something wrong with me”, Vanessa reached across and put her hand on his but before she could say anything, he continued.

“Somehow you have worked your magic and every time we are together my sun is shining. I feel happier than I’ve felt in oh so long!” he reached into his pocket and pulled out a little box. He dared not look at Vanessa before he opened it, revealing a beautiful solitaire diamond ring which he placed in the middle of the table.

The waiter approached with the dessert and stopped when he saw Allan go down on one knee.

“Will you marry me, Vanessa Fenchurch?” he said looking up at her. She was smiling at him, but her eyes were wet with tears.

Epilogue

He had leapt out of the car, leaving the door open and the handbrake off so that it journeyed on without him into Grafham Water. He could hear the sirens heading fast towards him. He ran like the wind towards the surrounding wooded area. He knew how to survive under the radar, and he would survive just like he did before. He smiled to himself and ran faster. Now immersed in the dense undergrowth he allowed himself time to catch his breath. He could hear the police cars arriving and the Detective Inspector's voice shouting. He laughed silently. They would never catch him. It was a stroke of genius allowing that stupid cow, Fran Cooper, to hear that he would commit suicide if he thought he would be caught. He had known she was eavesdropping. Absurd ideas, he would never be caught, and he would never commit suicide. Anyway, he was sure that she would have made some deal with the police to save her own skin as much as possible so the chances were great that she would have blabbed this nonsense to them thus causing them to think it was case closed.

He moved off again in the direction of the open fields. Once he was across these, he could pick up the unremarkable Ford Focus that he had parked there some time ago covered in foliage to avoid stray joy riders taking it for a spin. In the car he had several sets of false number plates to muddy the waters while he was on the run. He had a stack of cash carefully hidden in the bodywork along with false passports. He trudged on smiling to himself. They had no idea, the police, who they were dealing with. His intelligence was streets ahead of them.

He reached the car, grabbed the key from the back left tyre and got in the car. It fired first time, and he shot off heading south. Whilst driving, he thought about all those years ago, about his parents who didn't understand him, didn't understand his brilliance. His mother's face when she and his father had found him covered in the stupid cat's blood. He wanted to find out how its system worked, and they were worried about the poor little cat. He smirked. What they hadn't known was the enjoyment he had had stabbing the cat so that it couldn't escape and hearing its cries of pain. That had excited him, then when he had had enough of hearing its squeals of agony he had gone in for the kill and stabbed it through the heart. After that incident, his parents hadn't been the same with him and he knew that they had to go. He had heard them planning his downfall. His father in particular was going to investigate those rumours at Cambridge. If he hadn't been coming down the stairs at that moment he might never have known, and things could have been much more difficult for him.

As it was, he had plenty of money, some of which he used for expensive extensive plastic surgery altering his bone structure completely. This, together with blue coloured contact lenses and hair blonded with a bottle of peroxide, changed Qiáng's whole appearance. Even his own mother would have had trouble recognising him let alone a rather inept Detective Inspector.

He had earned his wealth through a particularly brilliant scam that he had implemented in his last year at Cambridge. It was amazing to him how easy it was to cream money off these pensioners who had more money than sense. Give them a nice, well-educated voice exuding total confidence in their non-existent financial vehicle and a beautiful fake authentic-looking website and the money just fell in your lap. It nearly went sour though when another Cambridge graduate, the little toerag holier than thou Peterson stumbled on it. He was going to ruin everything but unfortunately, he had a nasty accident when he fell out of the window of his second-floor rooms.

At the thought of Allan, a terrible expression crossed his face, and his mouth ruptured into a cruel smile exaggerated by the curve of his upper lip. He thought of the fire after watching a film on television and had expertly carried out his plan.

It had been a stroke of luck when he met Freddie Cunningham at Cambridge University. Freddie had the same mentality as he although Freddie had shied away from hurting his parents, so he had had no alternative but to play along. Freddie had tried to persuade Piers to go along with their plans using the family business as a front, but his father, wouldn't have any of it, so he had signed his own death warrant and along with his own, that of his wife's.

Then poor Freddie himself had become a liability. So, he had to go!

He grimaced as he thought about the recent events. Detective Inspector Allan had thwarted his well thought out plans for now but soon, very soon, Allan would come to regret his short-lived success.

Yes, he thought, Allan had made a big mistake, but not as huge as his own parents' who made the deadly decision not to accept and act, when they knew in their heart of hearts, he was a brilliant, dangerous, psychopath.

THE END?

Printed in Great Britain
by Amazon

52635848R00220